The Unpretentious
Philosopher

The Unpretentious Philosopher; Or The Rare Man

A Physical, Chemical, Political
and Moral Work
Dedicated to Scientists

by
Louis-Guillaume de La Follie

translated, annotated and introduced by
Brian Stableford

A Black Coat Press Book

ISBN 978-1-61227-136-1. First Printing. December 2012. Published by Black Coat Press, an imprint of Hollywood Comics.com, LLC, P.O. Box 17270, Encino, CA 91416. All rights reserved. Except for review purposes, no part of this book may be reproduced or transmitted in any form or by any means, electronic or mechanical, including photocopying, recording, or by any information storage and retrieval system, without permission in writing from the publisher. The stories and characters depicted in this novel are entirely fictional. Printed in the United States of America.

Introduction

Le Philosophe sans pretention, ou l'Homme rare. Ouvrage physique, chymique, politique et moral. Dédié aux savans, here translated as *The Unpretentious Philosopher; or The Rare Man: a Physical, Chemical, Political and Moral Work, Dedicated to Scientists*, was initially published under the by-line "M. D. L. F." in Paris by Clousier in 1775. Someone has expanded the final two letters to "La Folie" in the Bibliothèque Nationale's copy, reproduced on its *gallica* website (taking it for granted that the first two stand for "Monsieur de"), and that is how it is catalogued in the BN; it is unclear whether that is a mistake, or whether, if it is a mistake, it is accidental or deliberate. The book's author usually rendered his surname La Follie but spelling was rather haphazard in the 18th century, and the author might have used the double l in his more serious work to avoid the implication of "folly" contained in the single l, although he or someone else might have wanted to preserve that very implication, ironically, for the purposes of a satirical *conte philosophique* that embraces a calculated eccentricity for rhetorical purposes.

The first point that needs to be made about the nature of the book and its translation is that the translation of the final word of the title, *savans*, as "scientists" is inevitably dubious. In 1775 the word "scientist" did not exist in the English language—it was coined some fifty years later by William Whewell, and could not have been used in a contemporary translation, which would inevitably have preferred "scholars" if the translator did not want to retain "savants." In French, the word *savant*, equipped with a new orthodox spelling, continued in use with multiple meanings, usable to refer to all kinds of scholars without any separation of those engaged in scientific endeavor, although it increasingly became seen as primarily synonymous with the English "scientist."

The whole point of the argument contained in La Follie's book, however, and the core of his motivation for writing it, is to make the discrimination that the French language never quite completed. He wants to popularize a notion and an image that only exist, as yet, in embryo, in order to define himself, his protagonist, and a host of philosophers yet to come. His book is propaganda, not merely for scientific knowledge but for the scientific method, for the adoption of that method by all true philosophers, and for the recognition of a class of individuals who are routinely engaged in scientific enquiry by means of practical experimentation—i.e., *scientists*. It would therefore, be inappropriate now to use any other word in translating the title.

The purpose and innovative ambition of La Follie's book actually goes one step beyond that, because it also attempts to embody, and ultimately to make explicit, a plea for a particular method of communicating scientific ideas and attempting to make them persuasive. That aspect of the text is, in essence, a plea for the popularization of science, and an argument to the effect that it is wholly appropriate to use entertaining fictitious devices in the service of that aim; in brief, it is a plea in favor of "science fiction"—another term that was unknown at the time, and would not be invented for generations to come.

La Follie and his protagonist are sufficiently conscious of what might eventually be done in that regard to employ as the story's initial narrative hook the idea of an inhabitant of Mercury who employs a spaceship powered by electricity to undertake a voyage of exploration to Earth, and then becomes stranded when the ship crashes, forcing him to embark on a long search for the exotic materials required to repair it. That supposed predicament gives him an opportunity to communicate his advanced theoretical understanding of science to an inquisitive earthling—a didactic quest that takes up about two thirds of the text, before it returns to a plot that turns out to be rather more convoluted than was initially implied—but it is also a challenge in its own right, appealing to scientific discovery as a means of facilitating a practical endeavor.

This particular combination of literary ambitions was new—so new, in fact, that it eventually turned out to be some way "ahead of its time." Nothing else like *Le Philosophe sans prétention* was produced for a further fifty years, and by that time, La Follie's pioneering endeavor was forgotten. The novel was not included in the massive 36-volume collection of *Voyages imaginaires, songes, visions et romans cabalistiques* assembled by Charles Garnier in 1787-88, which became the chief reference-point for later writers with similar ambitions—most significantly Camille Flammarion, who became the leading figure in the boom in the popularization of science that occurred in France in the 1860s, and who similarly experimented with the use of fictional devices. Any writers of that later period who had come across the book would probably have rejected it as an uninteresting text, because they would have paid far more heed to the theories it espouses than to its ambition and method—and the theories it espouses had, by 1860, been proved utterly wrong—but they would not have been wholly justified in making that judgment.

1775 was, in fact, at least a decade ahead of the time when anyone had the slightest chance of selecting theories in chemistry for popularization that would actually endure, because the chemical theories current at that time turned out not merely to be mistaken but spectacularly erroneous. The novel might potentially have been followed up by a similar exercise based on better theories in the 1790s, but the revolution in science that was taking place then was overshadowed in general consequence by the much more flamboyant political revolution of 1789, whose unwinding consequences deflected literary attention in other directions for a further generation, and helped to delay the renaissance of scientifically-based philosophical fantasies until the 1830s, leaving La Follie's work historically isolated.

In terms of its scientific and science-fictional ambitions, *Le Philosophe sans pretention* unfortunately turned out to be a classic example of the manner in which elaborate and ambitious reasoning from a couple of mistaken premises can produce a vast web of ingenious absurdity. Indeed, it is such a perfect example of ratiocination from false premises that the text now has a rhetorical and esthetic charm quite different from the one intended by its author—but it is, admittedly, an esoteric charm that can only appeal to connoisseurs of the exotic. From the viewpoint of most modern readers, the primary interest of this translation will be the plot of the novel, and the manner in which the author deploys his fictional devices—a deployment that has several interesting features in the context of the "prehistory" of science fiction.

Louis-Guillaume de La Follie's "more serious" work consisted of papers published in the prototypical scientific journal, *Journal de Physique* [Journal of Physics] which were concerned with applications of recent discoveries in chemistry to the dyeing of textiles. His family, which belonged to the petty aristocracy, was heavily involved in the textile industry, and he became a researcher in chemistry with the specific aim of lending assistance to that concern. Whether his research contrived to increase the profits of the family firm is unclear, but he certainly had high hopes for it, and for the emergent class of professionals to which he thought he belonged. Not everyone, of course, was sympathetic toward the emergence of a new breed of experimental scientists primarily interested in possible industrial applications of their work; La Follie's endeavors do not seem to have looked upon kindly by the Académie des Sciences, which rejected the papers that ultimately ended up in the journal; he is, however, still on record as one of the first people to deposit a sealed claim to a new invention with the Académie, in order that it might serve as proof of priority of discovery, in the days when patent law was still highly uncertain in its effects.

La Follie was ultimately a victim of his own enthusiasm—some might say hubris. As the text of *Le Philosophe sans pretention* makes clear, and his scientific papers confirm, he developed a particular interest in "oil of vitriol" [sulfuric acid] and was fascinated by reactions causing effervescence, conflagrations and explosions. Given the imaginary practical uses to which the hero of the novel puts oil of vitriol and "marine acid" [hydrochloric acid] when he is forced to call upon his scientific knowledge to enable him to survive in dire circumstances—enterprises that it would be extremely unwise for readers to try at home, let alone if they are ever trapped underground—it is by no means surprising that he eventually died in a laboratory accident in 1790, in his forty-first year; it is rather astonishing that he had not contrived to kill himself sooner. Had people of the era not been willing to carry out experiments that we can now see, in retrospect, to have been horrendously dangerous, however, the rapid progress that soon obliterated all of La Follie's theoretical convictions would not have been possible.

La Follie was, therefore, a true martyr of science—and, as a true philosopher in his own definition, surely could not have thought of any better way to die. It would surely have a sadder fate had he fallen victim to the Terror, as he might well have done had he not made an earlier exit; *Le Philosophe sans pretention* also leaves no doubt that he was a supporter of the monarchy, although the necessity of obtaining a royal warrant to license publication for the book might have contributed to the protagonist's insistence on that point, especially in an era when another significant imaginative work embodying some scientific speculation, Louis-Sébastien Mercier's *L'An deux mille quatre cent quarante* (1771, but extensively revised in subsequent printings; tr. as *Memoirs of the Year 2500*), was in the process of becoming an underground best-seller in spite of its lack of a warrant, and raising censorious hackles in consequence.

Although La Follie was, in effect, the first "professional scientist" ever to put quill to paper in order to write what would nowadays be thought of as a "science fiction novel," his endeavor was not entirely without precedent, and can be seen as a logical development of a tradition of work with which he would have been familiar. It is necessary to remember that the *Journal de Physique* in which he published his scientific papers was a radically new endeavor, and that science had been making progress for more than two thousand years (unsteadi-

ly, to be sure) without the aid of the system of publication that it now standardized and taken for granted; most
previous scientific reportage had been presented in the
form of treatises, although some important works had
been livened up by giving them the form of dialogues,
and it was not unnatural that a would-be popularizer of
science in 1775 would be initially attracted to that form
of discourse.

The establishment of the dialogue as a principal
form of philosophical representation for didactic purposes dated all the way back to Plato's adoption of the So-
cratic dialogue as the principal teaching method of his
Academy, and it was Plato, in the dialogues he began to
write on his own account having concluded his mere
repetition of what Socrates had taught him, who first
began to experiment in earnest with the use of fictional
devices as a means of popularization. The most obvious
examples of Plato's uses of fiction are the apologues
included in the *Republic*—the story of the ring of Gyges
and the "Story of Er" that concludes the dialogue—and
the imaginary history of Atlantis, which he began to de-
ploy in two unfinished dialogues, the *Timaeus* and the
Critias. It is, however, in the *Symposium* that he is perhaps most ingenious, not only in making all the partici-
pants in the dialogue drunk, and hence indiscreet, but in
crediting one particular flight of fancy—the account of
the hermaphrodite—to the comedian Aristophanes, with
the clear intention of signaling that it was a joke.

Unfortunately, these pioneering endeavors were in-
hibited in their further evolution because Aristotle, who
set up a rival school, the Lyceum, thought it necessary as
a matter of principle to disagree with everything that
Plato said and did, and thus refused to have any truck
with fictional devices in his own works, casting a long

shadow over subsequent scholarly endeavor whose obscurity was slow to clear. When modern science underwent its first major surge in the 17th century, many of its promoters, including Isaac Newton, were solidly embedded in the Aristotelian mold, unprepared to make any efforts in the direction of popularization in their published works. Galileo, however, did appreciate the value of characterization in his own dialogue concerning the rivalry between the Copernican and Aristotelian theories of the solar system. Having been instructed to give the last word to the Church, he did so—but took care to make that last word ironic by characterizing the Church's representative within the dialogue as a perfect fool. Galileo was right to favor the Copernican model, and manifestly so, but that did not keep him out of trouble, and his difficulties in contention Papal authority also cast a long shadow over subsequent endeavor, which was almost as black in Catholic France as in Italy. That shadow formed the backcloth for all of La Follie's significant predecessors, and was one of the principal reasons for the renaissance of the kinds of fictional devices that Plato had pioneered, including flamboyant fabulation, utopian invention and drunken comedy.

In France, the dialogue that took over where Galileo left off in popularizing Copernican theory in the teeth of dogmatic opposition was Bernard Le Bovier de Fontenelle's *Entretiens sur la pluralité des mondes* (1686; tr. as *The Plurality of Worlds*), which—as its title suggests—converts its philosophical dialogue into a sprightly series of conversations, far more amicable, stylish and witty than any predecessor, and in so doing not only helped the book avoid persecution but also made it into a best-seller. It was already obvious by 1686 that if the Church attempted to fight that particular ideological battle to the last ditch it would suffer a defeat that would severely injure its authority, but combatants on other battlegrounds did not get off so lightly. Benoît de Maillet was unable to publish his ingenious dialogue *Telliamed* while he was alive, and the posthumous version published in 1748 was heavily censored. It was not until the full text was published in the 20th century that it became possible to see that Maillet could not only have made a significant contribution to the development of uniformitarian geology had his work been more widely read, but that he would have become a shining example to evolutionary theorists, by virtue of arguing that the evolution of life on Earth had taken place over billions of years, and even sketching out a primitive version of the theory of natural selection while hypothesizing about its mechanism.

By the time *Telliamed* appeared in bowdlerized form, however, a new and more aggressive generation of philosophical popularizers was emerging, who deployed every possible weapon to take on established orthodoxy. The regeneration of the *conte philosophique* is primarily associated with Voltaire, who was both the most flamboyantly fanciful and the most scathingly satirical of its exponents, but the greater impact was probably that of Jean-Jacques Rousseau, who employed a more modest didactic method in *Julie ou la Nouvelle Héloïse* (1761) and *Émile* (1762), taking his literary models from the English novel rather than the mock-Arabian fantasy from which Voltaire borrowed so heavily. Their mutual friend Denis Diderot also joined in the game, completing a triumvirate of radical philosophical novelists who became strident champions of both philosophical and political orthodoxy. Not everyone inspired by their methods, however, agreed with their political views.

Although Voltaire produced the single most important *conte philosophique* anticipating the concerns of science fiction, *Micromégas* (1752) the one writer in the genre prior to La Follie who had had any considerable involvement in practical scientific work was the physician Charles-François Tiphaigne de la Roche, whose hobbyist interest in agricultural science had led him to take a keen interest in biological science, and who produced two remarkable works including elements of scientific speculation in *Amilec* (1753) and *Giphantie* (1760).[1] Like Voltaire, Tiphaigne drew upon the imagery and narrative exuberance popularized by Antoine Galland's version of *Les Mille et une nuits* (1704-17), but he disapproved strongly of Voltaire's political views, and his works are, in part, counterstrikes as well as imitations.

As a petty aristocrat, La Follie was, inevitably, in Tiphaigne's political camp rather than the other, and he too employed the devices of the Voltairean *conte philosophique* with a different political slant, although he took care to include a slightly-disguised tribute to Voltaire's efforts in his text. Although he borrows from Voltaire in the mock-Islamic setting of the novel and the shaping of his narrative hook, however, La Follie's principal influence, as well as his principal *bête noire*, is Rousseau. Rousseau's ideas regarding the corrupting effects of civilization and the iniquities of monarchy are specifically attacked at several points in *Le Philosophe sans prétention*, but on one issue, La Follie and Rousseau are in perfect agreement, and that agreement plays a major role in forming the narrative component of La

---

[1] both translated in the Black Coat Press collection *Amilec and Other Satirical Fantasies*, ISBN 978-1-61227-033-3.

Follie's novel. Among Rousseau's various legacies in subsequent French culture was the growth of the cult of "*sensibilité*," which extolled spontaneous emotion as a behavioral guide, in opposition of social prejudice and conventional expectation, and which eventually had a considerable effect on the French Romantic Movement, and fiction in general; it became fashionable enough even in uptight England to call forth such satirical but ultimately self-sabotaging objections as Jane Austen's *Sense and Sensibility.*

Unlike Voltaire, Diderot and Tiphaigne, none of whom had much time for Rousseauesque "sensibility," La Follie is a wholehearted subscriber to it, and has no time at all for the notion that there is any inherent opposition between science and sentiment, either in theory or in practice. That ambivalent position, unusual in its day and still a trifle unorthodox even today, introduces a further peculiarity into *Le Philosophe sans prétention*, which adds yet another dimension to its originality. In order to appreciate the work fully it is useful to be able to see it as both a logical continuation of the burgeoning tradition of the *conte philosophique*, and also a deliberate step outside it. As a result of that step, the narrative element of the novel becomes almost as distinctive and peculiar as the didactic element, which is never fully integrated with it. Unfortunately, because of the space it takes up within the text, and the drastic error into which it was unfortunate to fall, the didactic aspect became an anchor dragging the whole work down into obscurity.

Many 18th century *contes philosophiques* remain comfortably readable today because the philosophical questions they address are essentially eternal and could not go out of date. Those dealing with scientific matters were on shakier ground, but most had the advantage of one secure victory on which to draw; no one was taking any real risks in championing Copernicus over Aristotle in describing the relationships between the planets and the sun, and whatever other cosmological follies they might commit, they always had that sturdy leg on which to stand. As Tiphaigne and La Follie illustrate with such tragic clarity, however, the matter was not so easy when speculators descended from lofty matters of cosmology to the nitty-gritty of chemistry and biology.

In *Amilec*, Tiphaigne sketches out his own theory of biological reproduction and embryology, building a scheme whose ingenuity is manifest, even though it is completely incorrect. Without the benefit of decent microscopes and several generations of difficult but careful observation, he simply did not know enough about cellular biology to have the slightest chance of anticipating the actual mechanisms of cell division and organic reproduction. In attempting to unify contemporary chemistry and provide it with a secure foundation in physics, La Follie had a lot more data on which to draw, including his own laboratory experiments, but he was also tackling a much vaster task, and he was tackling it at what was arguably the worst possible moment. He was the first writer of *contes philosophiques* to put the "hard" sciences of physics and chemistry at the heart of his endeavor, and precisely because they are the "hard" sciences, he was taking a much bigger risk than his rivals of not merely being disproved but made to look ridiculous.

1775 was a bad time for that kind of endeavor because it was only a few years in advance of some major discoveries and developments, which brought about to complete transformation of the entire world-view of the physical sciences. La Follie was well aware of being on the brink of some such revolution (as well as the other one), and his primary reason for writing his book, as he says in his preface, was corollary to his own attempts to think matters through, and to "instruct himself" as to the likely outcome of the impending transformation. In characterizing his eccentric hero, he was attempting to establish a hypothetical objective observer, from whose viewpoint it might be possible to unify physical and chemical science with the aid of a single omnipotent thesis. That was a laudable ambition, in spite of its impossibility, given the immaturity of scientific knowledge at the time.

Unfortunately, although entirely naturally, the notion La Follie took up as the lynch-pin of his unifying thesis is one that was shortly to be relegated to the unenviable status of the most notorious example of a mistaken scientific thesis: phlogiston. As soon as the idea of phlogiston was abandoned, it became an archetypal daft idea, ripe for and in desperate need of disproof and demolition; it survived in all textbooks of chemistry as a horrible warning of how one might go astray in trying to understand the world.

By the time the 19th century dawned, no one could any longer protest—however true it might have been— that phlogiston had seemed like a good idea at the time. It *had*, however, seemed like a good idea at the time to its proponents, and even if reading *Le Philosophe sans prétention* serves no other purpose, it certainly serves to remind us of that fact, and to illustrate why phlogiston seemed like a viable notion, in a scientific community that was not yet quite ready to let go of the classical theory of the four elements beloved by Aristotle, in spite of all the accumulating evidence that the theory in question was extremely unhelpful to a sensible understanding of chemistry.

The theory of the four elements, as promoted by Aristotle, was a tactful but rather paradoxical compromise. The whole idea of an element is that all material substance is ultimately reducible to one single principle. Different Greek philosophers however, disagreed as to what that ultimate principle might be. Some plumped for "water," others "earth," others "air" and others "fire." (The quotation marks are necessary because appointment as an element required a tacit redefinition of common terms, which left behind a considerable legacy of confusion, especially with respect to "earth" (*terre* in French), which continued to be used to identify soil, land (as opposed to sea) and the planet as well as the element). Rather than trying to arbitrate in a debate that was intrinsically impossible to settle, Aristotle was not the only philosopher to admit all four. We can now see that three of the "elements" correspond to the three easily observable basic states of matter—solid, liquid and gaseous—while the fourth plays a key role in negotiating their transformations and transitions within and between those states.

By La Follie's time, the anomalousness of "fire"—which, with reference to the element, was closer to signifying "heat" than "flame"—was fully appreciated, and discussions of its essential nature had already begun to link it closely to other concepts, especially light, and the phenomena of static electricity. In order to explain such phenomena as combustion, however, some further elaboration of the concept was necessary, and because it seemed obvious, at first glance, that combustion was a process of emission, producing flame and smoke, it seemed only natural to add a further "principle" to the elementary system that would identify and characterize that emission, and facilitate the analysis of all the different phenomena associated with combustion.

Phlogiston was invented in 1703 by Georg Stahl, who was modifying an earlier theory put forward by the proto-chemist (or "alchemist") Johann Becher. Becher had proposed a modification of classical elementary theory, which rejected fire and water as elements and substituted new forms of earth; water was replaced in his scheme by *terra fluida*, and fire by *terra pinguis*—an element that was supposedly not only responsible for combustible properties but also for "sulfurous" and "oily" properties; *pinguis* is Latin for "fatty" or "greasy." Stahl's phlogiston was a replacement for *terra pinguis*, and became much more popular among proto-chemists, although—as *Le Philosophe sans prétention* makes evident—variants of the older term did survive, usually with modified meanings.

Phlogiston theory was always controversial, and that controversy was thrown into sharper relief in 1772, along with the ailing theory of the classical elements, when the distinct properties of the residue of atmospheric air left after combustion were subjected to widespread study after its isolation by Daniel Rutherford. Rutherford initially referred to the separated component as "fixed air" or "noxious air," although others soon weighed in with "phlogisticated air" and "mephitic air" before Jean-Antoine Chaptal coined "nitrogen" in 1790, having determined that the gas in question was a major component of nitric acid. The negotiation between the terms was more than a mere competition of terminology, because the various concepts implied and embodied different theories—as the debate at the dinner table detailed in *Le Philosophe sans pretention* illustrates, although it would be overstating the case to say that it makes it clear.

Determined investigation of the supposed emission of phlogiston in countless different circumstances had already thrown up a host of anomalies, which had led some chemists to eject the theory, but it was not until the advent of "fixed air" that the accumulation and supplementation of those anomalies was ready to bring about a conclusive "paradigm shift," in which combustion came to be regarded as a process of absorption rather than emission. That now seems obvious to us, because we are perfectly familiar with the idea that the atmosphere is not a mixture of elementary air with "parts" of other elements, but a cocktail of gases, some of them elementary in the context of a much more elaborate scheme of "elements" and some compounded from other elements within that scheme, as well as the idea that one of those gases is oxygen, and that properly-defined combustion is really oxidation.

In 1775, however, the isolation of individual atmospheric gases had only just begun, and oxidation processes were still inextricably confused with other processes occasioned by heating. Oxygen had been isolated in 1773 by Carl Scheele, although the credit is usually given to Joseph Priestley, who was the first to publish the result he obtained independently the following year. The gas was not named, however, until 1777, when Antoine Lavoisier began the classic series of experiments that demonstrated the crucial role played by oxygen in combustion, and began hammering the final nails into phlogiston's coffin. Initially, the atmospheric component in question was labeled "dephlogisticated air," by contrast with "phlogisticated air." La Follie seems unaware of the isolation of "dephlogisticated air" and does not refer to it directly, but he is well aware that the amount of phlogiston supposedly contained in the atmosphere is very variable. In trying to defend phlogiston theory against the threat of the accumulating anomalies, albeit by revising it in an unorthodox manner, he is far more sensitive to arguments about "mephitic air," which derive from the then-unnoticed confusion of the nitrogen left behind by combustion and the gas we would now call carbon dioxide, familiar to La Follie primarily as a product of heating limestone.

The discovery of oxygen was not the only imminent development that would soon serve to discredit the unified theory that La Follie was trying to build. In 1783 the Montgolfier brothers launched the first successful hot air balloon, and they were rapidly followed into the upper atmosphere by scientists making measurements of temperature and pressure. The latter included the French chemist Joseph Gay-Lussac, whose scrupulous measurements, made in 1804, nearly cost him his life when he went up high enough to pass out because of oxygen deprivation. Again, this seems perfectly natural and obvious to us, but in 1775, chemists and physicists still had little acquaintance with the atmosphere beyond the limited effects observed when climbing mountains.

La Follie was admittedly somewhat behind the times in assuming that the extent of elementary air was infinite, and his eccentric interpretation of the theory of gravity was highly unorthodox even in 1775, but there was no very strong evidence then to persuade him that that Earth's atmosphere was a narrow layer beyond which there was vacuum, and the fact that he was a trained chemist enabled him to misunderstand the implications of Newton's laws of motion, retaining the already-obsolete Aristotelian notion of a innate tendency of material objects toward the earth, opposed by an entire illusory "centrifugal force," and a conviction that all motion is basically circular.

In the article on La Follie in his *Encyclopédie de l'utopie, des voyages extraordinaires et de la science-fiction* (1972) Pierre Versins points out the irony of the fact that, because La Follie designed his imaginary electrical spaceship before the Montgolfier brothers began the actual conquest of the air, his invention avoided the trap that almost all the imaginary space journeys undertaken in the next hundred years fell into by employing balloons as interplanetary vehicles. That sidestep was, of course, as accidental as the unfortunate error of trying to build a theory of everything on the basis of phlogiston, and was arguably spoiled by such follies as arguing that Mercury is habitable because the sun is not, in fact, hot (on the basis of a highly idiosyncratic and completely mistaken theory of light), but it is nevertheless true that La Follie deserves some credit for guessing the significance of the phenomena of electricity and anticipating an exciting future for electrical technology.

In sum, it is by no means surprising that the eponymous Philosopher not only gets everything wrong, but spectacularly wrong, in spite of his own smug self-confidence. Even though La Follie's endeavor would undoubtedly seem less crazy and more praiseworthy if his Philosopher had got a few more things right, it is by no means deprived of all interest by its errors, which are intriguing and revealing in themselves, if only in reminding us what vast strides physical science had made in less than two and a half centuries, and how immensely difficult it was, at the beginning of that revolution, to shake off the burden of the old orthodoxies, even for a man utterly determined to do exactly that.

The historical interest of the text is not, however, limited to the pattern of its errors, because its publication also represented a marked development in experimental narrative technique, which serves to illustrate the literary difficulties of inventing a fictional medium that would fuse science and fiction into a viable compound. La Follie's motive for attempting to do that was the same one that moved countless other would-be "popularizers of science" in the next two centuries: to make the scientific account of the world more easily graspable and more entertaining, in order to preserve it from becoming the exclusive esoteric preserve of scholars whose distinctive "misanthropic" characteristics were already becoming evident, and at which La Follie was keen to poke fun. Again, he deserves more marks for effort than actual accomplishment, because *Le Philosophe sans prétention* remains an exceedingly awkward hybrid of philosophical dialogue and sentimental melodrama, but it remains an interesting and enterprising endeavor.

Although its uniqueness is a corollary of its failures rather than its successes, *Le Philosophe sans pretention* still has a certain cachet by virtue of being the one and only significant work of hard science fiction based on phlogiston theory. We probably should not regret the fact that the discovery of oxygen led rapidly to an entirely different theory of combustion, which devastated phlogiston theory and consigned it to the dustbin of conclusively failed ideas, but it is worth noting the irony that it was La Follie's "hardness" as a proto-science fiction writer that led to his manifest obsolescence. Older, vaguer and more mystical ideas derivative of Classical atomic theory lived on in literature, as well as beyond the margins of science in the intellectual wilderness of allegorical alchemy, but La Follie's version of phlogiston theory was a genuine and quintessentially modern scientific theory, for which no such fugitive or cryptic survival was possible. When the theory was devastated, *Le Philosophe sans pretention* was promptly relegated to a new graveyard of ideas: speculative fiction based on subsequently-falsified hypotheses. It was lonely there for a while, but no longer lacks company today.

A grave in that particular cemetery of ideas might not be an enviable status to have, but nor is it entirely ignominious. Its originality warrants *Le Philosophe sans pretention* to a uniquely peculiar status within the history of the uniquely peculiar genre of science fiction, and makes it worthy of attention as a mutant text: a "hopeful monster" that is entitled to our sympathy and ironic appreciation, if not our admiration.

This translation was made from the copy of the Clousier edition reproduced on the Bibliothèque Nationale's *gallica* website.

Brian Stableford

DEDICATORY EPISTLE TO SCHOLARS

Gentlemen,

If, in this work that I have the honor of presenting to you, I have strayed from several principles adopted until the present day; if I have boldly followed my ideas; if I have drawn new conclusions, and claimed to explain many phenomena, good faith had guided my pen. I have no other pretentions than those of self-education. Prove my errors and you will receive nothing from me but thanks. You might perhaps criticize me for enveloping my dissertations in historical illusions. These are my reasons. A beautiful woman simply dressed rarely excites the curiosity of those some distance away, but if that woman advertises herself with an interesting costume, people hasten toward her. Her charms are recognized. People take notice of her. It is the same with Science. How many fine minds would attach themselves to it, and would make useful progress in it, if it excited their curiosity more. That reflection, gentlemen, has directed my plan. I desire that the diversity of objects might fix your attention, and not weary the mind of the enlightened Public, for whose suffrage I am equally ambitious. Then my desires will be fulfilled.

I am, with the most profound respect, gentlemen, your most humble and obedient servant,

D. L. F.

THE UNPRETENTIOUS PHILOSOPHER

Chapter I

Nadir, a rich inhabitant of Chrysopolis,[2] sometimes shut himself away in his library. It was by taste and not by ostentation that he had amassed, at great expense, the most numerous collections of books. Enjoying himself in their possession, he had been occupied for several years in making extracts from all that he had read.

Eventually, no longer finding anything new to extract, except for making continual repetitions, one day, he looked at his notes. Like his library, he had divided them into five parts, to wit: the Arts, Belles-Lettres, Various, Politics and Sciences. Suddenly, he became

---

[2] The city that the ancient Greeks called Chrysopolis has nowadays been absorbed by the urban sprawl of Istanbul, the successor to Byzantium and Constantinople, but retains the independent name of Üsküdar. The Greek name means "city of gold;" opinions vary as to whether it was so named because there was once a gold depository there or because of the way it shone when viewed from Byzantium at sunset. It was the scene of more than one significant battle in the long-running conflict between the Greeks and the Persians; in 1775 Üsküdar was one of three communities outside the city walls of Constantinople—a city that La Follie's novel calls Bisance (a variant of Byzantium) in pursuit of the same calculated archaism.

thoughtful; he reflected with the greatest attention; he became wrapped up in himself.

Finally, after mature examination, he said to himself: "That's enough; I need to get rid of a lot of books whose uselessness I now realize."

He rang. A few slaves came in.

Firstly, he indicated the section of the library that contained books concerning the Arts, and said: "Take all these Latin, Greek, Arabic and French folios, and all these more modern octavos and duodecimos; don't forget the marvelous secrets of Porta, Mizaud, Albert, Paxame, Africain, Alexis, Cardan, Varron, Tarentin, Hallerius, Silvius, etc., etc.[3] Take them all away. Only leave these

---

[3] This eccentric list of names mingles Classical writers with Renaissance writers, the latter including some who became notorious after their deaths, perhaps unjustly, for their interest in occult sciences; it is not obvious why they would be aggregated in the Arts section of Nadir's library, even though La Follie's "Arts" means something closer to our "technology" than "fine arts." The books in question presumably include Giambattista della Porta's *Magiae Naturalis* [Natural Magic] (1558); Antoine Mizaud's *Harmonia coelestium corporum et humanorum* [Celestial, Corporeal and Human Harmony] (1555); all 38 volumes of the collected works of Albertus Magnus; and Girolamo Cardano's *De Subtitlitate* [On Subtility—i.e., Transcendental Philosophy] (1552). No books by the Classical author Paxamus survive, the name only being known via secondary references, but he was credited, perhaps apocryphally, with a guide to erotic positions known as the *Dodecatechnon*. "Africanus" is presumably the Moorish diplomat Joannes Leo Africanus, whose geographical history of Africa, pubished in 1526, includes a probably-apocryphal account of the Alchemical Society of Fez. "Alexis" is presumably the Greek comic poet, none of whose works survive in complete form. The same fate befell almost all the 74 works of

two new Dictionaries, one of which, although very voluminous, only contains useful items. Wait a moment..."

Nadir got up, and opened those Dictionaries. He was about to rip out a number of pages, but the fear of damaging the binding caused him to abandon his project.

"Why," he exclaimed, dolorously, "has our Grand Vizier not settled the fate of a few celebrated Artists, who would then have been more faithful? The Scholars who have composed this immortal Work could not be universal, and their solicitations were encouragements too sterile for Artists."

To his slaves, he said: "Oh well, get rid of it all, completely. Take these books to the Dervishes at the Great Mosque; it's a present I'm giving them. Tell them that I make no claim of their amity in recognition; that it will be sufficient for me to be assured that they will never be my enemies. Go."

Immediately, Nadir rang. Four more slaves appeared. He rang again. Eight more slaves appeared. It was a matter of moving out the Belles-Lettres section. "Go on," he said to them, "Be brave. It's necessary to pick up and take to the Dervishes this curtain of books. From here to there, you see: sixty feet long by fifteen high. Go to work.

---

the Roman scholar Marcus Terentius Varro. Plato's friend Archytas, also known as Tarentinus, was reputed to be the founder of mathematical mechanics. The Swiss physician and naturalist Albrecht von Haller, or Albertus Hallerius, who was still alive in 1775, is an odd and slightly mischievous inclusion, presumably occasioned by his extensive contributions to Diderot's *Encyclopédie*, of which La Follie did not entirely approve. "Silvius" is presumably Aeneas Silvius Piccolomini (1405-1464), or Pope Pius II, a prolific writer sometimes known as "the humanist pope."

"In the meantime, let's see what I've put in reserve in this space of ten feet. Firstly, here are a number of excellent theatrical dramas. Good—all these books are to my taste. Today, the theater is the best school of morals. I've done well, of course, to send away a few productions keeping company with the Greek historians, as well as several gigantic cruelties as ridiculous as complaints against performance. I therefore only see in the collection, at present, the criticism of vice put into action, and that will always produce more effect than five thousand tomes of fastidious moralizing.

"Here is another genre of heroic examples of the most sublime virtue—examples more capable of educating and transporting heart than the thousand arid and monotonous thought convulsively emitted by a few atrabilious heads.

"Here are other poems, in which the unity of time and place does not hinder the authors at all, and whose outcomes are fortunate. The heroes punish vice and do good deeds. Good books! Excellent books! My choice in that regard isn't numerous, but it's well made.

"Journals...yes, journals; I was right to keep them; there are very good ones that bring to light the efforts of the human mind and appreciate them judiciously.

"Books of History...I've kept two authors on each subject, in order to be acquainted with the most elegant writer and the most insipid. Have I done well? I have, therefore, presumed that the latter is the more veridical...error, error! Each is equally likely to be the dupe of a feeble genius or a man of intelligence, and I prefer to be agreeably deceived. Slaves, you can also take away the two hundred volumes on this shelf.

"Let's go on. What! I've left novels here. Yes, novels. Let's consult my notes. *The moral is charming. In-*

vention full of genius. Features clearer and more convincing than all those folios of absurd and tedious metaphysics. But I see on my reserved shelves all the works of the Old Man of Nerfey, that old man who is still young, or, rather, still in the prime of life, whose fecund genius takes a thousand agreeable forms.[4] Academicians of Chrysopolis, who never cease issuing, in the matter of prizes, eulogies to authors that death has harvested, give me the satisfaction of issuing one to a living man. Believe me, the insult that is made to the modesty of an illustrious man is soon pardoned, and be sure that by following this advice, the rivalry and activity of working authors would acquire new force.

"With regard to Panegyrics, I've kept very few. Indeed, many writers in that genre have worked more for themselves than the subject they were treating. They have often sacrificed the truth to the charms of pompous hyperbolic phrases. They would have done better, when they produced their works, to have contented themselves with applauding their heroes.

"But what do I see? Here, in the reserve, a large number of fugitive pieces: tales, light-hearted epistles, love poems, sensual and erotic... My word, all that is charming. Is not Amour the master of nature? Is it not the play of the imagination that distinguishes us from the animals in that regard? Thus, I esteem these young poets, which light pen offers us agreeably varied scenes, and I laugh to see those severe censors, who publicly

---

[4] La Follie's contemporary readers would immediately have recognized a subtle transfiguration of *le Vieillard de Ferney* [the Old Man of Ferney], Ferney having been the location of Voltaire's residence since 1758, where he eventually died in 1778.

criticize works whose basis is delicacy, and which amuse themselves clandestinely with obscene trivialities."

Nadir urged his slaves on, and those men, who did not have a Bibliomaniac's respect with regard to books, were rapidly grabbing piles of quartos and octavos and throwing them into large baskets. Many items still remained to be moved out.

Nadir rang. Eight more slaves appeared. He showed them an immense section, containing more than three thousand volumes, concerning the different religions reducible to one great principle. All those authors had made, according to their whim, a little painting of the great principle, and each of them claimed that one could only see the Creator of the Universe clearly through the lens that they offered you. Nadir thought about how much harm the different visions resulting from all these lenses had done to the population and the happiness of States; how many intrigues, cabals, bloody wars, odious murders...

Engrossed in that horrible memory, he said, fervently: "Slaves, pick up this mass of volumes promptly, and take them to the Dervishes; if they ask what choice I have made among them, tell that that I have only kept one single book, that the book in question is my heart, and that it only contains two precise articles—but that in observing them, I shall still be the friend of the great principle, and of the Emperor and my peers.

"Let's see, what is this book in my reserve section? *Treatise on Tol...Toler*...but what's this? Six copies... Yes, I remember. So much the better. That book can never be multiplied sufficiently. I'd like all sovereigns to have one printed in letters of gold, and that those printed pages should carpet the steps of their thrones. One cannot distribute excessively a work that tends to the happiness of humankind. I'll have four copies sent to my wives."

Chapter II

A young princess brought up in Pannonia[5] had become the cherished spouse of the Emperor of Bisance, and since that time, everyone there had been convinced that the most charming bodies could be organized by the most beautiful souls. That truth was not new to Nadir, however. The amiable Mirza, his favorite, had often astonished him with judicious reflections, which characterizes the most elevated soul within her.

Three other agreeable wives comprised his entire seraglio—which is to say, his familial company, for he had no Seraglio. They enjoyed complete freedom of movement in the city. Why inhibit these charming beings, he said to himself, who only seek to please me; if, too occupied with the amiable Mirza to be in any state to distract myself with other wives, I can only offer them illusory amusements, I would be a barbarian to constrain their liberty further.

Nadir's house was, therefore, not the house of an Asiatic, but rather than of an intelligent Frenchman, who knows where pleasure exists. His meals, amusing suppers, at which the fair sex did the honors, often procured him the most agreeable guests, which the wives occupied themselves in pleasing.

---

[5] Pannonia was an ancient province of the Roman Empire, covering an area now distributed between Hungary, Austria and various Balkan States. The reference might have in mind Ayse Sine, the Bulgarian-born first wife of the Ottoman Sultan who had come to the throne in 1774, Abdul Hamid I; she was still a teenager in 1775.

Emerging from his library, Nadir went to Mirza's apartment. She was not there.

What? At eleven o'clock in the morning, Mirza was absent? She never went out at such an early hour. Nadir was anxious, but it was not the base anxiety that simultaneously makes for the martyrdom of the jealous and the torment of lovely women. No, more delicate sentiments were preoccupying Nadir when, at that very moment, Mirza came in vivaciously, followed by two slaves. They were carrying a quantity of prints and paintings.

"I've surprised you," she said to Nadir, giving him the most animated greeting. "Your first slaves told me about the removal of your library. I want to replace the items of which you are getting rid. Look, my friend, here is a spectacle more lively than a mass of sad writings. You can see in all these animated engravings the striking expression of an infinity of sentiments, Look, first, at this good father in the midst of his honest children, sometimes instructing them and sometimes receiving from them the support of filial love. Agree with me that these two prints cause more sensation than a hundred educational volumes by your writers, who have never educated anyone.

"Look at these storms, these shipwrecks, whose horrible beauty instantly provokes more reflections on the cupidity of humans than all those long works on the extraction of the world's wealth. Look at this new bride, whose naïve features offer a symbol of candor. Agree that this painting of Virtue is more seductive than a hundred volumes of moralizing nonsense. Look at these...but leave my paintings alone. Oh, you're very curious!"

"What, Mirza, you've bought so many pastel drawings! It's necessary to admit that you have confused trifles with beautiful things."

"Really, sir! Lovely portraits of women, trifles? Well, you shall not have them. But look at them, in good faith—is there anything more beautiful than the situation of this head? Look at those eyes, that mouth, that divine smile, the charming coloring. Admire the various poses of these other pictures. Think seriously, sir, think, that to paint a lovely women in all her attitudes is to paint the soul of nature with all its nuances. Agree, my dear Nadir, that you merit that lesson."

"Yes, Mirza, but you are my excuse. What painting, next to you, can...no matter; I accept these portraits; they shall go in my library. Besides which, beauty, in whatever form it might take, always reminds me of my dear Mirza."

Nadir proceeded, insensibly, to engage in even more expressive compliments, but Mirza, more tender than passionate, sometimes forbade Nadir compliments of that sort. She was in one of those prohibitive moods. "Come and see your wives," she said, taking him by the hand. "Come and see your friends. It's midday. You haven't been there yet; that's terrible; we shall be mocked and chided, so come along."

At first, Nadir was draw along reluctantly, but the impetuosity of his desires eventually calmed down and no longer slowed his pace.

Mirza had anticipated correctly. Fatima, Laure and Sophie all began to chide Nadir and Mirza. There is nothing in the world more charming than the union of four intelligent women. Nadir's choice was made, and yet the three unchosen wives had remained friends with Nadir and Mirza—friends devoid of pretentions, and without jealousy for the lot of their companion, who also loved them in good faith.

O liberty, what miracles you work in Chrysopolis! Four lovely women, sincere friends! But why, in Lutece,[6] where everyone is free, does one only find the phantoms of such a society?

Why, because there are very few Nadirs there, and inconstancy has multiplied pretensions there.

Someone observed to Nadir that hours are moments when one is enjoying oneself. Already, a few Bachas,[7] great friends of his table, had arrived in the drawing room and were waiting for the time to dine. The pleasure of having an open table was often an inconvenience to Nadir but it had been useful to him. Besides, when poor conversationalists had bored him, he had subsequently sought all the more eagerly, for the sake of contrast, the company of a few guests as crazy as they were agreeable.

That day's meal was not pleasant. First there were old reflections on good and bad weather, and then old news recounted in two hundred sentences, of which a hundred and eighty were redundant. Then there were details of the day's funeral orations, capable of furnishing their authors with new works, and finally reflections the uselessness of the science of heraldry, and the significance of a Bacha's coat of arms with three tails, etc., etc. Scarcely had the dessert been served than Nadir made a sign to his wives that he would leave them the care of following such uninteresting conversation, and he retired to his library.

He had reached the Politics section.

---

[6] An old name for Paris.
[7] La Follie's rendering of "Pashas."

"Let's see," he said, "what shall I put in the reserve on that subject? First, the regulations of our Emperor, his ordinances founded on constitutional laws. Very good. The constitutional laws of our country are very fine, but I hope that a few of them can be reduced to a single specification. In fact, in all countries belonging to a single Emperor, the laws ought to be the same, and it's ridiculous that, from one territory to another, it's the surveyor's staff or the situation of a Mosque that determines the fashion in which it must be obeyed.

"Here are excellent theoretical works on laws; there are very few of them. Here's the first one to put in the reserve and with distinction. Let's keep this one. This one? All right, but that's enough. The best of what there was in Antiquity has been extracted in these books, so I no longer need that original hotchpotch in all languages, in which a little common sense is mingled with so much extravagance. It hardly matters to me to see in an original that marks of consideration were once given in one country to the most skillful thieves, while they are presently given to a very different species. These few volumes on laws will suffice; let's get rid of all the rest.

"But, O Heavens, what a quantity of Commentators! Erudite gentlemen, I say to you that far from sensing the utility of your works, I see that your commentaries sometimes only serve as means of evading the law and have become the seeds of dispute. Believe that Calideleskers[8] are as capable as you are at interpreting the law according to circumstances, and I am not at all sure that your talents have not produced more harm than good; besides, I'm told that our young Emperor will

---

[8] This word does not appear to exist anywhere but in this single reference, so its meaning has to be deduced from context.

soon devote himself to the interpretation of certain articles of law, by means of articles that will be added to the law, and will serve to interpret them. Then there will be considerably less resource for bad faith.

"Let's have a look now at this prodigious heap of pamphlets. There are treatises on politics, financial projects, patriotic opinions. In truth, Authors, do you think that our accredited viziers occupying seats in the great Divan Hall don't have a field of view as extensive as you in your studies? Believe that if you had been able to give ten million sequins to our previous viziers, or that you had been able to assure them of the security of their seats, they might perhaps have effected the beautiful things that you have imagined—but with these fine thoughts on one side, and a hundred gold marks on the other, the balance is unequal. Furthermore, we now have a favorite of the Emperor whose intelligence and probity will never grow old; we also have viziers as enlightened and virtuous as their master. I therefore have no more need of all your tales. Get out of my house. Go occupy the Dervishes, for they dabble to some extent in everything."

Chapter III

Finally, there was the question of clearing out the section of the Sciences. Nadir was very embarrassed. He did not have sufficient knowledge to make firm decisions in that regard.

He has put in the reserve books of algebraic calculations, the elements of mathematics and geometry, but for matters of Physics, and the new elements of Chemistry—that science which embraces all of nature, whose theory always seems founded on experience but in which he nevertheless sees an infinite number of opposed opinions—he is suspended in indecision. He picks up a book, and put it down again. He picks up another, and puts that one down again. He walks around, he sits down. He thinks.

"Just as I expected," an unknown voice suddenly exclaims.

Surprised, Nadir looks up; there does not appear to be anyone there. His slaves have all gone. Convinced that the sound was only the effect of his imagination, he has resumed thinking when the same voice repeats the same words, distinctly. Then he springs to his feet.

He searches, and soon perceives, in a sheltered corner of his library, a man reading a scientific work.

That face was not absolutely unknown to Nadir; his library being open to all the scholars in Chrysopolis, he recalled having seen it there before, but the memory was vague. In fact, the man, a trifle taciturn, modestly dressed with a polite simplicity, had not been much noticed by Nadir, and even less so by the pretentious individuals who often came to spend time in the library in order to offer opinions on science.

However, Nadir found what the man had said to be very singular. "I would like to know, sir," he said, honestly, "what you think about the book you're reading."

"It's very good," said the stranger, looking at Nadir with an affectionate vivacity, "but I would say the same to the author as to you. This is why: he has clearly demonstrated the movement of the Earth and the other planets around the sun, but, still enslaved to general prejudice, he thinks that the sun is a fiery body; in consequence, when he sees by his calculations that Mercury is so close to the sun, he has difficulty deducing what quality the surface of that planet might have, in order that it should be neither consumed not volatilized by the sun. It was by reason of that embarrassment that I said to him, as I said to you, that it was just what I expected.

"Well, my dear Nadir, I want to render you a service. I can see your embarrassment in choosing between all your books of science. You shall soon know enough to appreciate each of these works according to its value. I am a philosopher, but a philosopher by taste and not by ostentation—so don't imagine that I owe my origin to your globe. I am, as you can see, an inhabitant of Mercury. It is with the aid of an ingenious discovery that I have risen or descended to the world that you inhabit. I say 'risen or descended' because, as you know, in the extent of the Universe, there is neither up nor down, nor center nor extremities.

"I will tell you, briefly, how I came to undertake my voyage.

"All the people of our globe are active. The climate is almost the same as yours, although it is closer to the sun; I will explain the reasons. Although out planet is fertile in men of intelligence, we nevertheless only have one Luminacy—that is what you call an Academy—and that Luminacy is only comprised by a dozen Sages or Incumbents.

"That small number will doubtless surprise you, but know that in order to be a Luminacian on Mercury it is necessary to have made either important discoveries in science or to have produced genuinely new works of literature. It is also necessary for a Luminacian to have renounced permanently the great display of petty prestige, the fury for making a name by means of erroneous theories, the mania of wanting to rise by debasing others, and, finally, those unsustainable pretentions that are sometimes presented beneath the veil of modesty. The number of aspirants is sixty. It is from among those aspirants that the replacements are chosen for Luminacians who return to the great principle of light, but in making those choices, no attention is paid either to the order of seniority or the quantity of published works; merit alone decides.

"I am one of those aspirants, who put myself forward for election at the recent promotion for work in science. The assembly had been convened. Already, the twelve Sages were looking at my work. They took extracts, comparing my reflections in summary, examining the connections between them, their verity and utility. I was quite certain that I had only exposed faithfully verified experiments, not imagined in order to present or support ridiculous theories. I was quite certain that I had stripped away, in that regard, all pretentions, and that, having sought only to educate myself, my reflections could only be more justified in consequence. I therefore awaited my fate with mild anxiety—which is to say, less anxiety that many of your scientists would probably have had if they submitted themselves, without self-regard, to a similar examination.

"The twelve Sages were in closed session; the aspirants, who had no place in that examination, were walking around in a nearby room, according to custom, when all of a sudden, Scintilla, one of our young companions, from whom we had already seen some good works, arrived hurriedly, knocked on the door of the Sages' conference room, and asked to be admitted.

"That request was contrary to the rules. It was refused.

"He insisted fervently. 'My friends,' he said, turning to us, 'help me—it's necessary that we should all go in momentarily. I only want a five-minute hearing.'

"The Sages immediately ceded to the fuss they heard, having, in any case, no arrogance—or, rather, the pettiness of believing that the infraction of the rules impacted on their authority or their merit—and granted the general audience.

"Scarcely had everyone gone in than Scintilla addressed the assembly. 'Gentlemen,' he said, 'as no mortals can be certain of the successive instants of their existence, I thought I ought not to delay for a single moment in making you party to an interesting discovery. For a long time, people have been seeking to discover be what mechanical means they might cross aerial spaces. I am glad to be able to tell you today of the success of my research.'

"He proffered a manuscript, saying, 'Here it is—but the manuscript is not sufficient. The theory, although quite simple, will perhaps not be sufficiently intelligible, with respect to such a new subject. Thus, before arriving at a theoretical conclusion, let us carry out an experiment. Two slaves have carried my apparatus on to the platform of out Tower. Let us go up there.'

"Scarcely had he stopped talking than our dozen Sages looked at one another with evident surprise, but without any hint of scorn. Several of us, by contrast, smiled, and, being more indiscreet than the others, I burst out laughing.

"Immediately, the doyen of the Luminacians criticized me coldly. 'Ormasis,' he said to me, 'we were unaware of this streak of arrogance within you, of believing that which you cannot imagine to be absolutely impossible. It is necessary to correct it. If Scintilla's discovery is sound, do not think it inappropriate that we occupy ourselves with him in preference to you.'

"'Willingly,' I replied, swiftly. 'If Scintilla's discovery is sound, not only will I not be jealous of Scintilla's merit, and render him all possible homage, but I promise, I swear, not to reappear in this august assembly until I have, with the aid of that machine, visited Hermione'—that is what we call the world you inhabit.

"Scintilla was not annoyed by my incredulity, because on our planet, scholars do not get annoyed. On the contrary, he came to grasp my hand amicably. 'I won't demand,' he said, 'that you keep your word. The author of such a perilous vehicle ought to run the first risks. I would be inconsolable if I deprived the Company of a member as useful as you.' He went out immediately, asking the assembly to follow him. We followed him.

"I went with the others. I reflected privately, calculating that the movement of levers to form a sufficient resistance—which is to say, to embrace a large volume of air—demanded a considerable force of power; that in consequence, the fulcrum of that force or power must be comprised of a very solid material, and, the specific weight of that substance thus having to be increased proportionately, that it would be impossible for such a machine to rise up.

"In sum, I imagined a machine with wings, in much the same terms as you have envisaged the canonical vehicle of which the phaeton is the earthbound model. How surprised I was, therefore, when I arrived on the platform, to see two glass spheres three feet in diameter, mounted on top of a small and quite comfortable seat.[9] Four wooden struts covered with sheets of glass supported the two spheres. Between the struts there were several springs, which I assumed to have the function of setting the globes in motion. The bottom section that served as the supportive of the seat was a plate coated with camphor and covered in gold leaf. The top was circled by metal wires.

"As soon as I had seen that new form of electrical machine, I became less incredulous regarding Scintilla's success. I remembered that he had already published interesting papers on that subject. He had rationally explained the electrical causes of certain effects, such, as, for example, the division of gold by the percussion of light, and its reassembled in its original form by a further movement. He had also demonstrated to us that the violet tint of litmus, converted into red by an electric pulse, was nothing but the effect of sulfurous parts contained in the air, which, decomposed by the inflammation of

---

[9] The notion of the glass spheres was presumably derived from La Follie's acquaintance with the Leyden Jar, a device for storing static electricity invented in the 1740s. Such jars were often connected up to increase the stored charge, into what Benjamin Franklin, who conducted an extensive study of electrical phenomena in the 1750s, called a "battery."

phlogiston, left the acidic fraction exposed, and sufficient acid to turn the tincture red. There had not been any decomposition of the air in that experiment, but only the decomposition of sulfurous parts contained within it. Finally, Scintilla had already explained to us an infinite number of petty phenomena similar to those that are now astonishing the scholars of your world, and allowing them to extrapolate consequences as far as the eye can see. I confess to you, therefore, my dear Nadir, that the closer I got to that machine, the more my surprise and credulity increased.

"I soon had no further doubts on the matter. Scintilla, whose body was as nimble as my imagination, slowly climbed into the machine, and promptly pulled a lever. We saw the two globes rotate with a prodigious rapidity. 'Gentlemen,' he said, 'you can see that in order to lift myself up in the air, my principal means is to annul the pressure of the atmosphere above my head. Observe that the percussion of the light is presently acting underneath my machine. That is what will lift me up without much effort, and, as the master of the motion of my globes, I can go up of down to whatever extent I choose. You can also see...'

"But we heard nothing more. His machine, suddenly surrounded by a luminous circle, had risen up at great speed. No spectacle so new and so beautiful had ever been offered to our eyes. We saw it remain motionless for a brief interval, then descend again, then rise anew. Finally, we lost sight of it.

"After our initial rapture of admiration, we reflected on the dangers that our friend was running. We did not doubt the solidity of his machine, but how could he withstand such a rapid flight without being suffocated?

"The doyen of the Sages set our minds at rest, however. 'Gentlemen,' he said to us, reflect on what we observed during the departure. Has he not assured us that he could nullify the pressure of the atmosphere above his head? Now, the effect of which he is making use is not that of vanquishing the resistance of the air by means of a force greater than that resistance, so I am confident that he is breathing with the same facility as us. I even believe that the rotatory motion of the globes must drive away from him the water vapor in the atmosphere that might have inconvenienced him, and I further presume that the same movement must maintain a warm and fairly agreeable temperature.'

"These judicious reflections reassured us. Indeed, after waiting for an hour, we saw Scintilla reappearing. His competent steering movements assured us that he was in possession of his mental faculties and his strength. When he came closer to us he descended more slowly, and set down in almost exactly the same spot from which he had taken off.

"You might perhaps think, Nadir, that our friend, on leaving his seat, would have been radiant with joy and pride, that he would have boasted of his importance by virtue of that of his discovery, and demand the tribute of our respects, like those petty individuals of Chrysopolis who, having presented their Luminacy with some minor saline compound, imagine that the Hippodrome is not large enough to contain them. Make no such mistake. Scintilla embraced us. We also embraced him with the greatest cordiality.

"'My friends,' he said to us, 'you would surely have made this discovery before me, if you had occupied yourselves with it, but the other objects that have excited our endeavors are no less important. This discovery

47

would be of very minor importance if we did not have the hope of traveling to the different globes of the Universe and augmenting our knowledge. I count on leaving tomorrow, and first plunging into the brilliant river that illuminates us, and from which we are not far distant. I want to discover, if possible, the principles of light.'

"'No, my dear Scintilla,' I replied, 'I cannot allow you to make such voyages. Your fecund imagination is too useful to our Company for you to risk your life. I shall go. Stay with our Sages, who will admit you to their number. I shall, as I promised, travel to Hermione. We have already presumed, by virtue of the ephemeral disappearances of that planet, that it is not luminous itself, since it is subject to being eclipsed by the interpolation of other opaque globes between itself and the sun. Now, the resemblance of that earthen body with ours tells me that there is little danger in visiting it. When I have explored that world, I shall pass close to the sun as I return, and then I shall make you party to my observations.'

"I went home immediately. I took a large provision of nutritive powder. I also took several of our phosphoric stones, but I only took them in order to furnish myself with light in case of need; I did not foresee then that those stones, very common on our world, would be of such great utility in yours.

"I returned to the platform. I found Scintilla there, who was instructing the assembly. I obtained from him the instructions necessary to regulate my progress as I wished. Finally, I left, with the admiration and regrets of my friends."

Chapter IV

"It was already night, but my flight in the direction of Hermione soon transported me beyond the projected shadow of our planet. The further I drew away, the more rapid my progress became, without my being obliged to accelerate my motion.

"Eventually, after five hours of flight, I found myself equidistant from the Earth and the Moon. I examined both globes carefully. Yours seemed to me to be larger, but otherwise, it presented the same spectacle as the Moon. I noticed that there were, as on the Moon, parts that were brighter than others. I deduced, rightly, that the parts of your globe were there were larger masses of cloud or water were reflecting the rays of the sun more vividly than those where there were no clouds, and I was not simple enough to believe that it was valleys and mountains that were forming those inequalities of light.

"In fact, by precipitating myself into the most luminous part of your globe, I soon perceived that I was surrounded by thick mist which obscured my view, because the rays of light, instead of being reflected toward me, were being intercepted. Imagine a diver who, walking on the shore, can hardly look at the water sparkling with light, when the sun's rays are reflected there, but who, when moving beneath those same waters, only enjoys a dim light. That, my friend, is the explanation of what are improperly called by you the moon's patches. That first instruction, my dear Nadir, is very slight, but I can easily, in all circumstances, free your mind from the error of prejudices.

"I soon perceived that it was necessary to counter a greater atmospheric pressure in order not to fall precipitately on to your planet. My machine was rotated into the appropriate position, and as I experienced increasingly greater weight, I increased the motion of my globes. Eventually, however, distracted by the spectacle that was presented to my eyes, which was a valley ornamented by a quantity of pleasant houses, I unfortunately fell on to a mountain with too much weight, and my two globs were broken.

"I was desolate, but in the end I conceived the hope of repairing the damage. For two years now I have been searching your planet fruitlessly for the metal with which those globes of electrical glass are formed on our planet. None of the new metals presently known to your scholars is the basis of that vitrification, exempt from bulges and furrows. I have taken every imaginable trouble in that respect. I have searched every country. I have even discovered an opening in one of your mountains by means of which I penetrated into the most profound cavities of your planet, without discovering the metal in question. I have not given up. I am still searching, and hoping.

"I shall not tell you now in unnecessary detail about the various adventures I have had since that time. I shall only cite one feature, which contains a few instructive reflections.

"You can easily imagine that my phosphoric stones, which were superb diamonds, furnished my needs abundantly. One day, however, I sacrificed one in a bad temper—which is to say, with the sole intention of punishing a man who deserved it.

"I developed a habit of going to visit all the authors whose books I read. Sometimes, I chatted with pleasure to reasonable men, but I often found men obstinate in their ideas, convinced that they know everything, dishonest, and thinking it impossible that they might be wrong. One day, I was in the home of one of these pretended and self-infatuated scholars, when he was brought the public news. He read therein that hard-working men had just assured themselves by various experiments that diamond could be volatilized by fire. Immediately, my man flew into a fury.

"'Is it possible,' he cried, 'that the public can be deceived by such dreams, and that someone had had the effrontery to pass conjuring tricks off as experiments?'

"'Gently,' I said. 'Calm down, sir. Reflect, I beg you, on the fact that diamond is a phosphoric stone, a substance containing a great deal of phlogiston, very little water and almost no air; and that, by that very reason, at the moment of phlogistic inflammation that splits all solid molecules, it makes no sensible explosion.'

"'Very good, Master logician,' he replied, "but tell me, what is your phlogiston? I don't know it myself, this phlogiston; it's just a word.'

"'Yes, I replied, 'it's a word, but I can take responsibility for explaining the word to you. I can at least take responsibility for explaining sensibly a principle intelligible to all the physicists in the universe, and the effects of that principle; afterwards, you can change the word, if you want to.'

"'Oh, damn it, I won't even listen to you; you'll only spout chemical nonsense.'

"'All right, let's not say any more about it—but I hope, at least, that you know a diamond when you see one.' I took one out of my pocket. 'What do you think of this one? Has it a beautiful clarity?'

"Instantly, I saw my man in admiration; he admitted that he had never seen one as beautiful. 'That's not all,' I added, 'show me that ring on your finger.'

"He confessed that it was nothing by comparison with my diamond, although it had cost him two thousand sequins. 'Would you care to pick up a fragment of crystal?' I asked. 'A topaz or a ruby—and we'll go into a dark place.'

"He came with me. I had hidden my diamond. First, I rubbed his with a cloth. My man was quite astonished that, by means of such a feeble friction, his diamond produced light. I then made him rub his other stones, which did not yield any light. 'You see,' I said, then, 'that your diamond is a substance more phosphoric than these other stones, and, in consequence, more phlogisticated.'

"At the same time I showed him my diamond, which, by virtue of the friction of the air alone, was emitting flashes of bright light. 'Let's go back into your apartment. Would you like us to put our two diamonds, in that fire, which isn't very fierce. According to you, they should be able to resist it.'

"'Willingly,' he replied. 'I'm not afraid, and I want to prove to you my certainty in that regard. Blow on it if you wish, there's no danger.' Immediately, that was done Suddenly, we perceived an exceedingly bright flash. My man then feared that something had happened but it was too late to remedy it. I bid him good day, asking him to investigate whether the rapid phlogistical combustion on my stone had accelerated the inflammation of his. He never saw me again, and I'm quite sure that he has not seen the two diamonds that I put into his fire.

"But I perceive, my dear Nadir, that I'm keeping you here for a long time, and perhaps contrary to your wishes."

"Not at all," Nadir replied, eagerly. "Your story has affected me singularly. Stay with me, my dear Ormasis. I will work with you. I shall educate myself. I too will devote myself to the search for the vitrifiable metal that is the object of your desire. I would like you to be entirely happy. You could not be more interesting to me. Stay with me. My heart, my purse..."

"Your heart, Nadir, I know; it is excellent. I accept your friendship. Of your purse I have no need. Be here tomorrow at the same time; I'll make a few introductions, and I shall be charmed if they amuse you."

Immediately, Ormasis left, with such promptness that, for a moment, Nadir scarcely perceived the separation.

The first sensations caused by a new and interesting story, are as seductive as the reading of certain books. Often, a reflective examination destroys the charms of the illusion. Dazzled by the scientific glimmers that Ormasis had inserted into his story, and carried away by the Philosopher's confident tone, Nadir had yielded entirely to confidence, but he soon hesitated to believe such adventures.

He went down into his gardens. There he encountered Mirza, who had come to enjoy the coolness of a beautiful evening.

"Dear Mirza," he said to her, "you find me pensive. Men are made to think, but your sex has the same rights. Share with me my surprise and my doubts. Raise your eyes. Look at those stars shining above your head. Look, in particular at the star toward the est. You know that it is the planet closest to the day star. Well, would you believe that it is inhabited nevertheless by humans like us? Would you believe that one of its inhabitants has come to our globe, that that rare man has just been conversing with me, that he has told me how he came to make his journey, with singular details…you're laughing. Wait a moment; we'll see which of us will be the more credulous."

Immediately, Nadir told Mirza Ormasis' story. He depicted all the circumstances for her with the same style and the same vivacity as the Philosopher. He added the same reflections to it, painted a picture of the dignity of the man who was proposing to instruct him, and who, accepting his friendship, had refused the offer of his purse.

In the end, Mirza was greatly affected by the story. "I no longer doubt it," she said. "This man's adventure has a character of truth that seduces me. Do not reflections as clear as his, in order to be perceived, need to rise above the shadows of imposture? My dear Nadir, retain the man tomorrow, in order that he can reside with you, and converse with us. I have many questions to ask him. Are the women of his planet lovely? How do they dress? Do they love as I love? Oh, my friend, if that man finally found the metal he desires, if he succeeded in repairing his machine, and if he offered to take you with him, would you consent? Would you be curious enough about those novelties to abandon me? My soul, as subtle as the electric fire that had raised you up, would soon catch up with you, but when you returned to our Earth, you would no longer find your Mirza here; at last, you would no longer find these animated organs, these feeble charms that you idolize, happy interpreters of my tenderness. Promise me, my friend, swear to me..."

"Yes," Nadir interjected, "I swear that my love will never make any sacrifice to curiosity. But my dear Mirza, you were making fun of this adventure a little while ago, as I predicted. Am I not the less credulous, for I think that the man is only a joker—but a very agreeable and learned joker? He ought to be all the more dearer to me for having given birth in you to fears regarding my fate, which you have expressed to me with the most expressive brush of sentiment. Divine Mirza..."

"My dear Nadir..."

Mirza sat down and leaned back against grassy steps, considering the countless globes that were above her head.

"Can there be any limit to the immensity of that creation?"

"No," Nadir replied, "and our greatest astronomer, if he were transported to one of the satellites of Jupiter, would be obliged to study a new sphere. See, Mirza, how small human beings are."

"That's what I can't perceive," Mirza replied. "Indeed, according to the principles of your Philosopher, everything can only be judged by comparison. There is, therefore, nothing great or small in Nature, since it has neither extremities nor a center. I therefore sense demonstratively that only comparisons can be drawn between one thing and another. Agree that I'm a good philosopher...but why are you amusing yourself staring at me. Look at the Heavens."

"I can see them."

"The light of those stars has a softness, a beauty..."

"Reflected in your eyes, it has much more interest..."

"I'm going to close them."

"Mirza...that's cruel...wait a moment."

"No, Nadir, I can't do it any longer. A delightful dream is lifting me up..."

Nadir and Mirza were having almost the same dream. The Philosopher's voyage was retraced in their imagination—but Nadir's dream was a little more occupied with details. Mirza dreamed that she had been lifted by Nadir into the Heavens of the Prophet. Nadir imagined himself touching the two agitated globes. He felt himself rising up, then descending gradually, then rising up again. In sum, the electrical movement carried him more than once into the Heavens of the Prophet.

Several voyages in one dream are sometimes tiring. Nadir perceived that a little before Mirza, but they awoke simultaneously. Their conversation, less animated than the dream, as nevertheless interesting. A similar awakening is the touchstone of spiritual beings. Nadir and Mirza had never known those hours of tedium which, in certain intimate confrontations, often succeed a few minutes of occupation.

Those hours, however, which were nothing themselves but the details of a dream, went by rapidly. They went back to the circle of their Company, but decided to keep the secret of the encounter with the Philosopher.

Chapter IV

Nadir waited impatiently for the moment that ought to bring Ormasis back to him, Having arrived at the rendezvous first, he walked around the library, looking at the clock from time to time. Already anxious, the fear that he might not see his Philosopher again tormented him—but Ormasis appeared, and joy was reborn in Nadir's heart.

"I don't know, amiable stranger, what charm your person exudes, but the anxiety that I have just experienced persuades me that your company has become a portion of my happiness."

"Your compliment is sincere, my dear Nadir, and yet it is still merely the effect of an illusion. Yes, motives of curiosity are what presently determine your friendship, but one day, I shall have other rights over your heart. Yesterday, after leaving you, I went to that opening in the earth that I mentioned to you. I judged by the heat of the vapors that there will soon be an explosion, and, in consequence, new openings in the masses of rocks. How glad I would be if I were able to find my metal there! I intend to continue my research after nightfall."

"Why risk yourself thus?" replied Nadir. "What light can suffice to guide your steps in those abysses? Are your diamonds luminous enough?"

"No, my dear Nadir, I have no need of them. Those profound cavities are illuminated by continual flashes of lightning."

"Is there not, besides," Nadir continued, "the kind of fire that is called the central fire?"

"Words, words," Ormasis put in. "There is only one species of fire in nature. First, I shall explain to you the truth of the great principle, regarding which there have been so many erroneous theories on your world.

"Your scholars have learned that fire exists in all the substances of Nature, but there are two questions that they have never had sufficient finesse to answer clearly.

"In the first place, is fire an element of another species than light, and ought one to believe that Nature has multiplied its operations in that regard?

"In the second place, why does movement develop the fire of substances? Why, for example, do two pieces of wood rubbed together produce fire?

"I shall reply to the second question first, because it will soon lead us to resolve the first.

"You are doubtless familiar with the experiments by which your scholars have demonstrated the laws of centrifugal force, and why, with equal force, one can throw a ball of lead further than a ball of cork. Observe, therefore, that the fire that exists in the atmosphere, as in all substances, being the lighter element, is less subject to the laws of centrifugal force than air and water are. Now, by rubbing any substance whatsoever, what is the result? The heavier elements, and, in consequence those most subject to the laws of centrifugal force, such as air and water, are displaced further from the bodies one rubs. Then the element of fire, which is lighter, becomes dominant, and more or less manifest therein, by virtue of the vivacity of friction that displaces a more or less considerable quantity of air and water. When the friction is continued for a long time, the parts of air and water that move away from the center of the body are reestablished there by atmospheric pressure."

"Permit me to interrupt you, Ormasis. How, then, do all the effects of electricity depend, as I believe, on the same principle? I've thought about that. In fact, while carrying out experiments on electricity, the air driven away electrified bodies is quite sensible. It's doubtless the same air that, being warmed by movement, and rebounding from a vase on which one has put dust or pieces of paper, lifts them up, drops them and occasions the agitation that seemed so surprising to me. It's doubtless the same air that activates the clappers of an electric bell. It also follows from the same principle that when the atmosphere is charge with vapors, and is in consequence heavier, it requires more considerable centrifugal forces to draw away the portions of water that impede the development of the fire.

"That is, in fact, what experiment demonstrates, since one can scarcely develop electric fire when the weather is humid. What seems to me to be difficult to conceive, however, is that fire develops at the very instant when I move my hand closer—or any other substance, whether it is a chain or an electrically conductive tube. What still surprises me is the shock I receive, and that a hundred other people receive at the same time. Where do these effects come from?"

"I shall satisfy your curiosity," Ormasis said. "First, observe that when anybody whatsoever is moved closer to the body of electricity, fire is more concentrated in the space where the two bodies have moved closer. It is, therefore, within that space that fire has to develop further, and, still by reason of that principle, the more the fire within the body is compressed, the more active it becomes. It is also for that reason that the harder bodies one moves closer to the electrical conductor are those that develop a greater proportion of fire, and the spark that escapes is indeed more vivid. As for electric shocks, they are no longer surprising, in view of what I shall explain to you.

"Fire is nothing but agitated light. When light has little motion, it illuminates without any sensible effect, but when it experiences an accelerated motion, the first effect of that element is the same as that of the other elements put in motion. It strikes the bodies that are close to it, and eventually, be reason of its subtlety, it penetrates them. When that percussion is repeated, it occasions the division of bodies, and these bodies, in dividing, decompose by the separation of their fractions of the bodies that are approaching them. This is what is called 'burning,' or 'combustion.' The easier these bodies are to divide, the more they are affected by that percussion; that is why essential oils, resins and wood are much more promptly decomposed by that percussion than stones and metals.

"The electric fire that develops on a body is, therefore, the primary effect of agitated light, and that effect can be compared to the effect of other elements that are agitated; but one observes that the activity of the course of the element compensates for the lightness of its mass, and supplies a percussion much more lively than the other elements provide, in spite of their greater weight. That subtle percussion can strike a hundred people simultaneously, in the same way that when a hundred ivory billiard balls in contact, scarcely has percussion been applied to the first, than it is immediately experienced by the last. When, while making an experiment with electricity, the friction is increased, the forcefully-agitated light carries portions of matter away with it, whose fragments divide or burn the objects that are moved closer to it."

"I understand now," Nadir replied, "and I see clearly that the air and water in the atmosphere, which exert a marked pressure on all the bodies of Nature, can be separated from a body by movement, and the element of fire, which is the least subject to the laws of centrifugal force, then becomes dominant in the same space, from which a quantity of air and water have been separated, and consequently develops there, and produces a more-or-less lively percussion by virtue of more-or-less powerful friction—but I glimpse a consequence of these principles that astonishes me greatly. Is it possible that there would no longer be any heat or fire if matter ceased to be in motion? Is it possible that the sun, that immense mass of light, would provide us with hardly any light at all if our globe ceased to be in motion?"

"Yes, Nadir, be certain of that verity. It is only the movement of the terrestrial corpuscles with which the air of your atmosphere is filled that accelerates the agitation of the light, in the form that we call fire. Can you not see that on those high mountains, where the corpuscles of earthen matter are less active, because they are not reverberating as in the valleys, that there is only a faint percussion—which is to say, a faint heat. Can you not see that the sun can scarcely divide the snow and ice there, although those terrains have a more considerable innate rotational movement by virtue of their greater distance from the center of the earthy?

"Do not be more surprised, therefore, that water rarefied by heat condenses when it rises to a certain height and falls as rain. If the sun were a mass of fire, how could you explain that condensation of water, that rapid formation of snow and hail? It would result necessarily that the higher the water rose up, the more rarefied it would become. It would never fall back to earth as rain, there would never be clouds, and the molecules of matter increasingly attenuated by the heat would continue rising indefinitely into the superior region by reason of the specific weights with whose laws you are familiar.[10] The effects of that electric fire named thunder would not be dangerous, since there would be no point of condensed matter there, whose fall and bursts cause such terrible explosions. Nights would not be sufficient intervals of time for all those condensations to be able to come into play. Besides which, it would result that rain, hail and thunder would only fall, so to speak, at night, and the portion of your globe that is illuminated by the sun for six months at a time would have been reduced to ashes.

"Notice too the effects of what you call apogee and perigee. You can see that the season in which the sun is furthest away from you is precisely the season in which you experience more heat. Why? Because the rays of light remain on your hemisphere for a longer time. If the sun were a mass of fire, that mass of fire being closer to the Earth in winter than in summer, at least agree that there would be moments, in the days of winter, when the sun would warm more than in summer; for remember that the rays of fire should not be assimilated to other heavy bodies, whose fall is more or less serious by virtue of the straight or oblique line that they might describe. Suspend a ball of red-hot iron from a brass wire and present a thermometer to it at the same distances in perpendicular and oblique lines, and you will see that the heat there will be exactly equal. Here, Nadir, are sensible principles; you will conceive them more easily than the

_____

[10] Specific weight is the weight per volume of a material; unlike density, it is not absolute.

terms 'inferior air' and 'superior air,' with which some men have cradled your ignorance."

Chapter VI

Nadir, although astonished by Ormasis' reasoning, nevertheless refused to yield to it; it is true that the weight of a generally-adopted prejudice sometimes overwhelms the strongest mind. He reflected momentarily.

"That is doubtless the opinion of the Luminacians of your planet," he said to Ormasis, "and I see that that opinion is entirely contrary to ours, but I beg you to respond to the following objection. How, by concentrating the rays of the sun with a glass, could one produce such a considerable fire if the sun were not itself a mass of fire?"

"Remember, Nadir, the principles that I have just explained to you, and you will see that the experiment in question is consistent with them and confirms them. I have told you that agitated light forms what is called fire, and that the more light is agitated, the more violent the fire is. Observe, therefore, that light, already agitated by the movement of the corpuscles of the atmosphere, then passing through a body denser than air, which is the glass, must be even further agitated. Besides, the inequality of resistances, relative to the various thicknesses of the glass, occasioning angles of reflection in a circular fashion, produces a multitude of concentrated rays. It is therefore at the point of the greatest convergence that the agitation of light must be very considerable. Finally, the sensible proof of the agitation of the light is the activity with which the same combined rays subsequently diverge. When, at the point of their combination, there is a body denser than air, which halts that activity of divergence, it is necessarily subject to the separations that are called heat, burning or combustion. These names are merely related to variations in the multiplication of the force of percussion.

"To complete the demonstration that it is that considerable agitation of light that produces fire, observe something that one of your physicist has discovered. He has noticed that, when rays of sunlight are passed through a glass lens, beyond the tip of the rays' cone of convergence, the cone of divergence produces more heat to the same degree as the other, although it is more distant from the sun.

"Finally, examine the phosphors that Nature presents to you, especially the phosphor sparkling with light created by your Scholars; in touching it you scarcely experience the slightest sensation of heat, but as soon as you agitate it and rub it vigorously, does not that light suddenly become a fire, whose effects are very violent? Fire is, therefore, nothing but the percussion of agitated light."

"Do all natural substances contain light, then," Nadir asked Ormasis, "Although it is not sensible to our eyes?"

"Undoubtedly," Ormasis replied, "and if you do not see that light in a large number of substances, it is because the tortuousness of their pores intercepts it. For example, when iron is heated to redness in a fire, does it not present more light, while burning the substances to which it is approached? Believe that the light within the piece of iron is still agitated, although it is no longer sensible to your eyes; be sure that that agitated light emanates over the objects one approaches to it, or the molecules of the iron itself, or those of other bodies that might have been drawn with them into the dilated pores of the metal.

"Also make this important observation: that the bodies that are darkest in appearance sometimes contain more rays of light than white bodies. In fact, the latter reflect the rays; the former absorb them. And is it not the case that of two men exposed to the sun, one clad in black and the other in white, that the one clad in black experiences much more heat than the other? The rays of light are not, therefore annihilated, and although they no longer appear to your eyes, they nevertheless exist in the most opaque bodies. Does not a man in a dark cavern who obtains fire from stones by striking them together have the arrogance of believing that he has created light? No, he agitates and develops the light within the bodies, but he does not create anything. I shall soon explain by virtue of what simple principles light, in spite of its subtlety, penetrates even into the most profound cavities of the Earth.

"It is therefore evident that the most opaque and blackest bodies nevertheless contain light, but that the light in question is intercepted by the tortuousness of their pores, and it is always a more-or-less forceful movement that develops it. It therefore follows that on the surfaces of bodies that have straight pores, it requires less movement to present the light to us. That is why that light, being less agitated, causes less separations, and there is no heat. In fact, when certain bodies, such as wood, fish, and even other animals, fall into decay, the light that you perceive on their bodies is developed by the agitation of their components, but that agitation is very weak. There is, therefore, no burning. It is the same with the glow-worm; the light of that insect disappears as soon as it is deprived of life. You therefore see once again that the light depends of the agitation of the constituent parts—but that agitation is not considerable. Besides, it is necessary to observe that in bodies charged with aqueous parts, the percussion of light is considerably weakened therein—which is to say that the effects of fire are almost insensible.

"You see, therefore, my dear Nadir, that on our planet we seek to understand the first principles of everything. If, for example, a Scientist of our Luminacy, in order to explain the phenomenon of phosphors, were content to say to us: 'phosphors are phlogistic acids that burn with more or less rapidity,' we would reply to him: 'Monsieur Scientist, you are not telling us anything. Indeed, whether the phlogistic acids are phosphors, or the phosphors are phlogistic acids, we have no more idea of the role played by light in the operation. Explain to us then, by means of intelligible physical laws, what phlogiston is, what its formation is, what its action on all bodies is, or admit that your knowledge is still quite sterile.'

"However, my dear Nadir, we know perfectly well on our planet what the principle your scientists call phlogiston is; I shall explain it to you shortly, and after that explanation, you will have a better sense of the verity of the definitions I am giving you. But before going any further, have you any more objections to make? Are you quite convinced that the sun is not a body of light or a body of fire?"

"Permit me," Nadir replied, "to communicate one more reflection to you. This is it. Why, in concentrating rays of moonlight by means of our finest mirrors, do we not experience any sensation of heat at their focus? Is not the rotation of the Earth during the night, however, the same as during the day? Is not the agitation of the atmosphere equally sensible, and ought it not, according to your principles, excite heat?"

"Very good, Nadir—but before explaining the reasons for that phenomenon, observe that it does not demonstrate in any way that the sun is a burning body. On the contrary, since eclipses demonstrate that the moon only borrows its light from the sun, why, if the sun were a burning body, would you not similarly receive its heat by the reflection of its rays? I shall explain these effects to you briefly.

"You know that the rays received directly from the sun are, so to speak, parallel, by comparison with the extreme divergence of those of the moon; that is why the light of the moon is so faint, and although it seems to you to be brighter at the focal points of your mirrors, you have every few rays by comparison with the quantity that comes to you directly from the sun, and, in consequence, less compression and much less agitation. In the second place, the faint heat that you can sense at the focal points of those mirrors is entirely destroyed by the aqueous condensations from which even the most beautiful nights are never exempt, which impedes the effect of the percussion of light, and consequently nullifies what is called heat. Finally, Nadir, do not doubt that the violent effect of mirrors is derived uniquely from the quantity of rays of light concentrated, whose agitation is then considerable, and that the effect is not derived from any effective heat of the sun. Do you not see that when the rays of an ardent furnace that is six or seven feet away, warming you much more than those of the sun, are concentrated by the same mirrors, they produce far less effect than the sun's rays?

"By virtue of what I have just told you concerning the lunar rays that do not produce any heat, you ought now to see why water extinguishes fire. In fact, fire being the percussion of agitated light, the progress of that percussion must be far more easily impeded by a body as dense, and simultaneously as supple, as water, which incessantly presents a considerable quantity of surfaces to the efforts of the percussion. You are familiar with the effect of a cannonball, which loses force in a bale of wool, when it would have smashed the thickest wall; there, my friend, is the whole solution of the problem; that is why water extinguishes fire.

"Do not think that fire and water are enemy elements; on the contrary, those two elements have a tendency to combine with the greatest rapidity. Then, the air contained in the water expands, and it is the noise occasioned by that rapid combination that has made people imagine that fire and water were contrary elements, while the components of fire so readily combine with the components of water that, if the combination did not exist, water would never rise up in vapors, there would never have been any animals or plants on the land—or, at least, none of those beings would every have been subject to metamorphoses.

"Never forget, my dear Nadir, the principles that I have just developed for you. You will find them entirely demonstrated in the subsequent course of our conversations. You will see that Nature acts with the greatest simplicity in all its operations; that it has, therefore, never created several kinds of fire or several kinds of heat, and that, far from having multiplied substances in that regard, fire and heat are themselves merely the variable effects of agitated light.

"Until tomorrow, my friend—I'll return here in the morning."

"Why?" Nadir replied. "Why this hurry to leave me? Stay, be the master in my house; you can live agreeably, at liberty. Does the society of four agreeable women frighten you? No, true philosophers love the beautiful works of Nature. Admittedly, perhaps I am speaking as a man in love, but if you knew Mirza— Mirza, the love of my heart, who gives it all its life..."

Nadir explained to Ormasis his way of life, his attachment to Mirza and his happiness. The Philosopher appeared to be softened by sentiment.

"You have known love, then?" Nadir asked him, excitedly.

"Have I known love? Oh, my friend, is there a thinking being that has not? But a cruel memory sometimes brings a melancholy into my heart...let us erase that image. Adieu, Nadir; I promise to stay with you tomorrow. Perhaps I shall reside here for a few days, and if my company can augment your happiness, I shall forget a part of my own chagrin. I cannot say more. Until tomorrow."

The Philosopher left. It was late.

More intrigued than ever, Nadir went down to the Company's drawing room. He was awaited there. A few friends from Chrysopolis were to be guests at supper. They sat down at the table.

Nadir reflected again on his friend's judicious reasoning; he was pensive. He was chided for it. Mirza was burning with impatience to question him, but it was not the right time. He was at supper without really being there. He was scarcely listening to the sparkling conversation, which often embodied little intelligence. He offered faint applause to the little allegorical sallies and meager epigrams whose authors formed them with effort, thinking that people would admire in them the intelligence that they were pursuing. He smiled distractedly at those trivia, the relaxations of great genius, which would have been the occupation and importance of many other petty individuals.

Nadir was, so to speak, in a bad mood; he would have liked Ormasis to stay with him. *I shall have the pleasure tomorrow*, he said to himself privately. *Perhaps I shall see how my philosopher conducts himself in the midst of such amusements*. Immediately, he invited the same guests to supper the following day, and told them that a foreigner from a very distant land would be present, whose pleasure he wanted to procure. Promises were made.

Finally, the company retired and Nadir's other wives went to their apartments. He was alone with Mirza.

"Now I can question you," she said. "How is our Philosopher? You can't imagine how much he interests me. So he's coming tomorrow—he has promised you that? You stayed with him for a long time. I forgive him; I forgive you, but on one condition. I want to be your pupil. Instruct me in my turn; yes, instruct me. Why do people have the mania of never offering women the knowledge of the abstract sciences? I believe that you scientists don't really trust women, because they aren't always content with words. But I have too high an opinion of you, Nadir, to think that…go on, Master, begin your lesson; I'm listening."

Delighted by Mirza's request, and glad to be able to occupy himself with her once again in such an agreeable manner, Nadir explained the Philosopher's first principles to her, with the same clarity with which he had received them. He perceived delightedly how much attention Mirza was paying, and with what intelligence she adopted all the ideas—but her enjoyment caused her to interrupt Nadir from time to time in order to ask rather flippant questions.

Finally, quite convinced that fire was nothing but the effect of the agitation of light, she said: "It is not astonishing that our Philosopher's planet, which you call Mercury and which is close to the sun, is not hotter than our Earth, for, that planet being much smaller than ours, if the rays of light are more abundant there, they are proportionately less agitated. In fact, if I rotate a large ball and a small one with a similar movement, I believe that the surface of the large ball would traverse more space than the other in the same time. The little ball would therefore experience less movement. Thus, since there must be less movement on the surface of Mercury than on the surface of our Earth, it is therefore not astonishing that the inhabitants of Mercury are no more discomfited than we are by heat, even though they are closer to the sun. Tell me, do you think I've explained it? I understand it, but do you understand me?"

"Marvelously, my dear Mirza, marvelously. I admire you. You're just resolved a famous problem, which our most skillful physicists haven't yet explained."

"Oh, Master, are you making fun of me?"

"No, I swear."

"Oh, you don't fool me, and I shall punish you. Good night. I'll reason on my own."

"One moment, Mirza; I'll come to join you in your apartment; I want to prove my good faith."

Immediately, Nadir ran to find a large folio on Physico-Trigono-Geometrical Elements, and came back to find Mirza. He opened the book on page 1590 and showed her an article conceived in these terms:

Corollary

The greater is the degree of longitude of a rectilinear line that departs from a center to a circumscribed circumference, the greater the velocity of that circumference has in its rotational movement, and that velocity increases in proportion to the square of the distance.

"Well, he said, examine and reread it. It's on that corollary that the judicious reasoning you've just carried out is based."

"What a joke!" Mirza replied. "I don't understand any of this incomprehensible verbiage, and you're claiming that I'm reasoning in accordance with it? Explain these big words to me, then. First of all, what is a corollary?"

"A corollary is an evident consequence of a demonstrated truth."

"Very good, Nadir. For example, it's demonstrated that you're lovable. I love you—so that's a corollary. Now explain to me what a rectilinear line is that departs from a center to a circumscribe circumference. Oh, there are many other questions in this book. What is this problem: *to find a tangent that simultaneously touches two circles of different diameter, one above and the other below*?

"In truth, that is a joke. Where would you find such a tangent?" Nadir nevertheless accepted the duty of explaining everything.

The book was very big. There were a great many diagrams to look at.

In the end, Nadir and Mirza spent the whole night discussing various points of Geometry.

Chapter VII

Already, dawn was announcing the philosopher's return to Nadir, and Mirza had formed the plan of hiding in the library, determined to listen carefully to the scientist's instruction, in order to give Nadir a surprise when he eventually came to repeat the same lessons to her.

One circumstance was entirely favorable to this plan. Nadir observed to her that he had reproaches to address to himself for having neglected his wives somewhat for two days.

"I want to make my peace with them," he said. "I think I perceived that they're in a bad mood. The Philosopher hasn't arrived yet; I'm going to see them. Are you coming with me?"

"No," Mirza replied. "I'd surely be drawn into the quarrel, and you're the only one deserving of criticism."

Nadir, therefore, went to his wives' apartments—but they were already in the gardens. They were breathing in the perfumes of flowers there. They were talking to one another, with considerable anxiety, about the coolness of which their husband seemed to be guilty, when they saw him coming to meet them. Their pleasure was sincere, but they resolved to offer him their reproaches.

Indeed, as soon as they saw him come within earshot, Sophie asked: "Is that a ray of sunlight I can see moving on that terrace?"

"No," said Laure, "it's something much rarer."

"That's true," said Fatima. "I did well, then, to buy that faceted glass known as a multiplier yesterday; even if we can only enjoy it for a few moments, we can enjoy it a lot." Immediately, she looked at Nadir through that glass, and passed it to her companions, who did the same.

"Oh," Nadir said to them, "I fully deserve to be chided, but your quarrels are so pleasant, that you make me happy with your complaints. It's necessary to confess to you that a stranger, a philosopher, has been occupying me in secret with amusing instruction—but I think that from today on he will reside with us, so our society can only become more interesting...yes, more interesting! Inept prejudice has excessively confused misanthropy with philosophy. True science enriches pleasures.

"Speaking of pleasures, yesterday I was a trifle thoughtful at supper, but I perceived that Selim and Osman were obtaining considerable pleasure in seeing Laure and Sophie. My dear Laure, my lovable Sophie, I hold Selim and Osman in high esteem. They have excellent hearts. If by chance, rising above the prejudices of the nation—which is to say, promising to leave you mistresses of your liberty while sacrificing theirs for you—that proposition gives you some interest in them, would you refuse their hands? Oh, believe that I shall make my happiness yours...but on one condition, that of seeing one another every day in the others' homes.

"As for my dear Fatima, if it is possible that..."

These reflections on Nadir's part caused Laure and Sophie to blush slightly. Selim and Osman were, indeed, pleasant fellows, whose proven love could not offer any offense to the friendship of Nadir; even so, they rebelled, became annoyed and quarreled—but Nadir was determined to stand firm and resolved to increase his wives' happiness.

"You see," he said to them, laughing, "that I think about you more than you imagine. Adieu—my Philosopher is waiting for me. I'll leave you."

Nadir reached the library just as Ormasis had arrived.

Young Mirza had not lost any time. Sitting on a self, she was a worthy replacement for eight folio volumes of *Critical Remarks on Antiquity*; she had pulled in front of her one of those flaps that take the place of the battens of a cupboard, but nevertheless contriving an opening in such a way as to be able to see everything without being seen.

Nadir and Ormasis came to sit down directly facing her. Scarcely had she set eyes on the Philosopher than she felt the keenest interest in him.

So that, she said to herself, *is the marvelous man. He's of a certain age, but his face is affable. I don't love him as I love Nadir. No, they're surely not the same sentiments that are affecting me, but...I don't know...I'm experiencing a tender sympathy that I can't define.*

Mirza only called a halt to these reflections in order to listen more attentively.

Nadir was the first to speak. "It's today, then, my respectable friend, that you will take up residence with me."

"Yes, my dear Nadir, but on condition that you don't raise any opposition to my nocturnal expeditions. Last night, I saw a new development in the masses of the Earth, which presented interesting curiosities to me. Yes, my friend, it's in those same places , in the bowels of the Earth, that an amateur has the pleasure of taking Nature by surprise, and not in mineralogical collections, whose principal items are often merely the products of cunning imposture. If you are genuinely curious to learn about

76

that interesting region and to help me in my research, it's up to you, but..."

"No, no reflections," Nadir interjected. "I'm delighted. This very evening, I shall go with you into the bowels of the Earth. A spectacle so new, so beautiful, will have a thousand charms for me. Will you now, my dear Ormasis, continue to educate me?"

"Gladly, Nadir. I had, therefore, made the observation that if there were not a veritable union between water and fire, water would never rise up in vapors. Now consider that vapors in motion considerably attenuate the portions of earthen matter that they encounter. A more intimate liaison therefore forms between the water and the attenuated portions of earth. Such is the origin of the formation of salts and oils. You can imitate that operation of nature in a laboratory much more easily now that scientists have imitated that of the formation of sulfur. You will even discover very singular effects, originating from the simple circulation of vapors over different earths, but it is of the greatest importance to observe the degrees of heat or percussion of light. You only require the degree of fire that will cook an egg, not that which will hatch out a chicken. The principle of this phenomenon will appear more evident to you when I have explained to you what phlogiston is, its formation, its conservation in substances, its diminution and reproduction."

"I hesitated for a long time," Nadir replied, "before accepting that fire and water could have an affinity—which is to say, a tendency to combine with one another—but I no longer doubt it. I appreciate that when one throws water over a fire, it is the percussion of light that separates out the air contained in the water, that that percussion consequently increases the volume of the air, and that it is the expanded air that strikes the organ of hearing. That's quite simple, my dear Ormasis, and I think I can find the truth of that principle in several experiments. For instance, if I throw a acid over an alkali, I immediately occasion an effervescence, but what is that effervescence—that swelling? It's nothing but the effect of the air suddenly expanded by the rapid friction caused by the combination of the two substances, and the light therein is similarly agitated. Now, Ormasis, give me the pleasure of explaining the principle of these affinities to me?"

"Certainly, my dear Nadir; I shall gladly continue my instruction at the pace your curiosity prefers. That is the means of increasing your interest in it. Enlightened scientists will have already given you notions regarding the principle of affinities; I shall explain it to you with greater clarity.

"You are firmly convinced on the basis of certain experiments that all bodies tend toward the center of the Earth, and that the force of atmospheric pressure is more considerable that the centrifugal forces originating from the Earth's rotational movement, which but for that pressure, would hurl all non-adherent masses, including human beings, immense distances. You are also firmly assured that all the fluid and solid bodies in nature have pores, and that these pores are variously configured. Thus, when one throws, for example, one salt upon another, the pores of which have a configuration related to the constituent components of the first, a fall necessarily ensues in the pores of that salt, which results in the separation of the air and an increase in its volume—and that agitation, which has been named effervescence, is more or less lively by virtue of the form and opening of the pores."

Very good, very good, Mirza said to herself, who was following the abstract conversation intelligently. *It is correct to say that everything comes together and falls apart.*

"So you see," Ormasis continued, "that what is called affinity is the tendency of one substance to penetrate another, and that the variety of that tendency depends on the variety of forms and weights. You need to understand forms and weights, my dear Nadir. Movement changes the forms of bodies; the forms of bodies occasion changes in weight. From that comes the modification of all living beings."

Yes, Mirza said to herself, again, *movement changes the forms of bodies. Indeed, it is by virtue of living and acting that I shall grow old, that I shall grow ugly. Perhaps Nadir will cease to love me—oh, if I believed that, I would never move again. The forms of bodies occasion changes in weight. I believe that when I grow old I will become heavier. From that comes the modification of all living things. Yes, I know that only too well. I shall cease to exist. But...what shall I become? What! Never to see Nadir again...never...no more hope...*

O, delight of my life, Nadir, charming being that I contemplate at present with so much pleasure, it will therefore be necessary for us to separate forever, both plunged into the chaos of an eternal night...

O Divinity, intelligence supreme, can one suppose such an absurd inconsequence? Would you have created thinking beings only to annihilate them? Infallible architect, can your works deteriorate? No—blush, scientists of Chrysopolis, who make so much effort to lower us to the condition of the vilest animals, and rob me of the sweet hope of living eternally with Nadir. You, Ormasis, honest Philosopher, I have the greatest desire to question you—but let's listen.

"Forgive me," Nadir said to the Philosopher, "if I cannot admit the opinion of the fall of parts of one body into another without asking you to resolve the difficulties I find therein. I know about the tangible pressure of the atmosphere over all the bodies on our globe, but when these bodies are divided into parts as fine as your constituent components must be, they must have the same specific weight as similar masses of air—which is to say that they must be as light as air. Then, the tendency of these same parts toward the center of the Earth no longer acts on them, so I do not understand how there is a fall of constituent parts of one body into those of another."

"I shall help you to understand that verity," Ormasis replied. When the parts of a body are sufficiently divided to give them a specific weight comparable to air, do you think that the increase or diminution of their elevation, in consequence of the other bodies they encounter, does not produce exactly the same effect in their air that I have just explained? Be sure that the effect is the same. There is always a fall of one substance upon the other by virtue of the relative weight of the two substances. What does it matter that the substances become more elevated, even if they rise up to the height of the highest air? They will still act upon one another.

"But, you might say, there is then no tendency toward the center of the earth, and it is, therefore, the ascension of bodies that similarly has the principle of affinities. No, my friend, it necessary always to start with the principle of the fall of bodies, which is the dominant principle, and reflect that if a heavier body than another obliges it rise up, it does not follow that the latter no longer conserves its tendency toward the center of the Earth.

"Until I explain the primal cause of the gravity of bodies—which is to say, their tendency toward the center of the Earth—be assured in the meantime that if the division of a body produces parts that rise up into the air, that effect still originates from the dominant principle that is atmosphere pressure, and those same parts only rise into the air by virtue of there being other parts that have a greater tendency than them toward the center of the Earth, by virtue of their mass and their form."

"Ah!" exclaimed Nadir, "you're causing me to make some very interesting reflections. When I believed that the sun was a burning body, it was impossible for me to sense all these truths; it was impossible, for example, to imagine how the varieties of atmospheric pressure originated; now, I'm no longer embarrassed. I understand why all vapors of any kind condense when they reach a certain height. I also understand that the air must be agitated by the fall of these condensed bodies, and that it is that agitation which occasions tempests, thunder and meteors. I can easily conceive that the bodies that are the most divided can, in condensing, form new masses of a different nature. Finally, the sun not being a body of fire, I can conceive that not a single atom of earthen or aqueous matter can escape our atmosphere.

"I can see clearly now the entire inconsequence of the system of downward tendencies; I sense all the pettiness of the reasoning by which it has been supposed that our globe will one day be vitrified. I understand marvelously that a conflagration in one part of our globe immediately occasions a fall of water, because the masses of water that are rarefied occasion the condensation of similar masses of water higher up in the atmosphere, and in consequence, their fall upon the earth, sometimes close at hand and sometimes far away, depending on air currents. Given the immutable laws of specific weights, it is therefore proven that the general conflagration of the world is physically impossible.

"Presently, the more I reflect on these continual condensations, the more I see that the division of bodies that nature operates, although considerable, is not infinite, as it might have been—in consequence of which, the extraordinary subdivisions imagined by some of our scientists, by virtue of which some have drawn the conclusion of intelligent substances, are merely puerile reveries. However, Ormasis, deign to enlighten my judgment, is it not natural to believe that our intelligent faculty is a property of matter?"

"Can it be," replied Ormasis, "that Nadir, who has just formulated a perfectly correct chain of reasoning, can terminate it with such an absurd question?"

It seemed that Nadir's ideas were still in concert with Mirza's desires. He had asked that question of the Philosopher, and it was precisely that question on which the tender Mirza ardently wished to be instructed. Charmed by the beginning of the reply, she was scarcely breathing, in order to listen more attentively.

"I could ask you why," Ormasis continued, "if intelligence is a property of matter, stones and trees do not possess that intelligent faculty—but you would tell me that it is because mineral and vegetable matter do not have the forms of animal matter. Well, my friend, what do forms matter? If intelligence is truly, as you say, a property of matter, all matter ought to have that property, no matter whether its parts are triangular, rectangular or obtuse, spherical or semi-spherical. So, my friend, trees and pebbles, according to your principles, ought to possess the intelligent faculty—or, at least agree, that a good lapidary, in giving stones infinite figures, would encounter the intelligent faculty in some of those varied forms."

"I feel the weight," Nadir replied, "of the ridicule that you heap upon those principles. Consider, however, I beg you, that in the animal kingdom there is much more movement than in the vegetable or the mineral, and that, the matter being considerably divided, it is therefore matter in that state that has the property of thinking."

"I shall enable you to see the triviality of those observations," Ormasis said. "Matter considerably divided, according to your ideas, would have the nature of a subtle alcohol, of an ardent quintessence, which circulates around the pineal gland, or floats over the fluid of your brain. In that case, your system would be contrary to all physical laws. In fact, if rather coarse vapors rise so strongly above your globe, by virtue of specific weights of which you know the immutable order, how do you imagine that the soul, being assumed to be a highly-divided matter necessarily disengaged from weighty matter, since it acts with so much speed, could remain enclosed within a vessel as porous as the human body?

"You might perhaps tell me that there is a continual loss of animal spirits, which are carried away, but that humans continually make up for that loss by the transmutation of the nutriments they absorb. Very well; here, then, is the atmosphere, continually filled with small portions of matter, which probably lose their intelligent faculty in the open air—for if they did not lose it, it would follow that human respiration would create millions of sylphs every day. However, my friend, necessity dictates that there is in every human one of those small portions of matter that is more securely fixed than the others, and which commands them. Indeed, without that, how can you explain, for example, the act of will by means of which you recall one idea or another on demand? How do you define that act of will? There would, therefore, be one portion of subtle matter that commands other portions of subtle matter and arranges them methodically within your brain. See, I beg you, how many subtle materials it is necessary to admit in order to deny the existence of a substance more perfect than matter.

"One of your famous Materialists has sensed that it would be inconvenient for your system to admit a Divinity. He had therefore taken the decision to deny the existence of that Divinity. The order of nature is only due, according to him, to chance, and does not announce the existence of an intelligent faculty. According to him there are thoughts because, he says, it is a property of matter to think. Look at that great reasoner; he is five feet two or three inches tall. The circular movement of a little fluid running through his little body therefore produces within him an intelligent faculty, but the movement of the immense fluids of all nature does not advertise the existence of an intelligence of more consequence than his own. It is thus proven, according to his own principles, that there at least exists a material God—but does not the continuous order of the movements of nature announce that the intelligent faculty in question is the sovereign of matter? In consequence, that faculty must have a substance more perfect than mater. It is thus physically impossible that it should be composed of earth, air and water, because a part of the whole cannot be superior to the whole."

"Presently, Nadir, be persuaded that the Divinity could have created an infinity of substances more perfect than matter, but which nevertheless have connections with it. The more considerable those connections are, the less distinct intelligent faculties are. Such is the situation of animals; such is also the distinctive state of the genius of certain humans. In sum, my dear Nadir, it is because those connections still exist in you that it is impossible for you to conceive of the nature of that thinking substance, but it is even more impossible to conceive that a thought might be formed of earth, air and water. During the time in which your scientists have decomposed the bodies of nature, dissected light and contrived a vast number of combinations, have they perceived that more or less earth, more or less water or more or less air or light has ever produced any degree of intelligence in their composites?

"Finally, Nadir, to complete your conviction that thought is not an effect of the action or rarefaction of matter, make the following observation. A man can agitate himself, undertake some violent exercise; you must know from experience that in those moments he is incapable of forming sublime ideas. When, on the contrary, that man walks slowly, or when, shut up in his study, he meditates in tranquility, he senses that his ideas are more elevated, and that there is, in sum, more clarity in the functions of his soul. The soul, therefore, is not the effect of a rarefaction of matter, or it would be in the moment of agitation when it would be most exalted. Now, since it is evident that a man who wants to meditate seeks tranquility, and that that moment of tranquility is that of the greatest elevation of his ideas, judge how the soul entirely disengaged from the senses must acquire knowledge, and perhaps pleasures, that it had previously been impossible for it to conceive.

"Those, Nadir, are reasonings within the range of our soul, in its present state. They are only physical reflections founded on common sense, but do you not find that those physical reflections, universally adopted on our planet, are worth more that the contradictory metaphysical conclusions of yours?"

"Yes," Nadir replied, "I concede, and concede with conviction."

"Me too!" cried Mirza, tearing away the sliding door that hid her from their view. "No, Ormasis, no, you are not a mortal; you are a guardian angel who has come to augment my happiness and the price of my existence. Receive the pledge of the most sincere amity."

Mirza had already run toward the Philosopher, and, having embraced him with the honest expression of the keenest gratitude, suddenly threw herself into Nadir's arms.

"My friend, my lover, my all, do you sense, like me, the pleasure of living incessantly? The moment of our separation will therefore be the one that will reunite us with greater sensibility. If you leave me first, I shall not be long in following you. The soul of Mirza united with yours…I imagine that that enjoyment must be divine. In the purest moments of sensuality, have we not sometimes desired to fuse with one another? Were our souls not striving to unite? There exists for them, therefore, a pleasure even more delightful! Oh, my friend, from this day forward I shall enjoy an unclouded happiness. Assured of living again with you, I shall no longer dread anything."

Imagine the Philosopher's surprise, and that of Nadir. What vivacity! What expression! What sentiments! What other response could Nadir have made? He covered her with kisses.

The Philosopher, moved to tears, was not about to be the first to interrupt such a touching scene.

"My dear Ormasis," Nadir said to him, finally, "You see her…judge for yourself how I must love her. Be our friend, our father—yes, our father; the one who instructs us, truly gives us a new existence. You have enabled me to sense the nobility of my being. Enjoy yourself one of the great pleasures of the soul, that of making people happy.

"By the way, my dear Mirza, do you remember the honest villager who, burdened with children and ruined by unforeseen circumstances, could not obtain delays from the miserly Emir who is pursuing him? It's today that the poor man ought to send us his response; he only wished to accept our offers as a last resort. Perhaps he's waiting. Perhaps our slaves, often very busy…."

"I'll go see," Mirza replied, swiftly, "and it will be running from one pleasure to another."

Indeed, Nadir confided such missions to Mirza from time to time, and he only gave her the most agreeable ones. Then she savored the joy of kindness, the delicious sentiment that one cannot define.

Scarcely had she gone than Ormasis said to Nadir: "I can see the extent to which virtue rules within your hearts. Well, my friend, how do your Materialist Doctors pretend to explain the joy of the benevolent soul?"

"It is, they say, because of the visual ray of compassion; the sensation of compassion results from a material knowledge, and that sensation affects us materially by analogy, in presenting the material image of well-being and ill-being, which is painted in our brain."

"What nonsense! First of all, what is the origin of the material knowledge that produces the sensation? No reply. In the second place, supposing that the brain were a collection of images, how could those images be judges?"

"But one judges by material comparisons, they say."

"Agreed, but what is the power that judges? No reply—and much confusion. Let us therefore forget these men who are trying to debase themselves, and, if it makes them happy to believe that their intelligent faculty must one day be converted into smoke, let them be happy. Let us pass on to other things."

Chapter VIII

"A long time ago, your scientists perceived that there exists in all the objects of nature an active substance that serves for their formation, their growth and also for their decomposition. Some have called it the 'sulfur principle,' others 'philosophical mercury.' Others have called it 'the water that does not wet,' and finally, today, the word most in vogue among your scientists is *phlogiston*. Let us adopt that last word, phlogiston—but as they have neither explained the principle of it nor its effects, I shall satisfy your curiosity in that regard. Pay attention, Nadir, for we are about to treat the most interesting subject for human knowledge, and in order for you to sense it fully, I shall sometimes repeat myself.

"I have clearly demonstrated that fire is nothing but the effect of the percussion of agitated light. I have explained why water extinguishes fire. You have also been able to understand why oil catches fire while water does not. In fact, light must be much more agitated by the friction of earthen masses combined with water than by water alone. You have understood these verities all the more easily became you have seen with your own eyes the familiar experiment, that the hardest bodies rubbed together are those which produce the most heat.

"Following to these principles, you will therefore easily understand that molecules of earth, being strongly divided and rounded, are susceptible to great agitation by the rotatory movement of the globe and atmospheric pressure. They therefore agitate light keenly, and the percussion of that agitated light is more or less powerful by virtue of the quantities of aqueous parts that impede the separations. Such, my friend, is phlogiston; it is a quantity of tiny portions of highly-divided and rounded earthen matter, whose multiplied movement agitates light.

"You know, Nadir, that when two pieces of wood are rubbed rapidly against one another, they catch fire. Well, my friend, it is by virtue of the same principles of movement that you see a piece of wood catch fire and light another—but the latter inflammation is more prompt, because there is, in fact, no movement more lively, and in consequence more communicative, than that of flame.

"Bearing in mind and carefully considering that common experiment, by means of which two pieces of wood are induced to catch fire by rubbing them together, imagine how a quantity of small bodies rubbed together rapidly would be capable of producing fire when there are few aqueous parts to weaken the effects of the percussion of light.

"It is easy now to resolve the problem of why animals contain more phlogiston than vegetables and minerals. It is because the portions of earthen matter they contain are in a divided state and possess a much more considerable movement. Vegetables move less than animals; you can also see that they contain less phlogiston. Minerals move even less than vegetables; again, note that they contain less phlogiston—and if the phlogiston contained in minerals and metals sometimes occasions such terrible explosions, it is not because it is more abundant there but because there are fewer aqueous portions. Consequently, the percussion of the light is not weakened as much as it is in vegetables and animals; you can appreciate that when that percussion is considerable, the resulting dilatation of the air must be rapid.

"Among animals, too great a quantity of phlogiston occasions separations in their constituent parts and kills them, but without causing any detonation or inflammation. Why? Because the aqueous principle, being abundant in animals, impedes the violence of the percussion of the light.

"A man who has breathed the phlogiston of coal is relived when he is exposed to open air; that it because he then breathes aqueous portions which inhibit the effects of that phlogiston—which is to say, the percussion of light—and, in consequence, the division of his blood. You can also see that the more a man has of what is called a humid temperament, the less harmful the vapors of coal are to him. It is the same as the contagion of some diseases, to which some people are more susceptible than others. In sum, my friend, the more you reflect, the more you will recognize the verity of the explanation I am giving you."

"Yes," Nadir replied, "but you also make me perceive, after your comment on explosions, some very interesting verities. I have been told that the air enclosed in a body, finding no issue by which to escape, breaks that body when it is exposed to fire, and that the effect results from the expansion of the air by the fire—but I could not see why the fire dilated the air. Now I can see that it is the percussion of the agitated light that divided the air, and that the divided air, increased in volume, causes the separation of resistant parts. I can also see quite clearly why, under the recipient of a pneumatic machine from which a large quantity of air has been removed, powder burns without explosion; it is because the air contained in the powder that is lighted, although suddenly divided by the percussion of light, also finds an empty space relative to the increase of its volume.

"I shall return to the definition of phlogiston. It is singular that our modern scientists have claimed that phlogiston is pure fire; I confess to you that I did not agree with that definition at all. In the first place, they had not given me the slightest idea of the formation of fire. In the second place, I found contradictions in their principles. For example, it was impossible for me to see how, in calcinating a metal by fire, I succeeded in removing its phlogiston, because, the phlogiston being, according to them, nothing but fire, I thought it ridiculous to say that fire was expelling fire. Even less could I see how black coal sealed in a vessel and exposed to intense fire did not lose its phlogiston, while when it was exposed to the slightest fire in the open air it soon lost it. I now see that the free or ambient air draws away the last aqueous parts of the coal, because they conform with it in specific weight. I see that it is not the same in the closed vessels where the air is more rarefied and where the vapors with greater specific weight cannot rise up. It therefore results that those aqueous parts, which remain in the coal, suppress the movement of the little balls—which is to say, the percussion of light—and, in consequence, there is no inflammation.

"I see with pleasure, my dear Ormasis, that the solution of this problem becomes general. Indeed, it tells us why inflamed bodies are extinguished as soon as they are derived of air, which is commonly known as 'stifling a fire.' I can also see that niter, to which some phlogisticated matter is added, only burns in closed vessels because it contains a great deal of air, the resulting explosion being a very striking proof of it. When, on the contrary, sulfur is boiled on its own in the narrowest and most tightly-sealed vessel, there is no explosion. So that substance, although highly phlogisticated, never caches fire in sealed vessels. All these principles are demonstrated reciprocally. But Ormasis, is it possible that metals also contain aqueous parts? Our scientists would surely consider me a visionary if I ever tried to make such an assertion."

"Well," Ormasis, "make it, and be firm in that opinion. You know how difficult calcareous earth[11] is to calcinate, and with what force it retains its least aqueous parts. You know too that argilous earth,[12] exposed to intense fire, similarly retains its aqueous parts, with even more force than chalk. Is it surprising, then, that other metallic earths can contain aqueous parts, and that they retain them even more intimately. Must it be affirmed that they do not contain them because no one can extract them? Witness, however, the ridiculous consequences to which conceit and the lack of examination draw the majority of men. They see that metal bars are elongated to shortened in proportion to the degree of heat or cold, but they do not want to admit that there is aqueous fluid in metals; but how, without that aqueous fluid, can the expansion and malleability of metals be conceived? How can the liaison of the constituent parts be conceived? If, according to their principles, the pure fire that they call phlogiston were sufficient to operate that liaison, it would require that metals had a sensible degree of heat in order to conserve their malleability; rather, be certain

---

[11] Limestone, in our understanding, does not "calcinate"—by which La Follie means "form a calx," not "take on calcium"—because it is already oxidated, but because it undergoes manifest changes when heated, many phlogiston theories assumed that those chances must be of the same kind as those that other objects undergo when heated or burnt.

[12] i.e., clay.

that a quantity of phlogiston that is found in an earth entirely deprived of aqueous parts would catch fire by the slightest augmentation of movement, and that a similar combination, far from forming metals, would occasion a continual thunder.

"Finally, if mercury did not contain aqueous parts in addition to its phlogiston, how could the fact that it solidifies at very low temperatures be explained? Why would that same mercury become fluid again as soon as the temperature is raised by a few degrees? By certain, therefore, my friend, that metals are like all the mixtures of nature; they are composed of earth, air and water. It is true that there are mixtures that contain fewer parts of air and water; you will understand the reason for that when I explain the principles of their formation."

Chapter IX

Nadir was becoming increasingly interested in the philosopher's definition; at first he had only regarded it as an agreeable theory, but he soon saw a system founded on physical and constant principles becoming a certain principle itself.

"I have a clear sense," he told Ormasis, "of the play of the little portions of rounded earth that agitate light. I understand that they are continually activated by the rotatory movement of the globe. It therefore follows that these tiny portions of matter that penetrate and circulate within all bodies agitate light, and that the percussion of that agitated light varies in intensity and causes varying degrees of separation, by virtue of the quantity of parts of water that weaken them. But when the movement, being considerably multiplied, occasions inflammation, I do not understand what becomes of these tiny balls after the inflammation. For example, when one has detonated or set fire to niter in sealed glass vessels, what has become of the phlogiston? Those little balls have surely not been able to escape, or at least must remain in large measure. Why do they no longer produce fire? Why do they not agitate light with as much force?"

"I shall explain these effects, Nadir, by means of a tangible experiment. Put into a vessel a quantity of little balls of earth and shake the vessel vigorously; is it not true that those little bodies of spherical form will warm up much more rapidly than if they were cubic in form? In fact, the same degree of movement that will agitate the balls hectically, will hardly stir the cubes. It follows, therefore, that the balls heat up more rapidly. Pay close attention, Nadir to what I am telling you. Suppose now that, the balls being agitated to the point of inflammation, or a violent inflammation is communicated to them, then a quantity of the balls will lose their spherical form by virtue of the percussion; several might even be bound together by fusion. Then the mass, no longer being an assembly of tiny balls, is no longer as susceptible to movement, and, in consequence to inflammation.

"That, my friend, is the explanation of what is called the loss of phlogiston. It merely involves, as you can see, a change of form.

"A curious individual took it into his head one day to ask one of your scientists why some bodies that have been inflammable cease to be inflammable. What did the scientist reply? Because those bodies lose their inflammable principle. Why does opium cause sleep? Because it has a soporific effect. I have seen many reputable men laugh at that comic bankruptcy, and yet be objects of the satire themselves.

"Now, Nadir, consider that the loss of phlogiston does not always suppose the effects of detonation or inflammation. No, those little agitated balls that we shall continue to call phlogiston can increase or diminish within a body by virtue of the quantities of aqueous parts that retard their course, for then the little balls are susceptible to condensation when their movement weakens, and can become solid bodies again, in the same way that the parts of a solid body can become phlogiston by division and movement. What I am telling you might seem extraordinary, but there is, my friend, nothing more true; such is the march of Nature. Such is the origin of all the changes it brings about, that of the variety of forms and of specific weights.

"Let us take a very simple example; consider what occurs in the milk of animals, and that observation will serve to convince you. You see that the most phlogisticated part, the lightest, rises to the surface and forms what is called the cream. That formation is more or less prompt according to whether there is more or less movement in the atmosphere, but the substance in that state is still not inflammable; you will try in vain to evaporate the aqueous parts by fire, you will never achieve inflammation. What is happening? One beats and agitates that cream to form what is called butter, and that butter is then a very flammable substance. You see, therefore, that the phlogiston has been increased in that same substance, at the expense of the parts that compose it. It is sometimes the simplest observations, Nador, that lead us to great truths."

"Yes, Ormasis, I am acquiring a better understanding of Nature and the effects of phlogiston—but you have told me that phlogiston is related to the weight of bodies; I cannot imagine what that relationship might be."

"What, Nadir, you do not sense it? Here it is. The more phlogiston a body acquires, the less it weighs; why? Because the interior movement it experiences in its parts, although insensible to your eyes, still diminishes its tendency toward the center of the earth. You know that the movement of rotation of that the user of a sling has given to a stone before launching it throws it much further because that movement has already caused the stone to lose a part of its gravity toward the center of the earth; my friend, all these experiments have faithful connections between them; it is only a question of appreciating them.

"The more phlogisticated a body is, the less it weighs—and, in fact, do you not see that metals provided with phlogiston weigh less than when they have lost a part of that phlogiston through calcination? Essential oils are lighter than greasy oils. They contain more phlogiston, and those same greasy oils, which contain more phlogiston than water and are lighter than water, become heavier than water when they have lost their phlogiston by decomposition. A very simple observation that has escaped your scientists will render this demonstration even more evident.

"There is no one who has not amused himself by lightly pouring wine into a glass containing water, in such a way that the wine, which is less heavy than the water, does not mingle with it and can float upon it. But why is the wine lighter than the water? It is because it contains more phlogiston than water. The proof is that when the same wine, by a further process of fermentation, has become vinegar, it no longer floats. On the contrary, it falls to the bottom of the vessel without mixing with the water. It has become heavier than the water—and it is necessary to note that this increase in weight can only come from the loss of phlogiston, and not from that of light spirits, for the best and heaviest vinegar is that in which one has added or retained more exactly the most spirituous parts.

"In sum, you will not see any experiments that falsify this principle; all concur in demonstrating it—and is any, by chance, appear to advertise a contradiction, the slightest observation will dispel it.

"It is by virtue of the changes in weight occasioned by more or less phlogiston that the same substance can affect our sense of taste variously—for be certain that the five senses are merely modifications of a single sense, which is touch, and that the variety of all those modifications depend not only on the variety of forms but the variety of weights that cause it.

"You see, therefore, that wine that has lost its phlogiston increases in weight, and it is also for that reason that it affects your senses of taste differently. In fact, the diversity of the weights and forms of bodies occasions the diversity of their fall circulation on the nervous excitations of the human body, in the same way that the variable flexibility of those nervous excitations will occasion a diversity of sensations in two people who taste the same substance.

"You also see that greases, oils and butters, those substances so mild to the sense of taste, affect it very differently as soon as they have lost their phlogiston, when their acidity becomes sensible. You know too that sulfur, a substance which does not affect the sense of taste at all in that state, is converted by the loss of phlogiston into an extremely corrosive acid called oil of vitriol, which can be transformed once again into the state of sulfur by combining it with phlogiston emanating from other mineral, vegetable or animal bodies.

"You see, therefore, my dear Nadir, that phlogiston is the same in all bodies; that it can escape from one body, that it can pass into another, that the air is itself charged with a large quantity of phlogiston, that several of those little molecules ambient in the atmosphere combine with a superabundant quantity of aqueous parts when the air is laden with them; that they then condense, fall to the earth and become constituent parts of other bodies, where they can be transmuted once again into phlogiston by a new division.

"Such, Nadir, the continual march of Nature; I cannot stress this principle enough, from which, as you can see, a host of consequences result."

Chapter X

Far from being bored by such an abstract conversation, Nadir found new pleasures therein.

"I understand," he said to Ormasis, "with more evidence than ever, your definition of phlogiston. In the first place, the great mobility of that substance tells us that the form of its parts must be spherical. Why? Because the bodies that have that form are the most susceptible to movement. In the second place, it must be of earthen nature, because, being much less supple, they conserve their form better and strike light more sharply. It is therefore demonstrated by all the laws of physics and common sense that your definition is accurate.

"I can also see that phlogiston is of the same species in all bodies. There is doubtless more of the same phlogiston spread through the atmosphere, which, agitated by the movement of clouds, occasions those explosions called thunder. I am now in a position to explain effects that I never understood before, because no one had ever defined phlogiston for me.

"I had often seen in the atmosphere a multitude of lightning flashes succeeding one another rapidly, without there being any outbursts or explosions, and our physicists told me that there was no thunder or explosion because there was not enough phlogiston in the clouds. I listened to them, but that continual inflammation seemed to me to contradict their response. I understand now that it is possible for the atmosphere to be filled with a large quantity of phlogiston and yet only to present light without explosion, when the percussion of that light is impeded by the aqueous parts that are present in the same space as the inflammation. But when a similar or even lesser quantity of phlogiston is agitated in a space that contains few aqueous parts, I understand that the percussion of the light must be infinitely more active, and that the subsequent dilatation of the separations and their percussion must be scarcely weakened by more considerable volumes of water. It is the same with the electric shock. When the atmosphere is charged with aqueous portions, and there is in consequence a great deal in the same space as the inflammation of the phlogiston, the percussion of light is very weak.

"Our scientists have already perceived that the effects of electricity and that of lightning are unleashed consequences of a single cause, but I could not divine what that cause was. I understand it now. I still have before my eyes the principle that light is, like all the other bodies of nature, subject to being agitated by other bodies; that fire is the effect of agitated light; that the separations occasioned by fire are merely a consequence of that agitation or percussion; that that percussion is more or less enfeebled by more or fewer aqueous parts, because water is a subtle body, and that it presents a quantity of surfaces, incessantly renewed, which impede or greatly weaken that percussion, in the same way that a bale of wool weakens the force of a cannonball with much greater success than a harder body the cannonball traverses rapidly, or by virtue of which it experiences a considerable movement of repercussion.

"Yes, I perceive increasingly why water impedes the effects of fire, and, in fact, many detonations only take place after the departure of a quantity of aqueous parts. For example, one can dissolves sulfur in oil without an explosion resulting, but when the mixture is heated for a long time, many of the aqueous parts are caused to evaporate, and then a terrible detonation occurs.

"Greasy oils contain more water than essential oils, so one can only set fire to them with nitric acid by adding vitriolic acid, which removes the superabundant water. Essential oils themselves experience a desiccation before detonating.

"I see that all the effects of nature derive from the same causes. However, Ormasis, since water impedes the percussion of light, why does water thrown on to molten copper cause explosions as dangerous as those of lightning."

"This is the reason, Nadir. You know that fire opens the pores of all the bodies exposed to it considerably. The water that is thrown therefore penetrates into the pores of the metal. But as the pores of the copper, although opened by the water, are still very narrow, the small quantity of air that the water contains, being susceptible to a rapid dilatation, then breaks the resistant parts. A proof of this verity is that water thrown on to molten gold does not produce the same effects, because the pores of the metal are much more open, and less in quantity than those of copper."

"I understand the connection of these principles," Nadir replied. "However, Ormasis, when one mixes iron and sulfur together, in order to imitate to some extent the effects of volcanoes, why is it necessary to add a little water to the iron and sulfur, to accelerate the inflammation of the phlogiston?"

"The reason is quite simple. Water only serves in that experiment to form a more exact mixture of the parts of iron and sulfur. What it demonstrates to you is that if, instead of enclosing that mixture in the earth, it is exposed to fire, one can see that the detonation only occurs after the evaporation of many vapors. This is, therefore, the effect that results from that mixture.

"You will see that it is always necessary to come back to the forms of bodies and the relative falls. The active parts of the acid salt, in falling into the interior of the tiny balls that we call phlogiston, increase their agitation; these multiplied frictions are, therefore, the origin of heat, and in consequence, the expansion of air known as effervescence; and that movement is increased as aqueous vapors are dissipated, to the point of separating the resistant parts and sometimes producing visible light."

"I understand now," Nadir continued, excitedly, "how acids divide metals. In fact, the active parts, being precipitated into the interstices of the balls known as phlogiston, augment the frictions and movement in the first instants of their fall, which results in the percussion of the agitated light, the dilatation of the air, and the separation of the resistant parts. But I also understand that, even though there is no evaporation of phlogiston, the movement of those tiny balls must be subsequently diminished by the interposition of those same active parts. It is, therefore, for that reason that the more acid is united with phlogiston, the less considerable its inflammation is. It is, therefore, for the same reason that sulfur, which contains so much phlogiston, but which contains a proportionately great quantity of acid, burns with so much tranquility. Besides which, you have told me that it contains aqueous portions and very little air, which prevents it from burning in sealed vessels.

"Forgive me, however, Ormasis...my Master...but I believe that some of our scientists would shrug their shoulders and make fun of us. These reasoners would say that they see nothing in our experiments except that sulfur is a compound of phlogiston and vitriolic acid, necessarily deprived of parts of water; that we have only succeeded in imitating that production of nature by combining phlogiston with an acid completely deprived of water. Now, can one claim that if sulfur does not burn in sealed vessels, it is because the aqueous parts do not evaporate, because there is not enough air to form specific weight with them? Where are these aqueous parts, then? I confess, Ormasis, that these objections disconcert me."

"What! Is it possible, Nadir, that such objections embarrass you? Ask your scientists whether they have not told you themselves that salts are compounds or aggregations of earth and water? Yes. In that case, vitriolic acid, which they rightly regard as the principle salt of all the others, is not exempt from aqueous parts, in such a state of desiccation as thy suppose. Such is the consequence of their own theory. There is no other reply to make to them. Furthermore, if they want another, show them this striking experiment.

"One heats oil of vitriol with tin in a glass bottle. As the tin dissolves, the acid combined with phlogiston sublimates in the neck of the bottle and forms a true sulfur. You see, therefore, that there must necessarily be some aqueous parts combined with the sulfur, for it is surely not the most concentrated acid that ought to rise first into the neck of the bottle.

"Now, my friend, be certain that when sulfur burns, there are always some portions of decomposed acid. Your scientists are still to be convinced that the vitriolic acid has not decomposed, because they obtain a considerable quantity of acid after each inflammation—but just because they obtain a good deal of undecomposed acid, are they able to conclude that there was no decomposed part? See, however, where that supposition has led them. They have imagined that the loss of weight they perceive during the decomposition of sulfur is exactly determined by a loss of phlogiston, and they have even taken the calculation so far as to claim that the weight of the phlogiston contained in sulfur is approximately one-sixteenth; which is to say that into seventeen pounds of sulfur they have admitted a pound of pure fire, for that is how they define phlogiston. Now, how can they imagine that an element lighter than air can increase the weight of a substance? On the contrary—and that is too evident to require demonstration.

"The enlightenment that your scientists have communicated to you on other matters demands your esteem in their regard, but beware of blind prejudice, which can sometimes draw you into the grossest errors."

Chapter XI

The Philosopher was about to go into detail regarding the advice that he had given, but, perceiving that Nadir wanted to ask him a few questions, he listened attentively.

"I should like to know," Nadir said, "why a red-hot coal plunged into oil is immediately extinguished."

"The reason is simple, my friend. It is because even the most inflammable oil is not exempt from aqueous parts, for without those aqueous parts, which weaken the movement of phlogiston, the whole mass of that oil would catch fire, instead of which, all oils only catch fire at their surface."

"But what causes that phenomenon, Ormasis? Why do oils only burn at their surface?"

"This is the reason. You know that the movement of the atmosphere is much more sensible at the surfaces of bodies than in their interior. There is therefore more movement on the surfaces of those oils than in their interior parts. There is therefore more desiccation and, in consequence, it is on the surface that the inflammation of phlogiston takes place. In addition, that inflammation is entertained at the surface because, the most phlogisticated parts of the liquid mass being the lightest, they necessarily rise above the others when they experience the movement communicated to them by the flame.

"It is now easy to resolve that famous problem of why the inflammation of wine-spirit can be extinguished by blowing on it, but, on the contrary, blowing on burning wood augments the inflammation

"Do not lose sight of the verity that the percussion of a cannonball is weakened more by a supple body than by a hard one. The same effects are seen here. The lighter a mass of fluid is, the more supple it is, and thus it weakens the percussion of light to a greater extent. Thus, the percussion of the flame that is blown out by a breath reenters a fluid, is weaker there, and the more supple the fluid is, the weaker it is. It is not the same with the flame that, blown by a breath, reenters a solid body. Its percussion is much more considerable, so it further increases the movement of the phlogiston contained in the pores of the body in question, and, in consequence, its inflammation."

"Ah!" Nadir replied. "That reasoning is sensible; I was dissatisfied by the answers that had been given to me previously. I asked why blowing made wood burn more brightly, and was told in reply that it was because it separated out the fuliginosities or aqueous parts that were opposing inflammation. That reason was good enough, but it was not sufficient, because it did not explain to me why similar blowing extinguished burning oil, although it also separated the fuliginosities. Tell me, I pray you, why water that is thrown on to burning oil immediately increases the inflammation?"

"Nothing is simpler, Nadir. You have just understood why oils burn at their surface. Now, when water is thrown over burning oil, what happens? The water, which is heavier than the oil, raises up a quantity of parts in falling through it. The surfaces of the oil thus being augmented, the inflammation must be more considerable. In addition, the air contained in the water being suddenly dilated by the hear, also raises up portions of oil and further augments the surfaces. You can see, therefore, my dear Nadir, by what specific mechanism the water, which ordinarily inhibits the effects of fire, augments them in this circumstance, and you can see that the experiment does not falsify our principles."

"Indeed," Nadir replied, "I was sure that there would not be any contradiction in the effects of nature, but I had until now sought in vain for an explanation of why water, which extinguishes burning wood, augmented to some degree the inflammation of oily substances. I am satisfied.

"I will come back to your definition of phlogiston. The more I reflect on that commonplace experiment in which one sets fire to two pieces of wood by rubbing them together, the more I appreciate that a quantity of small bodies rapidly rubbed together might agitate light and occasion a percussion and a considerable inflammation. I also understand that the flame which appears to our eyes is a development of the agitated light. I therefore understand, now, why spirit of niter poured on to an essential oil causes a detonation and a prodigious inflammation.

"In fact, the acid, by its fall into the phlogiston, augments at that same instant the friction and movement of the little balls. The fewer aqueous parts there are, the more active the percussion of the agitated light becomes. In sum, the oil, divided by percussion, then presents a infinity of surfaces, which catch fire at the same time and dilate the air with great vivacity. We also see that the more concentrated the spirit of niter is—which is to say, derived of aqueous parts—the more sudden the inflammation is. Similarly, essential oils are more flammable than others because they contain fewer aqueous parts and more phlogiston. In all these experiments I see the verity of your principles."

"I am delighted," the Philosopher said, "that you have easily understood the action of phlogiston. Now, you ought to understand that the more abundant light is in the atmosphere, the more the percussion of that light will divide the little molecules of the materials distributed therein, the movement of which it then augments. It therefore follows that the more light there is in a portion of the atmosphere, the more the air is charged with phlogiston. It therefore follows that when a full moon is over a portion of your globe, the air must be more phlogisticated than it is during other phases. Reflect on this principle, and you can explain all the effects derived therefrom.

"You know that an augmentation of phlogiston in animals suffices to maintain in liquefaction a substance such as the marrow of their bones. You know that phlogiston accelerates the fermentation of spirituous liquors, and you also understand that those liquors sealed in vessels during the full moon conserve a more considerable activity and are more susceptible to explosion—which has been proved many times without being capable of explanation. It is also for that reason that certain plants collected during the full moon or the first moments of its waning have more specific effects than at other times. That activity of phlogiston, much more considerable toward the equator, also depends on attraction, of which it is necessary to know the principle.

"We shall talk about that."

Chapter XII

The library door was ajar, and Mirza listened to the friends for a few minutes, not wanting to interrupt them. The Philosopher had stopped speaking. Nadir was thinking silently about the influences of the moon, which had so often been regarded as fables, and which he now saw as the natural consequences of the most evident principles.

Suddenly, Mirza appeared; she told him that the poor but honest man who had initially refused his offers had finally come to accept them.

"He was waiting for me," she said, "I helped him without humiliating him. I saw joy gradually reborn in his heart. His gratitude was so expressive...oh, Nadir, the pleasure it gave me was more than repayment."

Then she addressed Ormasis. "I heard a part of your conversation, my dear Philosopher. I understood quite clearly that what is called phlogiston is the substance in nature most susceptible to movement. Is that not true?"

"Indeed, Madame. There is another verity, which is that the movement most agreeable to me is the one that brought me here."

"I see," Mirza said, "that a true scientist is not a misanthrope, and that an honest compliment is as familiar to him as a physical explanation. And you, Nadir, do you have nothing to say?"

"No, my dear Mirza, but I think quite seriously that the movement of phlogiston most fortunate for me was the one that gave you birth."

"What?" Mirza replied. "That too was phlogiston? But you've just told me something very tender. I shall occupy myself once again with my questions. Shall we go down into the garden? If Ormasis agrees, we can go to find Fatima there. You know that Fatima is a little more reasonable than I am, but she is at least as curious. I've just left her. She would absolutely love to meet Ormasis. I promised her that we would go to join her. Let's go. Is that agreeable to you, Nadir?"

Immediately, Mirza took the Philosopher's hand, and he went with her.

Delighted by Fatima's curiosity, which already appeared fertile for his plans, Nadir walked hurriedly, saying to himself: *If I can get Ormasis to stay here, I shall complete the joy of the amiable Fatima. Still beautiful, Fatima is no longer at the age of foolish passions, and her heart is susceptible to a reflective attachment. As for Ormasis, I hope that the graces of a beautiful summer might seduce him, for he is also at an age where a sane man fears to expose himself to the caprices of a younger season.*

Mirza interrupted Nadir's reflection to tell him that the people he had invited had accepted his invitation. "You are going to dine with two scientists who detest one another," she said to Ormasis. "That's all I've been able to understand in their disputes. One is a Chemist named Grasacido, the other Doctor Fixoventi; we also have another Physicist. But I would like to know why scientists sometimes put such bitterness into their opinions. Do you become annoyed too, Ormasis, when someone does not share your opinion?"

"Never, Madame; it is of little importance to me whether someone adds faith to my principles—and when men find pleasure in persisting in the most false ideas, why should I oppose their happiness? They are no less my friends. A man of common sense never gets angry about opinions and tastes. For instance, one of your worthy writers might convert his elegant and bold pen into a mechanical and servile pen, and find happiness therein; so much the better for him. He might persuade himself that the theater, which is today the school of morals, and not, as it once was, that of ferocity and libertinage, is a poison that is spoiling the human species, Let us allow him the pleasure of criticizing a part of its works. He regrets no longer being in the so-called primitive state of humankind; he would like to be therein. Let us allow him his desires. He would like never to have read, and believed that he knows nothing because he has read a great deal. If the opinion amuses him, why fight it? He no longer want to read any works because he is convinced that they will not tell him anything new. Is that conceit on his part? Let us once again allow him that agreeable sentiment, which cheers him up. In truth, Madame, I would like all beings to be happy, and if a man's felicity almost always depends on his imagination, why try to put shackles on that when it poses no threat to social order?"

"Oh, that is a sane morality," said Mirza. "I can, indeed, see that tolerance ought to extend to opinions of every sort."

It was while moralizing thus that they arrived in the garden path where Fatima was. She perceived Ormasis with interest, and even with a kind of embarrassment. The rapid eulogy that Mirza given her on the subject of the Philosopher had traced itself in her heart.

"What!" Nadir said to her. "Fatima here. We've arrived very fortuitously. We did not expect to find you here alone. Where, then, are our two friends?"

"I'm annoyed with them," Fatima replied. "They were keeping some secret from me this morning; I was in a bad mood and left them. I met Mirza. She told me that I would find you here; I am certainly fully compensated."

"Madame," said Ormasis, "these little quarrels between friends do not last long, and I have perceived in my own case that some advantage often results from them."

"Yes," said Fatima, "they are promptly repaired, and the need in that regard becomes a pleasure when it is satisfied."

"But Mesdames," Nadir interjected, "you are not very comfortable here. These trees are not sufficiently garnished, and the sun's rays..."

"You're right," said Mirza. "Let's go into the shade. By the way, I should like to know why walking in the sun causes one to feel weary, and a strange heaviness.

"It's because it's warmer than in the shade," replied Nadir.

"But that is not sufficient," Ormasis said. "Explain to us now why that heat, and the sun's rays, weary a traveler. Perhaps you will tell us that the air, divided by heat—which is to say, by the percussion of the light— becomes lighter, and that the body of the traveler thus becomes relatively heavier.

"That reason is not applicable here. In fact, it is necessary to consider that a traveler is an active being. Now, the less resistance he encounters to his movement, the less fatigue he ought to suffer; as light air offers less resistance than heavy air, he ought therefore to be less weary when he is exposed to the sun. But as experiment produces an opposite effect, it is necessary to seek a different response. We will find it according to the certain principle that light necessarily exerts a pressure on all the bodies in nature, and that is what I shall demonstrate to you.

"You see, therefore, Nadir, that Mirza's question, apparently so simple might leads to curious explanations with regard to the weight of bodies. But I don't think I should go on. A true reasoner like me might only amuse Nadir and bore lovely women. Besides which, it's difficult to demonstrate clearly the origin of the gravity of bodies when one is occupied with their beauty." In making that reflection, Ormasis looked at Fatima.

"That," she said to him, "is a very honest excuse, but if you persist in it, it's a proof that you mistrust our intelligence."

That remark was an order for the Philosopher, and he immediately began the following dissertation.

Chapter XIII

"My dear Nadir, some Scientists, your contemporaries, as laborious as they are intelligent, have exposed interesting verities to their fellows; curiosity alone guides their work. Little distracted by conceit, their opinion is the result of a more reflective examination. There was a time when these Scientists were the ornament of your globe, and dissipated the false glamour of chimeras. For more than fifty centuries, stupid errors enshrouded in great words were the adornment of your philosophers—or, to put it better, there was no philosophy. Very little existed of the sublime knowledge that elevates humans above themselves, and penetrates them with a delightful sentiment.

"You know that your ancient astronomers believed that the sun revolved around the Earth, but that opinion, so powerfully accredited, having been submitted to the proof of a faithful calculation, entirely lost its credit. It was demonstrated, and very rigorously demonstrated, that, by reason of the distance to be covered, the sun could only make a circuit of your planet in 475 years—and that well-established demonstration provided the proof that it was the Earth that was rotating.

"After that discovery, your scientists judged, rightly, that the atmospheric pressure on all beings must be considerable, since human beings and other bodies not adherent to the Earth were not lifted up by that movement of rotation. Although they could not imagine what was the cause of that pressure of the atmosphere and that of the gravity of bodies, the consequences of their discoveries were nonetheless interesting. They observed that two stones equal in weight, released by two slings unequal in length, but whirled around with a similar movement, were displaced from their point of departure in inverse relation to the square of their distances from the center of the movement. That experiment naturally led them to posit as a principle that the higher bodies are elevate, the less they weigh. In fact, since the Earth rotates, it is therefore the case that the more distant bodies are from the center of the Earth, the faster they move through space. Then they have more centrifugal movement, and, in consequence, less weight-which is to say, less tendency toward the center of the Earth.

"After this observation, one of your ingenious scientists even calculated how much the weight that you call a pound on your globe would weigh on Saturn— and, indeed, it was sufficient for him to know the diameter of that planet to calculate the weight of a body at its surface, relative to the distance from the center.

"With the support of these principles, it was observed on your globe that the movement of a pendulum slowed down on the equator and that the movement accelerated toward the poles; now, as the isochronic movement of the pendulum depends on the law of gravity, one can draw the conclusion that, bodies weighing less on the equator and more toward the poles, the Earth must therefore be more elevated at the equator and flattened at the poles. Even if experiments had not confirmed that verity, there are certain reasonings whose force is, so to speak, that of a geometric proof. In sum, Nadir, believe without hesitation that the more elevated bodies are, the less they weigh."

"However," Nadir replied, "there is a victorious experiment in favor of the contrary theory. A balance was suspended at the top of a very high bell-tower. Beneath each pan of that balance was an iron wire that descended to some three feet above ground level, and which supported two other pans. The higher balance was loaded with equal weights, and the balance was equal. But after having brought the weight down from one of the higher balances and put it in one of the lower balances, instead of experiencing an increase in weight, there was, on the contrary, an appreciable diminution. It follows, therefore, that bodies, far from being heavier as they approach the center of the Earth, are, on the contrary, lighter... What? You're laughing, Ormasis. Am I mistaken? Is that experiment not true?"

"Yes, my friend, but it proves nothing, except that there is often, close to ground level, more vapor than at a higher level. Consequently, the weight, floating in a more resistant fluid, appears lighter. Moreover, your scientists have already refuted that apparent objection. It is sufficient for it to be demonstrated that the Earth is rotating, and to reflect on the immutable laws of centrifugal forces, not to doubt for a moment that the more distant an object is from the center of the Earth, the less it weighs.

"Reflect also on this other observation. If, according to your theory, bodies becoming more distant from the Earth become heavier—which is to say that they increase their tendency to reunite with it, it would result that all the globes in nature would fall upon the Earth, and that it would become the center of a universal mass. But since, on the contrary, those other globes, far from uniting with the Earth, rotate on their own axes, and the bodies that are on their surfaces similarly tend to their own centers, your theory is unsustainable."

"But after all," Nadir replied. "I can maintain, personally that the Earth does not rotate. I can maintain that a body as light and subtle as the sun could traverse a great circle as easily as the Earth might travel a smaller one in the same lapse of time. I defy you to prove to me by your calculations that the law in question is physically impossible."

"Those, my dear Nadir, are so many wasted words. Well, suppose for a moment that these ingenious calculations do not exist. It is by means of physical reasoning that I want to convince you. Yes, Nadir, it is physically impossible for the Earth to be a tranquil body. If the Earth did not rotate, there would be no mixtures of elements there, no compounds. Animals and vegetables would not exist. The Earth would not enclose in its bosom those various productions that only result from the mixture of elements. In fact, water, being much lighter than condensed earth, would never penetrate its bosom. Air, much lighter than water and earth, would always have floated over those two elements without mixing with them. Finally, light, that fluid so delicate, would never have penetrated anybody. Light can only penetrate into the Earth by virtue of a movement of rotation. Here is the invincible proof of it: I shall draw it from an experiment that is familiar to you. If one puts oil into a glass globe that already contains water, that oil, being lighter, remains constantly on the surface of the water so long as the globe is motionless, but as soon as the globe is rotated, the oil passes through the water, and penetrates to the center of the globe. You see, therefore, by means of this very simple experiment, that if the Earth did not have a rotational movement, water, air and light, being lighter than earth, would never have been mingled or combined with it."

"Now Nadir, reflect upon the essential consequences resulting from that experiment. One is that light is drawn by the movement of rotation toward the center of the Earth, which is one of the principal causes of the atmospheric pressure on all bodies .The velocity of its course compensates for the lightness of his mass. Do not be surprised any longer by the fact that the fall of bodies of air in hermetically sealed tubes, from which the air has been pumped, still exerts its pressure there and its tendency toward the center of the Earth. Do not be astonished any longer that rays of sunlight weary travelers. Do not be astonished any longer that the light of the sun slowing from the top of a chimney occasions smoke in an apartment; that effect proves the real pressure of a greater quantity of light.

"It is that pressure which, on striking the air, simultaneously prevents it from escaping upwards and occasions its reflux to the bottom of the chimney, in spite of the air current in the apartment, which forms a resistance. It is true that if that smoke does not find any issue for its reflux, then the percussion and repercussion of the light, in subdividing it, will eventually occasion its evaporation, and an evaporation all the more elevated because it has become lighter. It is thus that coarse vapors risen up from the Earth by night and precipitated by the first rays of the sun subsequently rise up again, in a state of division often insensible to your eyes, and fall again when the cold of the atmosphere has condensed them."

"Oh, my friend," exclaimed Nadir, rapturously, "you delight me with pleasure. What! It is with such simple reflections that I can solve problems that make our scientists go pale? Those laborious men have discovered that air weighs upon all the bodies of Nature. They have discovered that the Earth rotates, but have not reflected that it is precisely that movement of rotation that is the cause of the pressure of air and light—and yet they have seen, by decisive experiments, that the lightest bodies are those that tend more to the center of a rotating globe. The fall of bodies in the void makes them regard the origin of the gravity of bodies as something incomprehensible, because they see that the pressure of the air cannot have any effect on bodies placed in the void, but they have not reflected that light presses upon and penetrates all the vessels; that the light in question, by virtue of the movement of rotation, always tends toward the center of the Earth, and necessarily exercises a relative pressure upon all bodies; that that pressure must act equally upon different bodies placed in the void, because there is then less inferior resistance—which is to say, no repercussion of the air—that might cause bodies to fall unequally by virtue of their volume. That is why a ball of lead and a piece of paper fall in the void with the same promptitude.

"Finally, Ormasis, I now understand sensibly the origin of fermentations in sealed vessels. That intestinal movement is no longer an occult virtue for me. It is a natural consequence of the pressure of the light that penetrates and agitates all bodies. In fact, it is sufficient for me to know about that primary motor to reflect that agitated bodies, pressed one against another, can change form, weight, and, in consequence, taste; that the attenuated parts of these bodies can for emanations of different species; that these emanations can subsequently combine with other bodies. Finally, the principle of fermentations seems evident to me, the formation of phlogiston consequent on your precepts, and I have a better understanding of the play of light in all bodies.

"In reflecting further on the rotational movement of the globe, I understand how there can be light, air and phlogiston in the deepest cavities of the Earth, which I did not understand before. I understand that the rays of light that strike the Earth are reflected in varying degrees. I also understand that there is a large quantity of air repelled by the Earth that resists it, which also occasions its lateral pressure, and the light of these very varied reflections. I understand, finally, that the continuous impacts of air and light, by diversifying mixtures, occasion the changes that Nature makes manifest—which is to say, the successive compositions and decompositions of all beings.

"I presume," Nadir continued, "that the sun never loses its substance, in spite of the opinion of one of our scientists."

"My friend," Ormasis replied, "although I hold that scientist in esteem and admire several of his discoveries, I do not recommend that you adopt all his ideas. He does not recommend it himself. What would the loss of the sun's substance signify? Where would that loss go? What would become of it? Can you conceive that light might be annihilated, or even change its nature? In fact, it is not an element like composite bodies. How can one conceive of the metamorphosis of an element whose principles one does not now? However, it has been said that the sun would be reduced to nothing, if the comets that fall into the sphere in question from time to time did not repair its losses.[13] See how ridiculous it is, then, to compare the sun to an ardent furnace, since one is

---

[13] The thesis that the sun's energy was continually replenished by comets falling into it was popularized in France by the Comte de Buffon's *Histoire Naturelle*, whose publication commenced in 1745. He is presumably the scientist to whom the Philosopher is referring.

obliged to suppose that a few faggots fall into it from time to time to maintain the fire. It is, furthermore, in accordance with this false idea that it is supposed that Mercury, the planet nearest to the sun must be an uninhabitable world and much denser than yours, since it has not been volatilized by the intense heat.

"Reflect then that, heat being only the light agitated by the rotatory movement of the globe, it results that the smaller a planet is, the less distance its surface travels, and the less heat there is there. Do not, then, be surprised that animals can subsist on a globe such as ours, which, being twenty-seven times smaller than yours, is no warmer, in spite of being closer to the sun, and yet is warm enough, by reason of the large quantity of light that it receives."

Mirza made a sign to Nadir.

Ormasis perceived it. "Beautiful Mirza," he said to her, "I admit that excessively long explanations also exercise a fatiguing pressure on the mind. I should not have obeyed Fatima's orders. I confess to you, Ladies, that I dread boring you."

"Not at all," they replied, in chorus.

"In truth," Mirza continued, "you would not believe the pleasure with which I listen to you, and the particular attention of my friend is proof of the same pleasure. It was in order not to interrupt you that I made the sign; I was reminding Nadir of the explanation I gave him yesterday—an explanation relative to your last observation. I was very glad to see how similar it was to yours. So Nadir, in spite of all his compliments, was a little jealous, and to avenge himself he ran to fetch a large book of figures, and the demonstrations that it was necessary to make to me caused me to lose my reason more than once...

"But Ormasis, you have just picked a quarrel with us. My dear Fatima, it is necessary to avenge ourselves. Listen to me. To prove to him that we have given him all our attention, let us raise terrible objections."

"Gladly," Fatima replied, "but you're more learned than me; I leave that to you."

Chapter XIV

"So you claim, Master Philosopher, that light exerts a sensible pressure on all bodies. Good. But I don't believe that the strongest pressure of that light is that which tends toward the center of the Earth. One night, I was in my apartment; Nadir was not there, and yet I was not asleep. I was examining with a great deal of attention the flame of a candle. I determined to observe, and I believe that I saw that the flame in question, far from tending toward the center of the Earth, was always rising. My observation therefore lacked common sense."

"Forgive me, Madame, but the flame that you saw rising, and which does indeed rise over all burning bodies, was nothing but the vapors divided by the light and becoming lighter than the vapors surrounding it. As for the light that you see being agitated by the circular movement of the phlogiston, it diverges in all directions through the apartment, and the proof that the dominant movement of that light is not upwards is that, if your candle is set very low down in the apartment, it will nor light you any more brightly. You therefore see that it is necessary not to confuse the flame, which is a composite body, with the light, which is a simple body."

"Just a moment," Mirza replied. "Here's another objection. If light exerts a sensible pressure on all bodies, those bodies ought to be lighter at night than by day. In that case, the barometer, whose variation depends on different atmospheric pressures, ought to be more...Nadir, as soon as it gets dark, I want to see whether your barometer will fall. Oh, as to that, I don't believe it. Agree, Master Philosopher that that is a terrible objection."

"Madame, I shall leave Nadir the pleasure of replying. He is clever enough to get around the problem."

"In any case," Nadir replied, "if I were in a position to ask Mirza's indulgence, I'm sure..."

"I see," she interrupted, "that one has the resource of joking when one is in an embarrassing situation. I beg you to respond seriously."

"Very well, my dear Mirza, here is my very serious response. Although light exerts less pressure on bodies during the night than during the day, my barometer might well be as high by night as during the day. This is the reason: it is cooler by night, so the masses of rarefied water in the upper atmosphere condense and descend lower, which results in a greater pressure of the air that is below them; that is what compensates to some degree for the pressure of the light, which is less considerable during the night. You therefore see, my dear Mirza, that the barometer experiment does not falsify our friend's principles, in the same way that his principles do not falsify the ingenious reasons that some scientists have offered us for the variations of the barometer.

"There is another observation to make; it is that light, which does in truth exert less pressure during the night than during the day, nevertheless exerts a sensible one. In fact, what we call night is nothing but the Earth's shadow. Now, outside the projection of that shadow, light is abundant, and the movement of rotation, which is still sensible at that height, still draws portions of light, from which pressure results."

"Very good," said Mirza. "I like this serious philosophy, but explain that last observation to me a little more sensibly."

"Gladly, Mirza; come into the sunlight for a moment. Let us suppose that you are the Earth. The sun is behind you. Look at your shadow in front of you. That's night. Now, you can see that beyond the projection of that shadow, the light reappears with the same vivacity."

"Indeed," Mirza replied. "I understand your demonstration."

"That's not all," Nadir continued, "setting himself in front of Mirza. I compared you to the Earth. I'm an inhabitant of that Earth. You can see that the closer I am to you, the more I find myself in your shadow." Nadir drew gradually closer to her. "Ah!" he said, in a low voice, putting his lips to hers, "if a body as agreeable as yours formed an eternal night, plunged in that charming shadow, I would abandon light without regret."

"You're very amiable," Mirza retorted, "but be honest—you love light too much to renounce it. Remember that I've questioned you more than once..." She raised her voice and moved closer to the Philosopher. "Ormasis," she continued, raising her voice, what do you think of Nadir's indiscretion? Terminating a physical explanation with a kiss! Agree that that is lacking in scientific majesty. Of course, I have a good excuse for not retreating, because the sun's rays were pressing upon me and driving me toward my shadow. As for him, he has no excuse."

"No," replied Nadir. "I confess that, in order not to be humiliated. I would like Ormasis to be just as indiscreet with respect to Fatima."

The Philosopher was delighted by the cheerfulness of his hosts, and also by Fatima's beauty. That amiable woman had asked him to explain what isochronic oscillations were. He had already suspended a small stone from a silken thread. The thread was attached to the edge of the bench on which he was sitting. Having set the stone in motion, he demonstrated to Fatima that the isochronic oscillation of the pendulum was nothing other than circular movement—which is to say, a movement describing an arc of a circle.

"With regard to circular movement," I said, "I shall tell you a fact that might seem singular to you, which is that no linear movement exists in nature that does not obtain its origin from a circular movement."

"A good joke!" Fatima replied. "But if I advance my hand toward you in a straight line, that is a perfectly linear movement." And she did, in fact, advance her hand.

"Yes," countered the Philosopher, "but observe that the top of your arm is describing a circular movement. Notice now, beautiful Fatima, that your arm is extended. I take it, I raise it up. You see that it is again describing a circular path. I lean over; there's another circular movement. I kiss your hand; further circular movement, for it's impossible to open and close the mouth without a circular movement. You draw back; another circular movement. If you made a decision to run away from me, that would be another circular movement, but it would cause me a good deal of pain."

"Me, run away from you," replied Fatima, slightly disconcerted by that unexpected declaration. "You, Nadir's friend, for whom I feel all esteem..."

Nadir, delighted by what he suspected, hastened to save Fatima from a slight embarrassment. "You see," he said to her, "that our Philosopher is gallant. Don't think that I have admitted a misanthrope into our society. I've reflected, my dear Ormasis, on the singular truth that you have just enabled us to perceive. I know that all fluid bodies tend to adopt a spherical form, but I have never observed that in Nature there is no linear movement that does not receive its impulsion from a circular movement. In fact, in all the mechanical components that make linear movements, they always emanate from a circular movement. If, for example, in windmills there are rammers that go up and down in a straight line, it is always a circular movement that activates them. If I throw an object perpendicularly, the mechanism of my arm, which throws it, describes a circular motion. The bullet that escapes from a firearm is also impelled by the circular movements of phlogiston and the dilatation of the air."

"How amusing that is," Mirza put in, laughing wholeheartedly. "Listen to me, Nadir, I have a question to ask you in secret. Excuse me Ormasis. Tell me, my friend; is it also isochronic oscillation that..." She completed her question in a whisper.

Nadir laughed uproariously.

Ormasis and Fatima, already instructed by what they had heard, also shared the joke.

But it was no longer the time for joking. Nadir perceived in the distance the arrival of Dr. Fixoventi and the Chemist Grasacido. "Come on," he said to Mirza. "Let's go to meet them." He looked at his watch. "I didn't realize that it was so late. Ask for dinner to be served, my dear Mirza."

Ormasis and Fatima advanced a little more slowly.

"It must be admitted," said Ormasis, "that the couple marching ahead of us certainly merit being happy. I cannot yet confide to you, beautiful Fatima, what particular interest attaches me to those two beings, but even if that interest did not exist, they would be no less dear to me. In the fifteen years since a terrible accident deprived me of an amiable companion, these are the first moments in which I have to some extent forgotten chagrins that the resources of science have never been able to vanquish."

"I cannot imagine the reason for your attachment to our friends," Fatima replied, "but for myself, far from being jealous of their mutual happiness, it becomes a part of mine. Nadir might have told you in what fashion we live together. However, he would like me to find a spouse who would leave me my complete liberty, and, in consequence, the pleasure of always enjoying his society. I don't know why my anxieties regarding that proposition are redoubled today, and I sense more than ever an invincible repugnance for it."

"But after all, beautiful Fatima, if the friend that Nadir proposed to you were linked with him permanently; if he were to live here; if that man adored you; if, insensible for a long time to the sweetness of love, he found his felicity in you, would you refuse to make him happy?"

"At least," Fatima replied, "I would like to know him before making my decision."

"Yes," said Ormasis, "but if that man were no longer in the springtime of his life; if, sometimes, a residue of melancholy or reflections rendered him pensive, it is certain that your choice would never fall in his favor."

"Why not? To begin with, I do not have the conceit to believe that I am in the springtime of my life. In the second place, a touch of melancholy is almost always the proof of a sensitive soul. As for reflections, I would be scornful of a man who never made any. Besides, if those reflections sometimes extended to objects as amusing as they are instructive, oh, how much pleasure I would take in dreaming with him. Science gives true nobility to genius, and a man that possesses it experiences all its value."

"Well, divine Fatima, if, without aspiring to that nobility of genius, my feeble knowledge might sometimes interest you; if I were that friend; if Nadir..."

"My dear Philosopher," Fatima said to him, looking at him with the most tender expression, "we understand one another...let's go on, I beg you. I don't want anyone to perceive already that I love you—me, who passes here for the most reasonable and reflective of women..."

Ormasis then experienced a tender situation of the soul that is easier to feel than to express.

They thought that they were advancing very promptly, but they were hardly moving. A slave came to distract them from that sweet reverie, and told them that they were awaited in the drawing room.

Chapter XV

While the Doctor, the Chemist and the Physicist were conversing with Mirza, Laure and Sophie showed Nadir a letter they had received. As soon as Nadir perceived Fatima and Ormasis, he said to them with the greatest gaiety: "Come and read this."

Selim and Osman
to
Laure and Sophie.

You are two charming friends. We are two slightly dazed friends, but that is not from loving you. The union of Nadir and Mirza seems to us to be unalterable. The happiness of that friend, founded on confidence, is an example that seduces us. His one desire is to create converts to the same cause, to enable them to be as happy, perhaps to determine it; but without your permission we shall refrain making him any proposition. However, Laure and Sophie repudiated... 'Repudiated,' that term was not made for them. No matter, common usage has consecrated it. It will only serve to tighten the knots of our society, and that of our attachment to Nadir. We shall come this evening to learn the decision of our fate. We shall await it with impatience.

"So that," said Fatima, "was this morning's mystery. I had presumed that it was either a joke or delicacy. My amiable friends, I forgive you with all my heart. Judge by the pleasure I have in embracing you how much I desire your happiness."

"My dear Fatima," they replied, "we are surely very happy here. What more can we desire?"

"Read, then," Nadir put in. "Will Laure and Sophie count as trivial the satisfaction of making others happy? Yes, you will make others happy; however, in order that it will never be at the expense of your own felicity, I shall bind Selim and Osman with relevant promises. I will take charge of that."

Mirza had run to embrace her friends, and, soon informed on the subject, took the most sincere part in it. Laure and Sophie were not discontented. In fact, the finest sentiments are always in accord with something physical, and the most elevated soul cannot isolate itself from the impulsions of Nature.

They sat down at table. The meal was delicate. It was heartily welcomed. The appetizing dishes usually received sincere eulogies.

"In truth," said Grasacido, "I prefer a good cook to the most skillful chemist."

"Ah," said Ormasis, "that epigram against yourself does not convince us. Besides, the art of cuisine is itself founded on chemical principles. Pass me, I beg you, that ragout. For example, water and grease have no affinity to unite together, but by means of the intermediary of a mucilage such as flour, they have been mixed in such a way as to form this brown sauce, which is very good. You also know that the liaison of sauces is useful operation, if well done, because then the fats, being more divided, give the stomach less work to do. You also know that a quantity of spices in ragouts is dangerous, because the abundance of phlogiston they contain penetrates the pores of the sanguine vessels and tends to decompose the blood in rarefying it."

"It appears," Grasacido replied, "that the gentleman has knowledge of these subjects. For myself, I will tell you frankly that I have been seeking for a long time to imitate the sulfurs of our stomach. They are surely vegetal acids combined with phlogiston, but why do those sulfurs sometimes have the same odor that they have in base vitriolic acid? Why do they always make fluorine without the assistance of a concentrated alkali? Are there oils that…no, I won't go on about the object of my research. I see, however, that there exists everywhere an *acidum pingue*[14] that plays a major role in Nature, and presents its *latus*[15] in an infinity of different ways.

At the mere mention of *acidum pingue*, Doctor Fixoventi immediately abandoned chewing the wing of a partridge, of which his stomach was about to absorb the *fixed air*,[16] and looked at Grasacido disapprovingly. "In

---

[14] *Acidum pingue*, like 'Grasacido' means "fatty acid," but not in the sense that that term is nowadays used in organic chemistry; it was derived from Becher's *terra pinguis* by Johann Mayer in a textbook of Chemistry published in 1764, as a theoretical substitute for phlogiston supposedly compounded fire, light and an unknown acid substance. As Grasacido will shortly admit, the term was sometimes used to designate sulphur, but he wants to use it more ambitiously, in a fashion that he will try in vain to explain.

[15] *Latus* is Latin for "flank" or "side," usually used in the context of exposure; with respect to sulphur it could be used with reference to the substance's crystalline structure, or to its different isomeric forms, but again, Grasacido has higher ambitions for it.

[16] Although its use at this point in the narrative commentary is a joke, the subsequent discussion of "fixed air" reflects the disputes and confusions arising from Rutherford's isolation of de-oxygenated air, although the term had earlier been popular-

truth, sir, it's singular that one should wish to mystify scientists with a substance as impalpable as it is incomprehensible, and whose effects one pretends to explain by the touching of sides. Yes, the *latus*, the sides, the flanks, of an *acidum pingue*, of a substance whose form we do not comprehend—that's a joke, of course."

"Eh?" Grasacido replied. "Is it not more singular, sir, to pretend that there are airs that become fixed, heavy, and yet impalpable, and that those same airs become volatile again with the same facility. These inexplicable metamorphoses, contrary to the laws of physics, are certainly more inconsequential than my theory."

"That's false," the doctor retorted. "Nothing is more natural than fixed air, as I shall enable these gentleman to judge..."

He was about to go on, but he was interrupted by burst of laughter, of which the following was the object.

Nadir's cook was a fat Negro, thick-lipped and pug-nosed—in brief, the most comical figure. Having heard it said that her cook must be a chemist, and seeing him pass by the door of the room at that moment, Mirza had called him in. The Negro's great eagerness to obey his mistress had caused his foot to slip, and his head plunged into a dish of whipped cream that was being carried by another slave. Mirza, assured that he was not hurt, had greatly enjoyed seeing the performance.

"Gentlemen," she said, "I wanted to introduce you to the adept who merited your eulogies, but I did not know that he was also devoted to fixed air, to the point of making a mask of it."

---

ized in the 1750s by Joseph Black with respect to the gas produced from limestone by heating or treatment with acid. Fixoventi's name is, of course, a pun parallel to 'Grasacido.'

Everyone laughed heartily, and also complimented the Negro on his useful talents. Mirza was not unaware that in every estate, imagination makes the happiness of human beings.

The slave, delighted to have served the amusement of his masters and to have been complimented, withdrew with joy in his heart.

Sophie was not eating however, having distractedly detached the seal from the suitors' letter. She was amusing herself by rubbing the seal, to make it pick up little bits of paper.

"Yes, my dear Sophie," Nadir said to her. "You and Laure have the virtue of that seal. Those little pieces of paper are Selim and Osman."

"Oh, you're wicked," Sophie replied. "You're taking your revenge for our silence, but we ask for your grace for today. Besides, we're listening to these gentlemen with the greatest pleasure."

The Doctor was about to present his proofs, but the ever-curious Mirza addressed the Physicist, and everyone listened in silence.

"Sir," she said, "why does that wax seal, having been rubbed, attract little pieces of paper or other light bodies presented to it?"

"Madame, such is the property of all bodies whose surfaces are highly polished: glass, diamond and precious stones have the same effect, because friction acts universally."

"Very good," Mirza replied, "but why do the pieces of paper rise up to cling to be body that has been rubbed?"

"Madame, some of us have claimed that it is an 'electric fluid' that is in action, but as that new name has not provided any new explanation, and advertises similar effects by comparison, I therefore hold to the principle of attraction. It is by virtue of attraction, Madame, that these bodies come together."

"But in sum, Sir, what is attraction?"

"Attraction, Madame is…is the virtue by which two bodies attract one another, which, when the attractive virtue ceases, gives way to the repulsive virtue."

"But again, Sir, by virtue of what laws do these bodes have the attractive virtue?"

"But Madame, it is the occult qualities of Nature that…"

"I see," Ormasis interrupted, pained by the Physicist's embarrassment, "that the gentleman, too modest to develop his ideas, is contenting himself with the orthodox solution. But Sir, you have surely felt, as I have for a long time, that all these explanations are mere wordplay. You are doubtless aware that the atmosphere exerts a pressure in all directions on the bodies of Nature. Now, when one rubs a body vigorously, you can conceive that the air surrounding it is in large measure displaced by the movement. It is therefore at the moment when that air pressure is reestablished on the body that other small bodies are drawn to it. That reasoning is so simple, so natural, so much in conformity with true principles that it has surely not escaped your reflections."

"It is true Sir," the Physicist replied. "I have already had a few ideas in that regard, but this is a singular experiment, of which I have never been able to understand the principle. Ladies, would you have two small, very slender needles? Oh, here on this mantelpiece is a harpsichord strong; it is made of copper, but that doesn't

matter. I'll cut off two ends about three *lignes*[17] long—
that's sufficient. I set them to float in this glass of water.
They're about an inch apart. Look, please. The water is
presently quite tranquil. Notice how those two little needles are gradually drawing closer together. See how they
increase their speeds as they get closer, and suddenly
come together with the greatest celerity. Let us begin
again. You always see the same effects."

He looked at Ormasis. "Well, sir," he said, "there is
a sensible attraction; how are we to explain it? We have
not removed the air by movement, so it is not the reflux
of the air that draws those two bodies toward one another."

"Forgive me, Sir, you are too enlightened not to
sense that two bodies only come together because they
have more weight bringing them toward one another,
and that weight increases as the resistance there is between them lessens. That is the explanation for the experiment.

"There is only a distance of one inch between your
two needles, and a distance of more than two inches between your needles and the glass wall. The air that is
between your two needles reverberating more, since it is
in a narrower space, necessarily becomes lighter. There
is thus less resistance in the interval, and your needles
have a dominating weight toward one another because
the weight of the lateral pressure of the external air becomes more considerable than that of the air between
them. You therefore see, Sir, that I am content to apply

---

[17] A *ligne* was a measurement in use in France at the time,
corresponding to a twelfth of a *pouce*, which was the French
inch, here translated as "inch;" three *lignes* is therefore about a
quarter of an inch.

the law of gravity here. I am not innovating any new principle. I believe you understand me.

"One moment, however—here is my proof. I place the two needles two inches apart instead of one. Now watch. Are not the same needles that came together before moving further apart, toward the walls of the glass? That is not because there is a repulsive virtue between them, since, if I move them to a distance of one inch, they come together again. You see that these effects depend entirely on the variety of relative weights."

"I confess, Sir," the Physicist replied, "that your idea is a consequence of our accepted principles; it seems quite simple to me. We have already seen, in observations on physics, the reflections of one of our compatriots concerning the magnetic virtue. He reasoned in much the same way as you with regard to the experiment I have just cited. He has even extended his reasoning so far as to explain the origin of putrefaction, and why salts preserve bodies therefrom.[18] At first I thought that it was nothing but a series of theories, as we scientists do not like receiving new theories, I did not pay much attention to it at the time. I see today that reasoning in accordance with the laws of gravity are more essential than word-play. I understand now what that observer told us about the scent of liquids in capillary tubes. In fact, the less atmospheric pressure there is on a fluid, the more the fluid will rise up. That's quite natural. Now, in capillary tubes in which the air is greatly reverberated and rare-

---

[18] The reasoning in question originated with Isaac Newton, but the Physicist is presumably referring to Voltaire's citation of it in his 1734 essay on Newton, which popularized Newton's ideas in France.

fied, there must be less pressure than in a broad tube; in consequence, liquids must rise up further therein."

"That's exactly right," Ormasis replied, "and to convince you further that the agitation of the air is a sensible verity, all bodies whose pores, without being too widely pen, are nevertheless open enough for the air to circulate within them, are in fact the bodies that conduct most heat. For example, sponges and all spongy objects are the least cold bodies. Sugar, which is also a substance filled with capillary tubes, when rested on your hand, does not occasion the coolness of other salts, in which there are no capillary interstices. Take this piece of bread; put the soft side on your face and you scarcely experience and coolness; put the crust there and. Because the crust contains fewer capillaries interfaces, you will feel more coolness. Finally, the more capillary interstices a fabric contains, the more it warms you. A carded cloth procures you more warmth than one that is not carded, even if it is heavier. The warmth therefore increases by virtue of the capillary interstices being augmented. These observations are quite simple, but no less convincing for that."

"Upon my word, Sir," the Physicist replied, "if I did not have the certainty of skepticism, I would accept your reasoning."[19]

"What is this certainty, then?" exclaimed Mirza, swiftly.

"It is Madame," the Physicist said, "being certain that I doubt everything."

_____

[19] Skepticism remained a fundamental position of many French philosophers and scientists following René Descartes' famous meditation on the topic, published in 1637.

"Oh, Sir, I feel sorry for you; I believe that's a sad state—a state of inertia."

"No, Madame, it's the wisest state one can adopt, and the least vulnerable to sarcasm."

"Pardon me, Sir Physicist," Ormasis put in, "but it's a malady—a fashionable vapor—and you have too much common sense to be incurable. For example, do you doubt that you have had an excellent dinner?"

"No."

"Do you doubt that these are four amiable ladies?"

"Certainly not."

"Well, Sir, you see that there are truths that once cannot revoke into doubt."

"Very good, Sir Philosopher; I confess that you're convincing. I shall take pleasure in occupying myself with your principles. I see that by reflecting on the laws of gravity and different resistances, by reason of rarefactions of the air, that one can form a few certain reasonings with regard to tidal flux and reflux. I understand why, the closer objects are together, the greater is their tendency to approach one another.

"Now, I know that the Moon's equator is at an angle to the equator of the Earth. I know that at the Earth's equator, objects rise up more easily, by virtue of the centrifugal forces that diminish their gravity, and I can see that it is precisely at the point of the greatest proximity of the Earth to the Moon that the waters of the Ocean rise up. Sir Philosopher, you have suggested good ideas to me. I want to write a paper on tidal flux and reflux, which will concur entirely with the explanation that a great man[20] has already given us, but I shall render his

---

[20] Newton.

mechanism of attraction sensible without departing from his principles."

"I exhort you to do so," Ormasis replied. "I applaud your project in advance, and you will at least work to cure skeptics in that regard, whose state is absolutely desperate. But don't forget, Sir Physicist, also to take into account the effects of light on all bodies."

Very good, said the Chemist to himself. *Light is his agent; for me, it's* acidum pingue *that plays the central role in all these phenomena. I suspected as much.*

Excellent, said Doctor Fixoventi, for his part. *I'm sure that* fixed air *will one day explain the origin of attraction. We shall see what success their ideas have.*

Chapter XVI

Fatima was sitting between Ormasis and the Doctor. She took advantage of a moment when the latter was making a futile speech about his theory.

"I've understood," she said to the Philosopher in a low voice, "that the closer objects are to one another, the greater is the tendency they have to draw together, but I believe that you're mistaken, my dear Philosopher. At this very moment, as I offer you this pastry, I am very close to the Doctor, and thus more distant from you; however, it is certainly not the case that I feel a greater tendency to draw closer to him."

"Charming Fatima, that is a proof that the motor of your divine organs is not subject to the ordinary laws of gravity."

"In conclusion," said the Doctor, "the marvelous substance that produces all these metamorphoses is fixed air. It is by virtue of the aid of this fixed air that we have imitated the water of the bad mountain. If metal is calcinated by fire, it is because it is charged with fixed air. If limestone is calcinated by fire, it is because it loses the same fixed air. Nothing is more consequent. And it is not the loss and restitution of aqueous parts to which the effects of quicklime are due, as a few good people have thought."

"Doctor," Nadir replied, "as I am one of those good people, sometimes attached to old theories, liberate me, I beg you, from that servitude by means of novelties. To begin with, I have never understood what you mean by 'fixed air.' What is fixed air?"

"Fixed air, Sir, is a substance combined in the narrow pores of a substance, which can only escape it with great difficulty."

"Oh, I understand. What you call fixed air is, therefore, no more fixed than any of the other airs in the world. It is compressed air, bound within an object. Good. For a long time we've known what compressed air and free air are. We also know that the air compressed in a body can escape it when the pores of the body are opened by heat, and become free air. All that is not new."

"Forgive me, Sir; know, then, that fixed air always has the quality of fixed air, that it does indeed pass from one body to another, but that it communicates particular qualities to the other body. For example, when one throws oil of vitriol on to limestone, does not the fixed air that it gives off, and which one can collect, by means of an apparatus in common water, communicate an aerial quality to that water? Is that water not exactly similar to that of the bad mountain?"[21]

Grasacido, who was already biting his lips in fury, could no longer contain himself. "Of course," he said, "if one wants water well-impregnated with air, there's no need to go to such trouble. It's sufficient to attach a bottle two-thirds full of water to the blade of a windmill.

---

[21] The reference is presumably to naturally carbonated water, often produced in volcanic springs, but it is not obvious which particular "bad mountain" Nadir means. Artificially carbonated water had only recently become available in 1775, having been invented by Joseph Priestley in 1767; La Follie had obviously read Priestley's 1772 paper "Impregnating Water with Fixed Air," which describes a method using his beloved oil of vitriol to liberate the gas from limestone.

The air traveling rapidly through the atmosphere, which is trapped in that vessel, will penetrate the water by virtue of the motion and partly engage with it. But afterwards, the prisoner, in escaping, will soon renounce the pompous title of fixed air. At any rate, an aerometer will indicate the moment when that water is more salutary than that resulting from your preparations."

"I beg you not to interrupt me, Sir," the Doctor resumed, swiftly. "It is to the master of the house that I am addressing myself."

"Well, my dear Doctor," Nadir replied, "perhaps I haven't grasped your idea, but this is what the experiment tells me. I believe that the fall of the vitriolic acid in the pores of the limestone occasions friction, and consequently heat. I believe that the heat in question divides the parts of air and water contained in the limestone, which results in the dilatation and separation knows as effervescence, and, in consequence, the elevation of vapors. All that is quite simple. It's possible that the water charges itself with a greater quantity of air than it can contain. All well and good—but I cannot induce from it that the air is fixed, or was fixed there. I'm assured that the air is of the same quality as that of the atmosphere, and that by virtue of the rapid movement of effervescence, it has been able to draw with it a few selenitic or acid salts, and if I observe that the water in which the vapors have condensed turns blue litmus paper red, I cannot conclude from it that it is fixed air combining with the water that forms the acids."

"But do you not recall," the Doctor replied, "the experiment that made so much noise. One puts thirty ounces of limestone into a retort, and fits a recipient vessel to it by means of a sealed tube. Heat is applied, and yet one can only obtain an ounce and a half of water. It is only on opening the tube of the recipient that on hears escaping, with a hiss, and elastic fluid weighing thirteen ounces. That elastic fluid is fixed air, and if it does not escape the limestone will never be converted into quick-lime. It is, therefore, not the removal of water but the removal of fixed air that forms the quicklime. Is that conclusive?"

"Not at all, my dear Doctor. Here, in very simple terms, is the result of your operation. Limestone contains air, but it also contains, essentially, a large quantity of water. Now, when the vessels are sealed, why does dis-tillation only produce a small quantity of water? It is be-cause the vapors, in building up, prevent the evaporation of the remaining aqueous parts, which still have a pro-pensity to combine with the limestone that is in the re-tort. As soon as one opens the connecting tube, however, those vapors escape, making room for other vapors that also escape. I do not see anything in this experiment but that of the aeolipile,[22] in which water rarefied by intense heat escapes with a hiss, although it does not contain a large quantity of air."

"In truth," exclaimed Grasacido, "I do not know how he dares to publicize an experiment whose inconse-quentiality I have already demonstrated to him."

The Doctor pretended not to have heard.

"No, I don't believe," Nadir continued, "that in thir-ty ounces of limestone, there are twelve and a half ounc-es of air for half an ounce of water. I believe, on the con-trary, that there must be twelve and a half ounces of wa-ter for half an ounce of air. In fact, if a demi-gross of

---

[22] A device popularized by Heron of Alexandria but previous-ly described by Vitruvius in the first century B.C., in which steam is used to generate motion.

compressed air in a blowpipe causes such powerful explosions when it is given an issue, how can one imagine
that twelve ounces of air compressed in thirty ounces of
stone that there will not be explosions when one breaks a
few pieces of that stone? But that air has lost its spring,
it is said. How can it be that an elastic fluid, ready to
escape at the slightest fire, has no spring?"

The Philosopher was chatting to Fatima, while still
lending an ear to his pupil's reasoning. "My dear
Ormasis," Nadir asked him, "What is your sentiment
regarding the formation of quicklime?"

"I confess," Ormasis replied, "that I have the most
ancient sentiment in that regard. I believe that the priva-
tion of water is the essential characteristic of quicklime.
When one soaks the lime in water, the very sudden reunion of the water and the lime, through an infinity of capillary tubes, produces heat; such is the invariable effect
of rapid friction; that heat dilates a few parts of air, and
that air, suddenly augmented in volume, occasions the
separation of the resistant parts. Nothing is more natural.
But when the quicklime is simply exposed to air slightly
charged with vapors it becomes limestone again, slowly,
without heat or noise. Why? Because it charges itself
with water gradually, and the internal friction is less rapid. All these principles seem to me to follow."

"But after all, Sir Philosopher," the Doctor replied,
"you know that chalk renders the most caustic alkaline
salts. To what do you attribute those effects?"

"To what, Sir? To natural causes. To changes in the
saline forms that result from that reunion—such as, for
example, more trenchant angles."

"Oh, Sir," Grasacido interjected, "you don't believe, then, that it is *acidum pingue* that forms
causticum? Pay heed, then, I beg you, to the fact that my

acidum pingue is the agent of light, which carries it everywhere."

"One moment, Sir Chemist, one moment. You are too enlightened not to recognize that the agent of light must be composed of the most volatile and the most mobile parts of nature. Your *acidum*, however, does not manifest those properties. Firstly, the term 'acid' denotes a saline substance that is not among the most volatile. Secondly, acids seen through a microscope present to us a multitude of tiny points, and that form is surely not the most favorable to movement."

That observation made some impression on the mind of the Chemist. "I agree," he said, "that I ought to have selected another name, for example *circulum pingue*. Yes, *circulum pingue*—that name is far more majestic, and far more interesting; for, to tell you the truth, *acidum pingue* only signifies sulfur, and that term is not new. But I'm thinking: this *circulum pingue* will no longer have different *latus*. It would be necessary that its effects by uniform in all experiments, and that is no longer the case in the order of my theory, whose verity is, moreover, entirely demonstrated. For in the end..."

"Peace, sir, peace," cried the Doctor. Your *acidum pingue*, in spite of its *latus*, cannot be sustained and has been sunk by the following experiment." To Ormasis, he said: "You shall see whether or not this experiment is victorious in favor of fixed air. One puts lead under an inverted glass bell, plunged into water, and one then calcines part of this lead with a burning-glass. The water-level, which rose in the bell during the operation remains elevated. It is therefore evident that the metal, in being calcinated, has pumped or absorbed a quantity of air equivalent to the volume of water that has risen up. On the contrary, when, under the same bell, one recalls the lead to its metallic state, the water-level falls sensibly, certain proof that the lead has restored the air that it had absorbed. That is irrefutable."[23]

The Doctor had pronounced these final words in the most imposing tone. He was triumphant. Grasacido was embarrassed, and pretended to be distracted. Even Nadir seemed struck by this experiment, when the philosopher spoke.

"Sir Doctor, your experiment is faithful, I admit, but is your conclusion? Would you like to hear mine?"

"Willingly, Sir, but I'm convinced that..."

"I hear you. Well, you shall have the pleasure of criticizing me. Firstly, do you not agree that atmospheric air contains a quantity of salts and earthen molecules?"

"Yes Sir."

"Is it not also demonstrated that the more rarefied a fluid is, the fewer foreign bodies are sustained in the fluid?"

"Yes, Sir."

"In that case, when air is rarefied by heat, must it not allow to precipitate out the saline and earthen parts that are disseminated within it, and which then no longer form a specific weight with it?"

"Yes, Sir, that follows."

"In that case, Sir Doctor, the pores of a metal being opened by heat, is it not evident that the salts that are precipitated into the pores of that metal can cause divi-

_____

[23] The reference is to one of Daniel Rutherford's experiments; La Follie, the Doctor and the Philosopher do not, of course, realize that two different gases—carbon dioxide and oxygen—are in play in the contrasted experiments, thus seeing a contradiction where none really exists.

sions and separations there—in sum, what is called calcination?"

"Yes, Sir, I confess that that is possible; but why does the water-level rise in our glass bell when the metal is calcinated there?"

"Nothing is more natural. It is because the portion of air enclosed in the bell, being deprived of its saline and earthen molecules, no longer weighs as heavily on the surface of the water."

"In truth," the Doctor said. "I'm almost tempted to believe...but no, that's too simple. Besides, when one exposes powdered charcoal with the calcined metal under the same glass bell, why does the water level drop as the same time as the calcined metal resumes is metallic state?"

"It's because the saline materials that the calcined metal contains, uniting with a larger quantity of phlogiston, become more volatile, and rise up in the bell. Then the air in the bell, charged with these salts, exercises a more considerable pressure and caused the water-level to drop. Don't you think, Sir Doctor, that these chemical and physical explanations are more satisfying than the supposition of an air condensed by heat?"

Grasacido had regained courage, but he was more concerned to overturn his adversary's than establish his own. "That's not all," he said to Ormasis. "Not only is it claimed that air can be fixed in a body with the aid of heat, but it's also claimed that it becomes volatile by the increase of the same aid. Oh, Sir Philosopher, judge! What physics! It has, however, been necessary to resort to the ridiculous in order to adapt to that theory the experiment of mercury enclosed in a glass vessel, which successively loss and regains its fluidity by virtue of different degrees of heat. That experiment has administered a death-blow to fixed air."

"And you," said the furious Doctor, "how have you adjusted your flanks, your *latus*, to rationalize that experiment? It is, in fact, your explanation in that regard which is pitiful."

"Gentlemen, gentlemen!" the Philosopher said to them. "You both have talents. I'm sure that you hold one another in esteem. It is, therefore, only a question of reaching an understanding. Is there no means of reconciling you? Sir Chemist, when we have reasoned for some time together about phlogiston, you will see that it is unnecessary to admit an *acidum pingue*, and you will recognize, with the Doctor, that air acts considerably upon all bodies. You, Sir Doctor, without having recourse to the existence of a fixed air, a special air, which would, so to speak, be a new element, will have reason to assure yourself that air is one of the great motors in nature, but you will recognize with the Chemist that light acts powerfully on all bodies."

Grasacido listened to Ormasis considerately. The Doctor, more rebellious, became angry with the Philosopher. "Sir," Ormasis replied, calmly, "I am only seeking to instruct myself, and if your opinions can augment my feeble enlightenment, even if you offer them to me ill-temperedly, they will be no less precious to me."

"Well, Sir," said the Doctor, a trifled chastened, "explain to me how the mercury calcined by heat can resume its fluidity by means of the augmentation of the heat?"

"Nothing simpler, my dear Doctor. It's because the percussion of light, being more powerful, then removes the salts fallen into the mercury. That might seem to you to be contradictory, but there is a very simple experiment applicable to this object. Let us throw into cold water little wooden balls a little lighter than the water; they will float on the cold water. If we heat the water, they will fall to the bottom, because the water, dilated by the heat, will become specifically lighter than the balls. But if we boil that water, then a percussion proportionally more considerable than the dilatation of the water will lift up those same balls. Do you understand, my dear Doctor? Apply that experiment yourself, and reflect, at the same time, that, if water can never be condensed by heat, the same law must exist for the other fluids in Nature. At any rate, I do not expect you, in that regard, to adopt my principles; I only ask you for an explanation of yours."

"But in the end, Sir Philosopher," the Doctor retorted, "how can one not be seduced by the admirable experiments on fixed air that kill animals? All those little mice stifled by the fixed air of a candle, the plants, and the washing with water that rectify that air—is not all of that marvelous?"

"My dear Doctor, in order to respond to those experiments on the claimed fixed air—fixed air to which it has then been necessary to grant saline distinctions—here is a scene that I once witnessed.

"I was in the home of a scientist. He was one of those sane men who meditate calmly and who never fall prey to transports of enthusiasm. Two famous partisans of fixed air arrive. 'Our dear dreamer'—that is what he called himself—'we have come to tell you some quite extraordinary verities. We have found that coal vapors, woody gases, the mephitic vapors of mines and the vapors of fermentation all originate from fixed air.' Immediately, he takes us into his physics laboratory. They do experiments; they reason. My man watches the experiments tranquilly; says that he does not perceive anything new, and thinks in silence. They become impatient; they press him to explain.

"'Gentlemen,' he replies, 'I was reflecting on the immense multiplicity of odors produced by plants and flowers, and, being unable to attribute that odiferous variety solely to proportions of your fixed air. I therefore went back to simpler ideas. I imagine that all odors whatsoever are merely the contact of emanations from bodies that strike our sense of smell, for all the senses are reducible to one alone, which is touch. I imagine, of course that air is the vehicle of these emanations. I imagine that the air is more or less charged with these emanations. I imagine that these emanations can have an infinite variety of forms, and, in consequence, occasion a considerable variety of sensations. I imagine that these emanations, being highly phlogisticated, might kill an animal that breathes them in, because phlogiston in movement, breathed by an animal, easily penetrates the pores of the lungs, and gives such an activity to the circulation of the blood that it eventually decomposes if a prompt remedy is not administered.

"'I also imagine that the animal truck by these emanations, being exposed promptly to a current of free air, receives the relief, not only of air, but of aqueous vapors contained in the air, and sufficiently divided to penetrated into the pores of the lungs and reduce the movement of the phlogiston. I imagine by the same reasoning that the air agitated with the water loses its harmful character, because water diminishes the movements of phlogiston, and, besides, the majority of these emanations will be condensed or changed in form. The exudation of plants can also produce the same effects.

"'I imagine, therefore, that what you call 'mephitic air' consists of tiny bodies emanated by different substances. Some scientists call them 'miasmas.' I call them 'emanations,' but it comes to the same thing, and we need not occupy ourselves with words. I imagine that the air charged with a quantity of these emanations is what is called pestilential air. I imagine that people of a humid temperament, and whose blood and humors are more acidic, are less subject to the mortal maladies that result from them. I also imagine that acids promptly rectify that contagious air, because they temper the movement of phlogiston and inhibit its effects.

"Here is a very tangible example. Sulfur in mass is nothing other than phlogiston whose movement is enfeebled by an acid. Rub a rose with sulfur and it does not change color, but as soon as the sulfur is reduced to vapors, the phlogiston that it gives off promptly bleaches the rose; a proof that this effect is due to phlogiston is that on rubbing the rose again with an acid, the rubbed places recover the red color. One must believe, however, that the phlogiston that is given off is adherent to acid parts; if it were not, the air containing those emanations would be much more dangerous to breathe. We have the proof of that in the fact that, if sulfur in which there is a large quantity of acid is introduced into an alkali, the vapor exhaled is slightly warmed and entirely mortal.

"'I finally imagine, Gentlemen, by virtue of convincing experiments, and even more so by the evidence of reasoning, the true principle of the effects that you claim to explain to me by means of an agent more incomprehensible than the effects—which is to say, your fixed air. Thus, permit me not to believe that heat can condense the air that is in a vessel, curl itself up in a body and there form a substance that is invisible, and yet as weighty as your fixed air would be. And if, according to you, it is an error to believe that heat could never condense air, allow me my error.'

"Do you know, my dear Doctor, what the response was of the partisans of fixed air? They look at one another. 'Let us admit,' they said, 'in good faith, that the terms *fixed air* and *elastic fluid*, are nothing but the animated expressions of an agreeable delirium.'"

"I agree," said the Doctor, "that if I renounced fixed air, I would adopt your ideas, but not those of Grasacido."

"And I agree," replied Grasacido, "that if I renounced my *acidum pingue*, I would adopt this gentleman's ideas in their entirety, but never Fixoventi's dreams."

"Of dreams," the Doctor added, "there's certainly one... How, with regard to me, a Doctor...your superior..."

"Not you," Grasacido retorted. 'I know of no superior in the world but the man who is wiser than I am."

"Gently, gently, Gentlemen," Ormasis put in. "There are amiable women here who might not be amused by *acidum pingue*, nor fixed air, nor phlogiston. Let us admire those charming hands, which will pop the corks of that champagne."

Indeed, Mirza, Fatima, Laure and Sophie, each attacking her bottle, understood one another so well that the four pops occurred at the same time.

That sparkling liquid has more virtues than people think! Oh, Mahomet, you who forbade wine to Muslims, for having been the witness of a bloody scene of which it was the cause, had you been present at that dinner, the prohibition would have been rescinded from your Quran. Believe it. The Doctor and Grasacido were reconciled in good faith, and swore eternal amity. Such was the epoch of that reconciliation.

The frothy wine escaped in great waves.

"I confess," said the Doctor, considering these effects, that this is fixed air become very elastic."

"Oh, agree," replied Ormasis, "that light alone has been able to penetrate these bottles since the wine was sealed within them, and that it is, therefore, the percussion of light that has divided and dilated the air that is presently producing that effervescence."

"I believe, in fact," said the Doctor, after having drunk the glass of wine that had been presented to him, "that light acts on all bodies, and that it plays a major role in fermentations."

"I also see," replied Grasacido, "that air acts in an infinity of operations."

"Well," retorted the Doctor, having swilled a second glass of wine, "we were only arguing about words, then."

"In truth," replied Grasacido, "I believe that we ought to be ashamed of our disputes."

"Well, my dear Grasacido," said the Doctor, taking a third glass, "it's a means of reconciling ourselves."

"Yes," Grasacido replied, seizing the opportunity, "it's a means of forgetting everything that is past. To your health."

"To yours. But, my friend," the Doctor continued, "we're forgetting to drink to the health of our benefactresses, who are serving us so generously."

"That's true, Grasacido continued. "Ladies, accept our thanks." And the fourth glass had already succeeded the third.

One cannot imagine the pleasure experienced not only by Nadir's wives, but the Physicist, Nadir and even

Ormasis, in seeing the diverting scene that presented itself. The cheerful women served the two Bacchic athletes assiduously, and took care never to leave their glasses empty.

"Oh!" cried the Doctor, "this is surely an attack— but no matter; how can one resist he impulsion of a beautiful arm? The air, further deprived of its spring, will soon become elastic."

"And are the eyes not the primary agents of light?" Grasacido added. By comparison with those eyes, my *acidum pingue* is merely a sot."

"My word," said the Doctor, swilling another glass of wine, "we were great fools, me with my fixed air and you with your *acidum pingue*."

"I agree," Grasacido replied. "But one has certain ideas...and then it is necessary to sustain them. A certain reputation, you understand... To your health, my dear superior."

"What, my friend," the Doctor said. "You remember...it was just a joke, and..."

"For myself," said Grasacido, "I bear no grudge."

"Drink, then, to my health."

"Agreed."

"My dear Doctor, "it's necessary to be frank when one is a friend. Well, your fixed air is really a superior thing, although I've said a hundred times that you were nothing but a charlatan."

"And in the depths of my soul, my dear Grasacido, I thought the invention of *acidum pingue* admirable, although I've said a hundred times that you were an imbecile. Hold on...let's suppose...that I have fixed air in my glass, and you have *acidum pingue*. Let's switch glasses. See how much esteem I have for you. I drink it...never have I tasted anything so good."

"Oh, my friend," said Grasacido, "what courtesy!" He stood up, and immediately fell back in his chair. "Damn!" he continued. "I want to embrace you."

"Me too," replied the Doctor, performing the same ceremony.

"It's singular," Grasacido went on, "how securely one is held here. They're gentle chains...can you sing, my friend."

"No," the Doctor replied. "It's said that a scientist ought not to sing, and that gravity..." He made further efforts to get up, and continued: "But bodies are grave here, damn it..."

"What are you trying to do, Doctor?"

"Embrace you, my friend."

The two friends were facing one another. They raised themselves up sufficiently to take one another by the hand, and let go almost immediately. That transport of amity broke the two glasses that were in front of them. The misfortune was soon repaired.

"Oh," said the Doctor, "they are the two eggs of Castor and Pollux from which our amity is hatching out, of which...these...ladies...are...the vivifying...suns. You see, my friend, how weak I am."

"Yes, truly," Grasacido replied. "I particularly liked that Turkish saraband you were making with words."

"Oh yes," said the Doctor, "yes...yes...wait...there was a certain beautiful woman to whom I declared my languishing passion with majesty:

O you who burn me with a brilliant flame
You have the snuffer, lend it to me, Madame.

"Agree that that's beautiful...the brilliant flame, the snuffer. I won't seek to versify, myself, all those un-

158

known gods of fable. No, I prefer things that one ordinarily finds close at hand...snuffers...how naïve that is."

"Yes," replied Grasacido. "Snuffers—admirable. Oh, my dear friend, you're a great poet. For myself, I want to play a tune on the harpsichord." He tried to rise to his feet again. "But I want us to embrace."

Grasacido stood up, and fell back, but in falling back on his armchair a little too far forward, he slipped, and found himself lying under the table, without doing himself any harm. At the same moment, the Doctor, seeking to embrace his friend, headed in the same direction, and found himself amicably beside him. The others got ready to pick them up, but Nadir, perceiving that they were already sleeping peacefully, gave the order that pillows should be slid underneath them, and while they were tranquilly brooding fixed air and *acidum pingue*, the company went for a walk in the gardens.

Chapter XVII

"In truth," said Mirza, "We could not desire a more amusing reconciliation—but my dear Philosopher, you played a large part in it. When two people are not in agreement, I think the best means of bringing them together is to offer them criticisms and eulogies in equal measure."

"I believe, Madame," Ormasis replied, "that a spirituous vehicle presented by the Graces has even more effect."

"Yes," replied the Physicist. "Besides, those two scientists are from the same country, where cold and fog have rendered that vehicle necessary. How, with that primitive habitat, could they not surrender their reason to the efforts of beauty?"

"Oh, I swear to you," Nadir interjected, "that their last conversation was very reasonable."

"My dear Nadir," Ormasis continued, "let's not run the men down. They have merit, and they form their opinions in good faith—why criticize them? I have only debated with them in order to prevent myself from adopting their ideas, but if, after reflection, they persist in their theories, and if that stubbornness, whether well- or ill-founded, is a sensation of pleasure for them, let's not deprive them of it."

"Agreed," Nadir replied, "but my dear Ormasis, you won't prevent us from judging between you and them. When, for example, Fixoventi assures us that it is vigorous plants that rectify bad air and render it salubrious, and when that pretended discovery excited all the scientific Companies in the world, we others shall reflect that in our climate, where plants are vigorous al the year round, one experiences much more poor air than in the northern lands, where plants only subsist for a few months—but we shall not give ourselves for that reason to an opposite theory. We will simply observe that in cold countries there is more rainfall or snowfall than in ours, more condensation, les phlogiston and fewer dangerous emanations. That, my dear Ormasis, is the consequence of your principles, and we shall adopt them for preference. Isn't that true, Sir Physicist?"

"Certainly, Sir," said the Physicist, and continued: "I don't know whether Sir the Philosopher has once followed courses in chemistry and physics, but he has left all the harnesses of schooling far behind."

"Yes," Ormasis replied, "but I have retained the principal guides."

Meanwhile, Nadir's wives were walking a short way ahead and making reflections advantageous to their new guest. While the sensible Fatima was enjoying the double pleasure of praising the man she loved and hearing him praised, someone came to inform Ormasis that two slaves had just brought him a trunk.

"That's good," he said. "I'll be there shortly." Taking his host aside, he continued: "My dear Nadir, a traveler like me does not have much furniture; if you want me to use yours freely, accept the key to this trunk. Order that it be placed in your apartment. It's yours. I need to go back to my caravanserai and make a few preparations for our nocturnal excursions. I shall return."

Fatima, who glanced behind her from time to time, was the first to notice Ormasis' departure. The Physicist told her that someone had just asked for him. Nadir, drawing closer to Mirza, asked her to step aside with dear Fatima, because he had something to tell them.

The opportunity became very favorable. Sophie had just caught a butterfly on a rose, the colors of which were charming. The Physicist had a magnifying-glass with him, of surprising effect. The butterfly was placed under it. Soon, a small caterpillar that was agitating on an anemone leaf offered a new subject of examination. Laure and Sophie then had the pleasure of passing other objects in review beneath the magnifying glass, for the instrument presented novelties incessantly. At the same time, the Physicist explained to them the fashion of caring for the larvae of butterflies, and what precautions it was necessary to take with regard to the chrysalises. All these matters were worthy of discussion, and a person who thinks such observations petty ought to reflect that there is nothing petty in Nature.

Mirza and Fatima took advantage of the moment and followed Nadir. He had had Ormasis' trunk taken to his apartment. "This," he told them, "is a present that our friend has offered me; he demands that I accept it. He has given me the key to it."

"Give it to me," said Mirza. "Grant me the pleasure of opening it...but no, I'd deprive you of it. If, however, Fatima wishes..."

"Very good," Fatima replied "Come on, curious child, you'd be annoyed if I accepted. Hurry up."

Mirza immediately opened the trunk. "There's a lot of sand to remove," she said. "Help me, then, Nadir. Look at these pretty transparent pebbles."

"O Heavens!" cried Nadir, "it's a sovereign's present. No, Ormasis, I won't accept it. My friends, this is at least eight hundred marks[24] of gold dust. These peb-

---

[24] A mark, in this sense, was about eight ounces.

bles are uncut precious stones. There are several diamonds of the greatest beauty. No, I won't accept it."

"Why not?" asked Fatima whose emotion was inexpressible. "My dear Nadir, the man who is making you these presents is surely capable of offering more of the same."

"You're right, my dear Fatima," added Mirza, swiftly. "Accept, accept, my friend, what is offered to you. I'm overcome with joy. Oh, Nadir, can you imagine the pleasure of no longer being obliged to calculate our income?"

Nadir immediately embraced his friends. "I give in to your reasoning," he said, "but what gratitude could ever compensate...? Yes, I'll accompany him in his research. I owe him that. But I'm far from desiring its success. That electric machine he wants to construct no longer piques my curiosity, no longer heats my imagination. Let him remain with us. Are all worlds not formed in equal proportions? Happiness and misfortune exist everywhere, and if he can become happy with...why expose himself to dangers?"

"What!" cried the tender Fatima. "Can he...? No, I'm tranquil. I don't believe that such an amiable man would seek to impose on a woman who, in good faith..."

Fatima, suddenly falling silent, perceived that her secret had escaped her.

"My amiable friend," Mirza said to her, immediately, "don't be sorry; Nadir and I had guessed it this morning. We have also divined our respectable friend. Imagine how delighted we shall be to secure him with your chains. I don't know why I experience so much pleasure in thinking about that union. Listen to me: you surely have empire over his heart. Dissuade him from continuing his research. Make him cease his journeys into the entrails of the Earth. Besides, I don't want Nadir to accompany him. Oh, my dear Nadir, what if you suffered some mishap? I shiver at the thought."

"Mirza, my dear Mirza," Nadir replied, "reflect for a moment on the duties of friendship and advise me. At any rate, calm your fears; you can believe that our philosopher would not expose us to any dangers. I confess to you that I'm curious to see the works of Nature in the bosom of our globe. How much pleasure I shall have in telling you what I have seen!"

"Yes, Fatima put in, "but ought not Mirza to be apprehensive, as I am, about the consequences of that curiosity? All in all, if Ormasis plans to stay here, I can't see the reason for all this research. I'm determined to obtain some clarification."

Mirza supported Fatima in this resolution, and they went with Nadir to rejoin their companions.

Chapter XVIII

Selim and Osman had arrived. Laure's and Sophie's eyes had already assured them of success in their request, but they soon had a private conversation that completed their desires. The result was that they promised to allow their new spouses all the liberty they could desire; that, renouncing in that respect the customs of the nation, they would follow Nadir's example in every respect; and that, in the event that their wives had grounds for complaint, and that they persisted for three years thereafter in wanting to separate from them, they would have no further rights over them and would be obliged to repudiate them—which they swore to observe on the souls of their forefathers and all possible obligations.

Selim and Osman loved too honestly not to accept these conditions gladly. Besides which, they could only contribute to their own happiness. Often, the dread of losing the person one loves maintains love.

Nadir therefore promised them that they would go to the judge the following day to satisfy the customary ceremonies.

While the sensible Fatima and the tender Mirza discussed the nocturnal expedition and tried to reassure one another mutually, a young Emir and an old Sangiac,[25] friends of Nadir, arrived. The company reassembled in the music room. They were almost all skillful musicians.

---

[25] A Sangiac, or Sanjak, was one of the administrative subdivisions recognized in the bureaucracy of the Ottoman Empire, and hence, by extension the official in charge of the region in question.

Nadir's wives had talents of that genre and Nadir played several instruments successfully himself.

The Physicist saw that they were preparing a concert. He was not very passionate about music. The lugubrious sound of the monochord[26] pleased him as much as the most beautiful arietta. He went home, to dream skeptically about the attractive principles that sounds can occasion, being only percussions and repercussions of agitated air.

Grasacido and the Doctor, after having slept for some time, woke up, looked at one another, meditated together on the great events of life, and calculated that they would be much better off at home until the next day.

Three hour had already gone by since the Philosopher's departure, and Fatima was singing the harmonious piece "Cruel, you flee from me, etc."[27] She rendered it with the most touching expression. Mirza, who was accompanying her on the harpsichord, was the first to perceive that the Philosopher had come into the room.

"There he is," she said, in a low voice, to her friend.

Immediately, Fatima, forgetting eight bars, came promptly to the passage: "Ah, I see him again, etc." and Mirza smiled. The accompanists took it badly. The old Sangiac was plucking the strings of his bass furiously. They were, however, busy trying to repair the transition. Although the Philosopher had come in with the delicacy

_____

[26] The ancient instrument in question, in which the length of one or more strings is varied by movable bridges, is sometimes held to have been originated by Pythagoras; it was more widely used in scientific demonstrations than making music.

[27] It is impossible to identify this piece from the lines quoted by La Follie, which score no hits on Google.

and silence of a music-lover, Nadir, who noticed him, finally called a general halt.

"I fear," he said, addressing Ormasis, "that this amusement might not be to your taste."

"My friend," the Philosopher replied, beauty, precision and harmony are the three graces of Nature—how can one be insensible to their charms? I have always loved music, and if that harp you are holding were not in such good hands..."

"Oh, my dear Ormasis, please..."

"No, I shall not disarm you..."

Nadir insists; Ormasis accepts—and Fatima, condemned to begin her arietta again, sees with pleasure that her friend possesses agreeable talents.

Surprise soon follows. Ormasis plays a prelude. The quality of the sounds, the precision of his hand, the accuracy and multiplicity of the chords reveal a superior talent, and announce to the symphonists that their parts have become unnecessary. They listen in silence. Ormasis, much more at his ease, is no longer required to follow the composer's accompaniments strictly. He yields to his imagination, and that imagination is fecund. He follows with an infinite artistry not merely the inflections of the voice but the characters of the expressions.

Sometimes plaintive and stifled sounds present the image of dolor; sometimes faint sounds are lost in the distance; one listens, and doubts that they still exist. Gradually, other, more assured sounds gradually bring back sensations of hope; the chords and harmonies multiply, and finally characterize the most animated joy.

The arietta had never previously been what it seemed then, and Fatima had never sung with as much soul.

Oh, divine melody, when your charms are presented with so much verity, the most poorly-organized being—which is to say, one whose nerves are taut with the greatest dissonance—will always be seduced by the impression they cause! Imagine how enthused the listeners were.

The old Sangiac, a great music-lower, could not find compliments sufficiently impressive. Nadir, delighted by pleasure and astonishment, had to endure the old Governor's questions. "Who is that man? Where does he come from? What does he do? Where is he going? He's an angel! Oh, Sir, that was divine. Tomorrow, I'll talk to the Emperor. One ought to bestow a dazzling fortune on a subject of such consequence."

"There's no need, Governor. Besides, his talent is nothing by comparison with his merit. He's an exceedingly enlightened philosopher..."

"What quality of sounds!"

"Who has principles of a clarity..."

"Yes, sounds of such clarity..."

"Can one be grateful enough for sublime instruction that elevate the soul..."

"Yes, Sir, he has elevated me..."

"But we're talking at cross purposes, Governor. I tell you that he's a true philosopher, a great thinker."

"Ah!" the Governor replied. "I understand...a philosopher...that's of no consequence. What harmony, Sir! Ask him to play again."

Mirza and the other women were already begging Ormasis to accompany them in an arietta too. He gladly yielded to their insistence, always with the same success, although in different genres.

Seeing that he was amusing everyone, Ormasis offered to play a solo in the garden. The moonlight was beautiful. There was a breeze. That was what he wanted. He asked that a small stage be set up, about five feet above the audience, which was soon prepared.

Scarcely had Ormasis begun his piece than everyone was gripped by a new pleasure. The waves of the air caused surprising effects. The sounds, agitated in the atmosphere, formed a marvelous harmony. Sometimes it was an angelic murmur that was scarcely audible in distant spaces. Suddenly, it was a noisy concert, whose energetic and divine chords would have transported the most insensitive soul. In sum, those harmonious waves caused inexpressible sensations. People were afraid to breathe. They experienced that sweet oppression of which the least musical of humans is sometimes not the master.

The old Governor could no longer contain himself. Scarcely had the piece finished than he threw himself to his knees. "O my God," he said, "if it is true that we experience such delightful pleasures in the other world, take me—I am no longer afraid to die!"

That transport greatly amused the company. Ormasis was heaped with thanks, and the fear of importuning him had difficulty overcoming the desire that everyone had to hear him again.

Chapter XIX

They strolled for some time. The company split up. Ormasis and Fatima found themselves. The more delighted Fatima was to discover the Philosopher's qualities, the more annoyed with him she became. Finally, she quarreled with him with regard to his research, which only tended to separate him from her. Her reproaches were sharp, but they assured the Philosopher increasingly of the possession of a tender heart.

"Charming Fatima," he said to her, "I promise you that this expedition will be the last. I would have been able to dispense with it, but I think it useful to Nadir's happiness. Not only do I want the journey to put him in a position never to fear a reversal of fortune, but it's appropriate that he enjoys, at least once, a very interesting spectacle. As soon as we return, I swear to you never to leave you again without your permission."

Nadir was expecting two more guests for supper, but having received information that they would not be there, they sat down at table.

The old Sangiac continually interrupted the conversation in order to hold forth on the effects of music. "It matters little to me," he said, "whether music is ultramontane or antemontane. I want character, expression, and the expression to be relevant to the subject. For example, is there anything more ridiculous than seeing a hero expire with a cadence in which his fury is expressed to the tune of a rigadoon? Is it not even funnier to see a lover make a passionate declaration with intermittent roulades? What would a pretty young woman think if her lover threw himself at her feet to say an *I love you* punctuated at every syllable by thirty or forty sounds? If she didn't take him for an imbecile, she'd at least think that he as making fun of her. It is therefore natural not to interrupt expressive phrases. It is necessary to reserve for crowd scenes the multiplicity of sounds and the great efforts of the Art."

The music lover could have continued similar reflections for a long time, but his imagination was gradually deflected toward other objects.

Mirza was delighted with her guest; she had seen him at odds with Fatima. When she perceived that her companion seemed satisfied, she recovered all her gaiety. "My dear Philosopher," she said to Ormasis, "I've always wanted to ask you how the women of your country dress. Are they pretty?"

"Madame, their costume is very similar to yours, but in this circle, their beauty would be completely eclipsed."

"Sir is not from our country, then," put in the old Sangiac. "I suspected as much. On the subject of beauty and costume, our young Empress appeared before her people yesterday. You know how enthusiastically she is always applauded, and how she merits it—well, can you believe that I was almost disappointed."

"What!" said the young Emir. "Disappointed? I don't understand. How, when the most sincere joy animates all those who have the good fortune to look at her, when the entire nation adores her..."

"One moment, young man, one moment; we're in agreement. Let's understand one another—I'll explain. It was by way of distraction that I paid attention to her costume; she was, I admit, well dressed in the greatest elegance. Damn, I said to myself; I would be truly furious if she thought there was any need for such assistance to appear to be what she is."

"Oh, my dear Governor, an honorable reparation. Why, that's as clever as can be."

"Not clever at all, I beg you; I intend no finesse."

"Very good," said the Philosopher, then. "I offer all of you very sincere compliments. I have traveled through many countries, and the young emperor who governs you is admired everywhere. Thanks to philosophy, it is no longer horrible carnages, disguised under the name of victories, that render a monarch illustrious. No, the happiness of his people is the true thermometer of his grandeur, and if, attacked by an enemy, he is sometimes obliged to redress the injustice, it is always reluctantly that he advertises his valor in order to have his rights respected."

The old Sangiac looked at Ormasis with an astonished expression. "Sir," he said, "I think that morality is very good. I'm told that you're a philosopher. Is philosophy a good thing, then? It's claimed that it instructs people and tends to their wellbeing—so do some philosophy for me, I beg you. Oh, if I could philosophize as well as you on a harp, I'd burn my bass tomorrow."

Selim and Osman had just raised a question, on which their opinions were divided. Selim claimed that luxury was useful to the wealth of a State. Osman claimed, on the contrary, that it was a destructive vice that had ruined many great empires.

"Gentlemen," Nadir replied to them, you are both right. A single distinction in that regard will bring you into agreement. When the luxury of a realm subsists at the expense of foreign products, you are right, my dear Osman; it is a destructive vice whose progress the sovereign cannot stop too soon. But when a kingdom encloses

172

in its own bosom the manufactures that furnish the maintenance of luxury, you are right, Selim; then luxury is truly essential to the realm. It maintains the circulation of wealth, it furnishes subsistence to an infinite number of the unfortunate, and always contributes to the happiness of the people. For example, foreigners arrive in our court. The adornment there is carefully planned; festivals are held there, and it is necessary to raise the tone of our manners. They leave their gold and take away our trinkets. If our young empress adopts some new fashion, she is not unaware that the benefit of an infinity of workers will result. Do you not see old dowagers who, obliged to change their accessories, put into circulation, involuntarily, a part of the wealth that they had locked away? Is it not necessary also that rich lords relieve the active indigent? Is it not natural that virtuous men, enriched by the benefits of a prince, should distribute them in their turn? Is it not also appropriate that rich merchants, to adorn their wives and mistresses, should restore to laborious industry that which a more tranquil industry has enabled them to acquire? Yes, my dear Osman, that circulation is a good. If I were the emperor, I would give letters of dishonor to those who, at great expense, will travel a hundred leagues to transform cash into investments, but as investments are found in all countries, I would approve even more disproportionate exchanges in my realm. What do the expenses of fantasy matter, when the numerary value remains within the state? What I say about investments can apply to many other objects. I don't even except the raw materials that our climate refuses us, and whose value is augmented by our industry."

"I yield," Osman replied. "I see that it does not require either historical citations or wordy volumes to resolve these questions."

"My word," said the old Sangiac, "that's well said. But gentlemen, I believe that if you get mixed up in it, you'll produce books. I'll ask you another question. Do the sciences contribute to the wellbeing of a State? Personally, I don't believe it. Our old Caliph Omar burned the famous Library of Alexandria and forbade the use of books, in order to maintain the ignorance of his subjects, because it appeared to him to be precious. Rashid, his successor, on the other hand, had books introduced. He wanted the philosophers of all lands to come. What was the result? Internal wars ravaged the empire?"

"I ask you for one favor, Sir," Ormasis replied, "and that is not to profane the name of philosophy. What you call philosophers here are merely sectarians. The difference is considerable; here it is:

"A sectarian is a man filled with ambition who lacks talent but wishes that people should pay heed to him. His genius, too small to rise to beautiful knowledge of Nature, crawls for some time over the absurd notebooks of a host of imbeciles. He brings together different statements devoid of common sense and extracts new consequences therefrom, as ridiculous as the principles, and suddenly produces an unintelligible dogma that he claims to be respectable. The less he understands it himself, the more the explanations demanded of him render him furious. Intelligent men, unfortunately, pretend to support his system in order to satisfy particular hatreds against those who oppose it. Cabals form, blood flows, the empire is weakened and the sovereign sometimes becomes the victim of the most stupid errors.

"A philosopher, by contrast, contemplates in silence the beauty of the Universe; he admires the majesty of the Creator. The march of Nature occupies his genius. He attempts to discover a few secrets. The slightest discovery affects his soul with a delightful sentiment. He converses tranquilly with his friends. If their opinions are divided, those sorts of quarrels never trouble the State. Never is blood spilled in order to demonstrate whether it is pressure or attraction that agitates the Ocean. The philosopher does even more for the happiness of human beings and the maintenance of social harmony; a leader is required who enforces the obedience of laws, and as laws are respectable, that leader, that sovereign is therefore, for him, also a truly respectable being. Does the sovereign have a few weaknesses? 'Perhaps I would have even more,' he says to himself, 'if, like him, surrounded by flatterers, I were only enlightened by the torch of my will.' If, on the contrary, the sovereign only has virtues, the philosopher, glad to have such a master, adds to the respect that he owes him the most sincere admiration. In sum, whatever the circumstance might be, he is always the faithful subject of a monarch."

"My word," cried the old Sangiac, "your reflections are luminous. The Mufti can issue a fatwa and fulminate against philosophers; is they come to my Sangiacat, they will be tranquil there, even if I have to use my scimitar to form the electric rod that protect against lightning. Yes, from this moment on, I declare that I am a philosopher. I already feel that I love my prince as a philosopher, and not in the hope of obtaining a better Sangiacat."

"Marvelously stated," Nadir replied, "those are the first principles. In that case, we are all philosophers here." There was unanimous contentment and applause.

The old Sangiac was weeping with joy; he confessed that for a long time he had not savored a pleasure so pure. Perceiving that Nadir's wives were applauding too, he exclaimed: "So they are philosophers too! Excuse me, Ladies." He got to his feet and ran to embrace them.

Far from disapproving of this impulse, Nadir got to his feet too and gave the signal for that decent gaiety that is the soul of society.

"My friend," said the old Sangiac, addressing Nadir, "I want you to come and take your revenge. I'm leaving for my Sangiacat in a week's time. I shall take you all. I flatter myself that our great master, our great philosopher, will come with us. Ladies, I beg to persuade him, you who surely have power over him."

He addressed these last words while looking particularly at Fatima. These old courtiers almost always have a sure tact. They observe without being observed.

Everyone promised. "I'm not sorry, the Sangiac continued, that Cadmen and Almanzor were not here today; I wouldn't have been so amused. They're two agreeable hypocrites, but, I confess, they seem silly to me. They have such affected manners, their behavior is so false, they make such awkward gibes...but I've promised to be a philosopher; I beg your pardon, gentlemen, I wasn't thinking. By the way, Ladies, I'm very bold to take you home with me...my wives...no matter, they're no longer in the age of coquetry. I moan every day because, if the imprudent Aisha, the young favorite of our Prophet, had known either the discreet retrenchments of a boudoir, or the useful eloquence of an antechamber door, she would never have been surprised, and the inconstant Mahomet, on whom she avenged herself with so much pleasure, would not have extended her punishment to the entire sex. But my dear Nadir, thanks to your example, from which several of our friends will profit, the most agreeable cheerfulness will become the soul of our society, and the brutal joy that is the companion of debauchery will be banished forever."

"Governor," Mirza put in, "I will make you a confession; it is that I have never seen you as you are. I thought you were sad, very somber, particularly scornful of women, and then I took against you. But now I find you so agreeable that if my dear Nadir had never existed, I would have been reasonable enough to love you. What do you say, Fatima?"

"It is certain," Fatima replied, "that any woman whose heart had not been captured might easily decide on the gentleman."

Laure and Sophie made similar declarations.

"Very good," he said, "I see that if I had pretentions to form here, I would at least receive agreeable excuses. But also, Ladies, I would not be obliged to make them to you... Well, Ormasis, am I not a true philosopher? You can see it; I'm not boasting. However, I think it's permissible for philosophers to be amorous. I confess to you that, in spite of my age, if it were necessary, in order to be a philosopher, to renounce the pleasure of liking a pretty face, I wouldn't want to be one."

"Be tranquil, Governor. If the public honors with the name of philosopher men who render themselves unsociable by affectation or boorishness, the public is mistaken. The profession of faith of the true philosopher is: 'I love God, my Prince and Women.'"

"Marvelous," replied the Governor, "marvelous. 'I love God, my Prince and Women.' Oh, damn it, I'm a philosopher with all my heart. Now, my dear Master, tell me, I beg you, in what fashion do people make love in your country?"

"Gladly. Nothing in the world is more interesting. The two sexes have a singular vivacity. The frankness of our women renders the men happy; the humiliation of a suitor who, enchained in the retinue of a coquette, occupies himself in making every effort to be seductive, is unknown there. At first glance, one knows whether one is agreeable; love never makes futile progress. When two hearts are in accord, they soon perceive one another. The moment of realization has inexpressible charms for them, and compensates them with few sensations in the proof of it."

"What do you mean?" the old Sangiac retorted, immediately. "What! Few sensations in the proof? That's not possible."

"Forgive me, Sir. The inhabitants of my country only know, so to speak, Platonic love; they are so intense. The physical instant is so rapid that it becomes inappreciable."

"Oh, how singular that is!" exclaimed the Sangiac. "Ladies, what do you think of the lovers of our philosopher's homeland? Be honest."

That question occasioned details, amusing distinctions and delicate treatment by the agreeable women. In sum, the philosopher's joke furnished material for a very lively conversation.

All pleasures are temporary, however—or rather, for them to subsist, they require a sensible variety. The old Sangiac reflected that it was late. He got to his feet, albeit regretfully. The young Emir, Selim and Osman followed his example and went home.

Laure and Sophie were not long delayed in going up to their apartments, in order to occupy themselves with private conversations regarding the sincere passion of their future spouses.

Mirza and Fatima thus remain with Nadir and the Philosopher. They gaze at one another, silently. When one loves so tenderly, an adieu, of whatever sort, costs too much to pronounce.

The tender Mirza contemplates her dear Nadir. Tears shadow her beautiful eyes; Nadir get up to kiss her. Fatima abandons her hand to the mute adieux of her friend. They turn their eyes away.

Our two travelers take advantage of the moment. They set forth,

Chapter XX

The environs of Chrysopolis were ornamented by
fine roads—which is to say that those roads were well-
maintained, for their breadth was only calculated for
public utility and nor for ostentation. The calculation had
been made of how much a single fathom of terrain saved
on a fifty-league road would conserve the annual wealth
of the State. In consequence, they were all laid out in
straight lines, except for steep mountains. It is also true
that the graphometers were not gilded, and the engineers,
not being dazzled by an excessively bright light, did not
perceive any curvature of the line of sight. This resulted
in much more comfort for travelers, considerable savings
of terrain, immense wealth conserved, easier maintenance and less expense for the State. Nadir and Ormasis
thus followed an easy course by moonlight, only dis-
turbed by arriving at the foot of a chain of mountains.

Nadir tried to express his gratitude to the Philosopher for the considerable present he had received from
him.

"Tomorrow," Ormasis said to him, "you will make
me a similar present, and we shall be quits."

The two friends were chatting about dear Mirza and
the amiable Fatima when they perceived two men running toward them. Nadir already had his scimitar in his
hand.

"Don't worry," Ormasis said to him, "it's surely my
two slaves; they're anxious because we're so late. Yes,
really—you wouldn't believe how attached they are to
me. Well, my friends, here we are, turn around. You
were apprehensive about some encounter, then, my dear

Nadir, and had already put yourself on guard? Believe me, in that circumstance, never take up those murderous weapons; they are only useful on the battlefield. Among the unfortunates who steal on these roads there are some who, driven by necessity, groan themselves about the violence that they are obliged to commit. There is a surer means of protecting oneself from their attacks, without depriving them of life. Look at this weapon."

Ormasis took from his belt a sort of pistol without a hammer, whose barrel widened at the mouth. "Don't imagine that this barrel is loaded with powder and lead; it simply serves as a conductor of vapors. In this base, which is a trifle swollen, there are two compartments. The one that is directly connected to the barrel contains a mixture of essential oil of guaiacum and highly-phlogisticated powdered charcoal; the other compartment, which is lined with glass, contains highly-concentrated spirit of niter. There is a communication between the two vessels but it is blocked by a gold plug. As soon as I press this button, the channel is opened; the spirit of niter falls into the mixture, and it instantly releases a wave of flame and smoke, which knocks out all those at whom one directs it. Ordinarily, there results a lethargic sleep of two or three hours, sometimes shorter if the weather is humid. It is, therefore, with such weapons that I have often defended myself in the course of my travels; they have never failed me. When the unfortunates are lying on the ground, I put a couple of sequins in their pockets, in order that when they wake up they will at least find enough to furnish their subsistence, and I continue on my way with far more satisfaction than if I had taken their lives."

Nadir thought the invention of this philosophical weapon very ingenious. He confessed that he would gladly have taken part in a very curious experiment, but one of which they presently had no need.

Finally they arrived at the foot of the steepest mountain. Those solitary places, observed during the calm of the night, offered the imagination interesting scenes. The moonlight was brightly reflected from masses of white stone, and the shadowy opening of an old quarry was clearly distinguishable.

"Here," said Ormasis, "is the entrance to our palace. Follow me."

Soon our travelers found themselves under the mountain, and taking the path that was to their right, they perceived by the light of their torches their slaves and four horses, with a few provisions for the journey. It did not take long to dress; they abandoned their garments to don deerskins, tailored to fit their stature quite well. Bonnets of the same fabric covered their heads. They mounted the horses and followed a path by torchlight, whose slops was fairly gentler—but the descent was so long and tortuous that without the aid of the horses they would have been exhausted before reaching the entrance to the gulf.

Nadir, greatly astonished, looked in all directions, and did not know whether he was still looking at the work of human beings or that of Nature. He had heard it said in Chrysopolis that a cavern existed whose depth no one had ever been able to determine, but no one had been able to give any details of it.

Suddenly, he heard in the distance a sound similar to that of the loud clapping of hands. "You cannot imagine," Ormasis said to him, "where that noise is coming from. It is nothing but little drops of water falling on hollow stones. The loud noise comes from the disposition of a very curious chamber, which you shall see. You are familiar with the principles; we shall not waste time with them. Let us only enjoy the effects."

Our voyagers thus advanced sensibly. Soon they reached that interesting space, in which the faintest voice, similar to thunder, would have made the most intrepid man tremble had he not been forewarned. Other admirable objects presented themselves to Nadir's eyes. There were immense groups of shiny stalactites, whose forms offered the imagination the most various scenes. Those stalactites surrounded the chamber, giving the delightful illusion of a crystal apartment. It was in that chamber that Ormasis left the slaves, in order to penetrate into almost-inaccessible places whose paths he had discovered by degrees.

Our voyagers dismounted; Ormasis looked at his watch. "We have at least six hours," he said to his slaves. "You have some provisions—so much the better; you might have to wait longer. Immediately, they assembled a kind of sled, to which wheels were fitted. A lantern resembling a street-light was fitted to the front, whose lamps were lit. Nadir watched these preparations in astonishment.

"Well, my friend," the Philosopher said to him, laughing, "agree that this is a pleasant chariot. We can leave whenever you wish."

Immediately, the vehicle was taken to a narrow path, whose slope seemed very sheer. The slaves attached exceedingly long ropes to the rear of the sled.

Full of confidence, Nador, whose curiosity was gradually increasing, sat on the sled behind his friend. Ormasis placed a small box on his knees and took two iron-tipped rods in his hands. The slaves let out the ropes and our voyagers set off with an admirable promptness.

"Don't think," Ormasis said, "that I went so rapidly the first time I attempted this descent. No, these ropes certainly impeded my course and I went very slowly. I will make the observation that we will not be returning through the same opening, although I shall prudently leave my sled here until I came back to the chamber."

In a short time they found themselves at the bottom of the steep descent. The terrain was no longer sufficiently oblique to enable the sled to progress, and they got off. Ormasis opened his little box. He took out two bottles, two packets and an earthenware capsule. "You see in one of these bottles," he said to his friend, "a vinegar that has been concentrated by excessive cold, which results in a mixture of snow and spirit of niter." He took the stopper out of the bottle.

Nadir breathed in, with pleasure, an odor as sweet as it was penetrating, and, following his guide's example he rubbed his face with the acid. "That, I confess," he said, "is a well-intended precaution. This radical vinegar is of a singular purity; it procures me an agreeable well-being. It seems to me that it has augmented my strength. But my dear Philosopher, for what use are those two packets intended, that other bottle and the earthenware capsule that you're securing in your belt?"

"I shall tell you. Pick up that lantern. Let's walk... The smaller packet contains an alimentary powder. The powder is made with the nutritive part of a mass of paste, which one extracts under a trickle of running water. It is, therefore, that substance which is subsequently mixed with meat-extract, and as it becomes very hard, one pounds it and passes it through a sieve. A gross of that powder is sufficient to feed a man for twenty-four hours and give him a great deal of strength; it is, however, as well only to make use of it in indispensable circumstances, for its immoderate use can be dangerous, in that it derives of occupation certain secretory vessels of the human body, which eventually lose their spring and occasion maladies. The other packet is nothing but marine salt. The bottle contains glacial oil of vitriol. You will soon see how the last provision will be useful to us."

Nadir and Ormasis continued on their way. They discussed the operation by which vitriolic acid can be successfully extracted on a large scale in lead vessels. Ormasis observed that in the course of that large-scale operation several thousandths of that acid in vapor form had passed through a thin iron tube without corroding it. He explained that chemical phenomenon by pointing out to him that the acid, when it is above the point of deflagration, still contains a great deal of phlogiston.

In the distance, at the corner of the path, Nadir suddenly perceived a profound opening from which swirls of flame were emerging.

"Don't be frightened," his friend immediately said to him. "The closer we get to it, the more interesting the spectacle will appear to you."

Soon, Nadir perceived, beyond that opening, exceedingly wide pathways and vaults of the greatest elevation. Continuous lightning-flashes formed a very bright light in the bosom of these abysses. The curious Nadir, increasingly wonderstruck, forgot all the dangers and lengthened his stride.

"Just a moment," the philosopher said to him, stopping him. "We might perhaps perish, my friend, if we advance any further without taking precautions. The mephitic air of these inflamed routes is of the greatest subtlety. Our vinegar will not be sufficient to protect us from it."

So saying, Ormasis took up the earthenware capsule. He filled it with marine salt, and opened the bottle of oil of vitriol. Instantly, a smoke—or, rather, a cloud—enveloped our voyagers. Ormasis was still holding the fuming capsule in his hand. "Let's go on," he said, "and have no fear."

They advanced to the rim of the gulf. Nadir saw, to his surprise, that the flames parted as they moved and seemed to respect them. The effect seemed to him to be supernatural. He contemplated the confidence and activity of the Philosopher. He thought he was seeing one of those powerful gnomes who travel through their tenebrous domains in majesty, seemingly commanding the elements there.

"Well, my dear Nadir," Ormasis said to him, "does the effect of that operation seem surprising to you? This is the principle of it. Nothing is more expansive than marine acid reduced to vapors. Now, what is the result of our operation? The marine acid vapors that escape from our capsule and diverge around us provide impulsion from the center to the circumference, and repel the flames, which are only very light vapors themselves. Ours even extinguish them in part. At the same time, they rectify with the greatest success the most highly-phlogisticated mephitic air, and that air then ceases to be harmful."

"In truth," Nadir exclaimed, "I would never have thought that one could protect oneself from great dangers by means of such simple operations—but my dear Ormasis, why have our chemists, who have been using that method of manufacturing marine acid in closed vessels of a long time, not reflected that it might be useful in the open air, not only for mine-workings but also to inhibit the contagion of pestilential air?"

"My friend," Ormasis replied, "Something always escapes the most industrious of men. Gradually, the science will progress and humankind will gain by it. Don't imagine, my dear Nadir, that I have ever made a secret of that operation. On the contrary. One day, I found myself near the Persian border, where plague was beginning its ravages. Immediately, I went to see the Governor, to whom I prescribed what needed to be done. My operation was carried out faithfully in all the public squares. It soon produced a salutary fog, which covered the town for several hours. Far from troubling the sick, the fog gave them relief. All those who had not been afflicted were protected, and that expense, so useful for humankind, did not amount to twenty sequins."

Nadir listened to his friend with a kind of enchantment. He was walking, reflecting on these useful matters, when a frightful noise suddenly resounded in the subterranean caverns.

Ormasis perceived that a small opening to his right, by means of which he usually passed through these rocks, was brightly lit. Rapidly, he climbed with Nadir into a kind of grotto covered in sand, from which they could examine what was happening in other subterranean spaces separated by immense walls.

Nadir saw, to his surprise, different layers of earth agitating and producing reddish vapors.

"Consider these effects," Ormasis said to him. "Don't be frightened. Although the noise is very loud today, be sure that the solidity of these rocks in unbreakable."

Chapter XXI

Nadir admired these interesting phenomena with an inexpressible sensation.

"You see," Ormasis continued, that acid of sulfur is falling into the phlogiston of that ferruginous earth; the movement of the phlogiston is increasing, and it is increased even further by the evaporation of aqueous parts. Vigorously agitated light develops in masses of earth; its rapid percussion dilates air urgently, and causes explosions all the more powerful when they find more resistance."

Scarcely had Ormasis stopped speaking than a frightful thunder shook the vaults of the caverns; a torrent of fire inundated the vast abysses. Nadir considered with a fearful eye the sparkling waves that were rolling and multiplying impetuously. Then he saw, to his astonishment, masses of water following the course of the waves of flame at high speed and climbing with them over the highest paths of the subterranean mountains.

"You are looking," Ormasis said to him, "at the effects of a volcano, the eruption of which has occurred in the sea. You can see the waters of the Ocean rapidly climbing those steep slopes. You're familiar with the common experiment by which water is caused to rise in an inverted glass after having put fire in the glass to rarefy the air, rendering it lighter and consequently reducing its pressure. Well, my dear Nadir, what is presented to your eyes here is merely the result of the same principles.

"Observe at present that the water, by virtue of the rapidity of its flow, is lifting with it an infinity of seashells and other productions of the sea. Look at those pieces of wood, the sad debris of shipwrecks; look at that iron anchor attached to one of the pieces of wood, and which, dragged by the torrent, is climbing the steep slope with it. In thirty years that anchor will be found in the earth, a hundred leagues from the sea, and someone will maintain that the sea covered that portion of the land a thousand years ago, as if iron, which is the metal most prompt to decompose in the earth, could have subsisted there for a thousand years in that form.

"Those seashells will be discovered, and those fish, having become fossils—new subjects of error, for the belief that the sea covered the entire surface of this land. People will not reflect that, with the aid of fire, sea water can rise up even into the highest mountains. They will take extravagance to the point of imagining that the entire earth was covered with water before the formation of humans, and that those same humans had originally been marine animals; that the waters of the seas gradually diminished; that those marine humans then preferred the earth to the first element in which they had been born, and multiplied their species there by preference; that the waters of the sea are still diminishing; that the atmosphere is a gourmand what continuously takes water without restoring it, and mocks the laws of gravity; that that gourmand will swallow all the waters on your globe and will finally transform it into a veritable sun.[28] And

---

[28] This is a slightly garbled version of a thesis set out by Benoît de Maillet in *Telliamed*. It was echoed in several later works of French *roman scientifique*, including a striking episode in Hippolyte Mettais' *L'An 5865* (1865; available in a Black Coat Press edition as *The Year 5865*, ISBN 9781612271002).

what will be the proof of all these miracles? That oyster shells and other seashells have been found in mountains far from the sea.

"Another proof is that marine humans have been seen who do not care, in truth, like their distant ancestors to inhabit the earth, and who no longer, like them, have the faculty of articulating sounds; but there are nevertheless humans that have been seen swimming in the sea, that have been captured; and observe that that species of humans is very volatile, for none are ever conserved, in spite of the familiar means of preserving cadavers from putrefaction. Agree, my friend, that an author who lets himself be carried away by the flight of his imagination is soon precipitated into the chaos of error."

"Indeed," replied Nadir, "several of our scientists have criticized that theory. They have thought, rightly, that the sea always gains on one coast what it loses on another, and it even seems probable that in its displacements it travels over almost the same terrain, since cities that have sunk are sometimes discovered a few centuries later. Yes, I sense increasingly that the theory of land-emergences is unsustainable. I think that not a single drop of water is lost from our globe, and that water rises in vapors and condensed by the cold at a certain height in our atmosphere necessarily falls back on to the earth without any loss. Hence its filtration through the earth, the origin of torrents, rivers, streams, the nutrition and growth of vegetation.

"I sense that it is reasonable to compare the universal circulation of waters with what occurs in an alembic, but I understand that comparison better since you have demonstrated to me the existence of a refrigerant, for that of an ardent furnace, at the top of an alembic, such as the sun is supposed to be, appears to me to be contradictory to the effects of such an operation. With regard to the nutrition and growth of vegetation, I'm beginning to conceive..."

"Just a moment," Ormasis interrupted. "There are no more bursts of fire to fear; let's go through that opening now. You can see hardly any water, and it appears that only a little is flowing back. Have no fear, though; we're following the safest path."

Immediately, Ormasis crawled through the hole formed in the rocks. Nadir followed him. They went along a rather high ledge, walking with the greatest ease.

"You can imagine," said Ormasis, "that I have orientated myself here more than once with a compass. The Black Sea is to our left, but we are well below its bed. You may doubt that it is in that sea that the mouth of fire opens; we would then be in greater danger. The eruption must have taken place in the Gulf of Hormuz. You can understand that we are further from the waters of the Ocean here, by virtue of the spherical form on the earth; it is, therefore, by oblique paths that the fire raised up the water to our level and beyond. Don't be surprised now if the waters, in flowing back, do not bring back all the productions that they drew away."

"That's what I can't understand," Nadir replied, "for water coming down certainly has more force than that which rises up, whatever rapidity the fire communicated to it."

"My dear Nadir, that's another question, but I'm content to cite a very simple experiment. If you roll a ball in such a way as to make it climb an inclined plane, do you not see that the ball, at the limit of its ascension, is, so to speak, momentarily at rest before rolling down. It is the same for the water that has to descend again after rising up. It is during that moment of rest that the heavy bodies it contains fall on to the earth and are not carried away, as they would be lower down when the water has resumed the rapid movement of its fall. It is for the same reason that the tide does not always take back what it had brought to the shore of the sea. It is too obvious for us to occupy ourselves with it further. Let us pass on to other matters. What did you want to say to me on the subject of the nutrition and growth of vegetation? I remember having interrupted you on that subject."

"I was saying," Nadir replied, "that I conceive, not the principal motor, but at least the mechanism of that growth. In fact, the vapors of the Earth contain highly-divided parts of earth, which are doubtless deposited on the seeds of vegetables, and it is because these parts of earth are highly-divided that they arrange themselves around each seed, relative to the different forms. But my dear Philosopher, since the most limpid water always contains earth, is it not rather portions of that same water that are transmuted in the ground. I've reflected on that. Yes, I maintain that the transmutation in question takes place. Entire trees have become very large, having had no other alimentary principle than water. Now, as one cannot suppose that there is such a large quantity of di-vided earth in the water, I believe that the water itself is transmuted into earth. Another, even more striking, proof is that our scientists have distilled the same water a hundred times over, and at each distillation there is al-ways an earthen sediment, and that proof is incontrovert-ible."

"Incontrovertible, my dear Nadir—and yet here are a few replies. In a moderately heated apartment one fills a large glass with water, making sure that the external surface of the glass is very clean and free of all humidi-ty. One throws *sal ammoniac* into that water. Immediate-

192

ly, the surface of the glass, which was quite dry, is charged with a considerable dew. You know that that effect is due to the coolness communicated to the glass, which condenses the parts of water with which the atmospheric air is filled. Eventually, these drops of water evaporate as the glass warms up; then the external surface of the glass is tarnished. The air and water of the atmosphere are, therefore, charged with an infinity of earthen molecules, equally susceptible to condense.

"Now, if a solid surface such as that of the glass can be charged with such a large quantity of earthen parts, imagine how many of them a liquid surface would retain. And indeed, you will observe that water evaporated in the open air leaves a much more considerable sediment than the same water distilled in sealed vessels. After these observations, you will no longer believe that water is transmuted into earth because that water can make a tree grow. You will no longer be astonished that, in distilling the water many times, it still produces an earthen residue, since it is sufficient that every time, when the vessels are opened, the surface of the water receives the impression of a current of air, which communicates its earthen molecules to it. It is also probable, as one of your scientists has observed, that the continuous percussion of the boiling water divides a few portions of the glass containing it, without affecting its polish, by virtue of the gentleness of the friction."

"I can see," Nadir replied, "that you do not believe in the transmutation of the elements; you therefore do not think that rays of light can form masses of stone, and that those stones can then be transformed into light, although one of our illustrious scientists has voiced that opinion."[29]

"My dear Nadir, I do not believe what I cannot conceive. I see that the arrangement of the colors that form the spectrum is immutable. Now, given that there is no transmutation even in the rays, I cannot add faith to far more incomprehensible transmutations. One can, therefore, esteem a scientist without adopting all of his hypotheses. Besides which, a laborious man rightly permits himself a multiplicity of reflections, and it is sufficient for him to extract a single ray of enlightenment for one to testify gratitude toward him; it is, therefore, not scientists respectable by virtue of their work that I am attacking here. No, if I were susceptible to ill-humor of that sort, I would direct it at those singular individuals who, on reading a work, scarcely occupy themselves with experiments and ingenious reflections founded on sound physics, but determine to adopt a supposition with which the author has amused himself.

"These singular individuals therefore pose as a principle that there is only one sole matter in the universe. Agreed; however, that matter will always have four essentially distinct parts. Let us retract, if they wish, the name element, but the different sensations that light, water, air and earth cause them to experience will make them admit, however reluctantly, four principles. Let them be content, therefore, to examine the compounds resulting from the various mixtures of these principles, and they will have enough work to do, But if it is extravagant for a person to pretend to know the organic and constituent molecules of each of these principles, is it not even more extravagant to decide that these principle

---

[29] Newton, in *Opticks* (1717).

change their nature, and are transmuted into one another?

"I like the honest physicist who, induced into error by a mixture of air and water, imagines that air is nothing but rarefied water. However, he seeks to instruct himself. He heats an aeolipile full of water, from which it appears that only air is escaping, but on fitting a vessel that condenses those vapors, he recovers the same quantity of water therefrom. He carries out another experiment. He pumps air from the receptacle of a pneumatic machine, under which he has put a glass full of water. He sees the water boiling, by virtue of the air that it contains and the reduced pressure of the atmosphere, which causes it to rise within the glass. But he does not perceive any diminution of the water, not a single atom of water converted into air. He also observes that water penetrates bodies that air cannot penetrate: certain proof of the difference of form of the constituents of the two principles. Finally, he puts the damp cloths he has used in his experiments out to dry in the open air. A powerful wind is blowing, and the cloths are soon dry. Then he reflects that the great wind would not have dried the objects he has exposed to it so quickly if the great wind had only been a large quantity of water in movement; immediately he recognizes that his ideas were only errors and, renouncing any theoretical pretention, he adopts the existence of four essentially different elements or principles of matter, and although it is impossible for him to obtain them in the state of purity, he sees enough particularities that establish the differences of their species."

"The observations that you make," Nadir replied, "interest me greatly, but they do not convince me. In fact, reasoning inversely, ought one not to believe that everything is water, that everything can be converted into water, since all the bodies in Nature can be lique-fied. No, nothing can prevent me from believing in that transmutation—or, rather, the perfect identity of the two elements of earth and water."

Nadir was debating heatedly, and the inflamed air of the volcano had warmed him considerably. An ardent thirst was tormenting him. He informed the Philosopher of his condition.

Ormasis immediately offered him a handful of sand. "Here, my friend," he said, "slake your thirst."

Nadir, surprised, saw clearly that the sand, which required nine hundred degrees of heat to be fluid, was not water. Immediately, Ormasis took a hollow pebble and, collecting a few drops of petroleum oil that was oozing from a nearby mass of stone, he offered it to his friend.

Nadir understood immediately that a phlogisticated fluid, not becoming solid at the same degree of cold as water, was still not what he needed to appease his thirst. "I abjure my puerile reflections," he said to Ormasis.

Ormasis then showed him a spring of clear water behind a rock. Nadir, as he slaked his thirst therein, agreed that if all the bodies in Nature were susceptible to become fluid at different degrees of heat, that difference in the degrees of heat was sufficient to indicate their different species, and, in consequence, the distinctive character of the elements composing them.

Chapter XXII

Scarcely had a moment of calm succeeded the subterranean tempest than a distant roaring reawakened Nadir's attention. Thick clouds suddenly filled the immense caverns. The fires were snuffed out. There was no more mephitic air to fear. The marine acid fumigation became unnecessary to our voyagers, but their lantern was very necessary. Four reflectors were scarcely adequate to light their way.

"These clouds," said Ormasis, "these thick vapors that are condensing around us, are surely the sea-water that you saw rising up so rapidly. You know that the water in question rose up, and followed the course of the fire, because fire always rarefies the column of air ahead of it, but that the same water will be precipitate in the nucleus of a profound volcano. That is what is causing the roaring that is striking your ears, and the fog you can see is that same sea water, reduced to vapors by rapid boiling. Come and see the effects that the evaporation in question will have produced. There is no more risk of explosion. Let's climb up a little to our left, and let's walk quickly—it won't take us far from the terrain to which I'm going to lead you."

Indeed, after half an hour's march, our voyagers arrived close to the place where the nucleus of the volcano was. They only perceived that by virtue of the considerable heat that could still be felt.

Nadir saw, to his surprise, very bright white masses of enormous size. He reflected for some time. "I imagine," he said to Ormasis, "that during the evaporation of the sea-water, the salts were melted by the violence of the heat, and that is doubtless what his reduced them on a massive scale. But is that what is called gem-salt?"

"Yes, my friend, and you can see here the solution to a great problem. The formation of that salt on a large scale had seemed incomprehensible to your scientists. It is conceivable, said some, that parts of earth and water, agitated together and combined, might form salts in the bowels of the earth. But only crystallized salts in their natural form ought to result from that slow combination—or, at least, salts mixed with earthen parts, such as one sees in rocks and are incorporated with portions of earth. On the contrary, here are entire exceedingly shiny masses, without any apparent mixture and without any form of crystallization—from where do they come? Others had claimed that the terrain in which such quarries are found had the faculty of continually producing salt, but the streams of fresh water that run through the bottom of these abysses soon undeceived the partisans of that theory. Finally, your scientists, by dissolving and filtering that salt several times, found that the only difference between that fossil salt and sea salt was a few more earthen particles, and they were not mistaken, for if you care to melt marine salt with calcareous earth or seashells, those seashells dissolve in it and are incorporated with it, and you will then obtain a veritable fossil salt.

"You can thus see by what processes these saline masses have been formed. In several centuries these quarries will be filled with it, because the small quantity of water that will be able to filter through the earths will only attack the surfaces of these masses, and besides, the cold that will overtake these caverns will diminish the dissolving virtue—which is to say, the dilatation—of that filtered water. Let us now resume the route that will take us into terrains charged with minerals."

Our voyagers marched rapidly. Soon, they were obliged to slow down; it was necessary to follow a narrow and tortuous path with precaution. The narrow path skirted precipices whose depth could not be measured. A few trickles of water fell into these tenebrous gulfs, forming an alarming murmur—but the mists diminished, and the two friends, illuminated by their reflectors, advanced with sufficient assurance. Eventually, they reached less dangerous paths, and these new routes offered Nadir the most interesting spectacle.

"My friend," the Philosopher said to him then, "the earth that we have traversed thus far has seemed quite uniform to you; now look at its different layers. Look at these banks of yellow, red and blue clay. Examine these other calcareous earths, these marbles, these alabasters, these agates, these spars. Let us take a detour to our right. Cast your eyes over these shiny masses, look at these innumerable crystal veins and precious stones of every color. Consider, on the other hand, these matrices, these seams that present you with an infinity of branches of native gold and silver. Would you like us to pause here for a moment?"

Nadir could not have asked for anything better. Our voyagers immediately sat down in the midst of these immense treasures.

Fascinated, Nadir ran his eyes over those delightful objects. "What beauties!" he exclaimed. "O, my friend, what marvels!"

"Well," the Philosopher said to him, "I promised you that you would be in a position to offer me presents similar to those I offered you. Have I not kept my word? My dear Nadir, I'm older than you; I wanted you to profit from my discoveries. A benevolent heart like yours ought not to have any shackles. When you have shared your fortune with honest unfortunates, you will only have to come here to regenerate it and augment it according to the circumstances."

"What, my dear Ormasis, it's also for my own felicity that you have brought me here? How can I ever thank you?"

"My friend," Ormasis replied, "I am repaying a legitimate debt."

Nadir could not yet sense the force of that reply. Sitting on a rock, he suddenly looked down at the masses of earth that were beneath their feet, and saw there a prodigious quantity of gold powder mingled with fragments of quartz. "Here, then," he exclaimed, "one tramples underfoot the vile metal that makes the happiness of humans!"

"My friend," Ormasis continued, "abandon that epithet to the imagination of poets. A good naturalist will never call gold a 'vile metal'; there is nothing that has more real value. Not only does it resist for a long time the intemperance of the air without decomposing, but nothing in the world is sounder and more convenient than vessels of such a material, and one ought to wish, for the good of humanity, that it were more abundant. You see, then, my dear Nadir, that if vile men commit iniquities to acquire gold, it does not follow that the metal merits their epithet."

"Very good, Ormasis; one can therefore love gold for purely philosophical reasons."

"Yes, my friend; besides, the true philosopher does not scorn wealth, although he never resorts to baseness in order to acquire it. The fortune of others does not torment him. On the contrary, it amuses him greatly to see moralistic mud-slingers hurling their bile indiscriminate-

ly at all the Croesuses of the Earth, and affecting a cyni-
cal pride that does not fool anyone."

Chapter XXIII

While listening to his friend, Nadir examined a vein of sand in the rock on which they were sitting, and, perceiving a few bright gleams there, he poked the vein with the iron tip of his staff. The small shiny stones were soon more exposed, and separated from the sandy material. He recognized them as beautiful diamonds.

"You see," Ormasis said to him, "that we can take riches away from here without any difficulty."

"Yes, my dear Philosopher, and that's what I shall do—but my surprise is increasing with every passing moment. Can it be that Nature, merely by the proportional diversity of elements, forms such beautiful things? Tell me, I beg you, by what labor, by what progressions, masses of common earth can be subjected to such transformations. Enlighten me. What is the origin of the arrangement of the different layers of earth one atop another?"

"My friend," the Philosopher replied, "that arrangement in layers is nothing but the result of specific weights, with whose laws you are familiar. It is natural that the water that filters through the earths precipitates and transports equally earths of equal weight. There, in a few words, is the solution of the problem. You can therefore conceive that those who, examining the layers of earth in different countries, claim that it was the currents of the sea that formed them, have an idea of these objects upon which they have not sufficiently reflected. It is true that the sea transports layers of differently-colored mud in the countries where it forms some extension, but there are innumerable regions that the sea had never covered, whose earth is also layered. There are immense terrains, not only in Asia but in other portions of the globe, in which one does not find the smallest seashell to provide an indication that they have been inundated by the sea. Finally, my friend, the arrangements of clays that the sea has often transported in layers over several terrains, is similarly a consequence of the principle of weights that I just mentioned.

"Presently, I will satisfy your curiosity regarding the formation of the objects that offer themselves to your eyes. I will begin by developing for you the principle of metals. You will conceive at the same time the origin of precious stones and that of the transmutation of all earths—which is to say, of the changing of their makeup. This, therefore is the great question: by what agency do argilous or calcareous earths become metallic earths?

"Observe first of all that the sulfurous vapors that circulate in the bowels of the Earth are particularly abundant in metallic mines. Those sulfurous vapors might have attracted more attention from your scientists who have carried out research in that regard. You know, therefore, that sulfur is a composite of sulfuric acid and phlogiston. You also know by virtue of certain experiments that metallic earths contain more phlogiston than other earths. Well, my friend it is, therefore, by the intermediary of acid that the phlogiston combines with earthen matter. What effects do these sulfurous vapors have? These: they divide and attenuate molecules of earth as they circulate with them. When these vapors subsequently encounter colder portions of earth, they condense there, and these molecules of earth are reunited by condensation. The longer these molecules of earth have circulated, the more divided they are and the more susceptible their parts are to fit together exactly. Then they admit less air and water into their constituent parts, and become heavier and more compact. That is, in fact, how metallic earths are made. Observe also that the phlogiston that is always in action, being combined in these molecules of earth, circulates within the constituent parts and maintains their linkage by rarefying the internal air. Such, then, my dear Nadir, is the operation of Nature in the formation of metals."

"Very good," replied Nadir. "Those are physical arguments and principles that appear to me to be evident. But whence comes the difference in fixity between metals and minerals?"

"I will explain in a moment, my friend. The earths that have been combined with phlogiston by the intermediary of vitriolic acid and have become metallic earths are not fixed metals while that acid has not been removed from their constituent parts by a subsequent operation of Nature. Why? Because the sulfurous parts interposed in the constituent parts prevent their precise union and render them volatile to fire. Such is the condition of the semi-metals antimony, zinc and bismuth. Such is also the condition of several metals whose earth is more divided than that of semi-metals and whose molecules, being still mixed with acids, are entirely volatile for that reason. But when the earth has first been reduced into a state of considerable division by the action of sulfurous s vapors, and when the vitriolic acid is disengaged from the constituent parts without having removed the phlogiston, that divided earth, in condensing, fits together more exactly, and becomes a substance more fixed and compact the more divided it has been. Then fixed metals result."

"Permit me to raise an objection, my dear Ormasis. You claim that it is the acid that is the cause of the volatility or certain metals or minerals, but I attribute that volatility solely to phlogiston. For example, antimony is very volatile to heat. If I remove its phlogiston, a calx results known as pearly matter, which is very resistant to heat. It is thus evident that the volatility depends solely on phlogiston."

"Marvelous, my dear Nadir—but no matter how considerable a quantity of phlogiston I add to gold, it is impossible to ender it volatile by that method. It is therefore not the phlogiston that renders metals volatile."

"But my dear Philosopher, that is because gold is naturally fixed."

"Well, my friend, it is that 'natural fixation' that it is necessary to explain. Why is gold fixed, although it is highly phlogisticated? It's because it contains no acid in its constituent parts. Antimony, on the contrary, in spite of its calcination and washing, retains a quantity of acid. Now, when one presents phlogiston to that antimony calx, the acid it contains dilates, simultaneously dilating the constituent parts, and then the semi-meta becomes volatile again. It is the same with other semi-metals or metals, in which there is more or less acid engaged. Be certain that it is on this first principle that the variation in the fixity of metals depends."

"Ormasis, your principles are beginning to seduce me. I am no longer surprised, therefore, to see all these mixtures of metals in the same mines, in the same deposits. In fact, the molecules of earth divided by sulfurous vapors, being subsequently condensed, have formed metals of variable fixity by virtue of variations in the division that have experienced, or the variation in the acid that has remained in their constituent parts. However, my dear Philosopher, I still come back to the question: is it possible? What! Lead, mercury, those imperfect metals, are only volatile because they retain more acid in their constituent parts? That is what I cannot conceive. A hundred times over I have seen lead reduced by fire to calxes of various colors, vitrify therein and rise up in vapors. I have similarly seen mercury extracted from cinnabar form precipitates of every sort. I have also seen it, exposed to fire and open air, evaporate completely, without bearing the slightest sulfurous odor. There is, therefore, no sulfur in those metals. There is no acid combined with their phlogiston."

"Oh, I fully expected, my dear Nadir, that you were going to present that petty objection to me. Observe, therefore, my friend, that sulfur does not have any sensible odor when, in combination, it is united with a superabundant quantity of phlogiston. Your scientists have even given the name of nitrous sulfur to a more highly phlogisticated species of sulfur, which has indeed no odor, but the name is irrelevant. It follows that sulfur well charged with phlogiston has no sulfurous odor when it evaporates; such is the sulfur contained in mercury and lead. If the acid were extracted from those metals, their constituent parts would fit together more closely, and they would become fixed metals. Finally, I repeat, present to gold or silver as much phlogiston as you like, and it will never become volatile. It is therefore not phlogiston that is the sole principle of volatility. But if one succeeds in introducing sulfur into them—which is to say, acid combined with phlogiston—then one renders them volatile. That is what experiment demonstrates to us, and that is what Nature offers us in different mines, where gold and silver are sometimes found in a fairly considerable state of volatility. Again, in that state, the sulfur is not perfectly combined with the constituent parts, which is why they are easily recalled to their state of fixity."

Chapter XXIV

Nadir took a very keen interest in these further explanations. "With regard to phlogiston," he said to Ormasis, "I'd like to know why metals precipitated by the intermediary of other metals conserve their metallic brightness. For example, if I dissolve copper in an acid and then throw iron into the solution, my piece if iron is covered in beautiful sheets of copper. If, on the other hand, I throw into that solution a fragment of alkaline salt, the copper parts only precipitate out as a dirty powder devoid of any metallic sheen."

"My friend, that effect derives from a very simple cause; it is that the iron has furnished more phlogiston to the solution, which is not furnished by the alkali salt, and, the copper precipitated by the iron having retained more phlogiston, its more closely-knit parts reflect light—which is to say, conserve their metallic brightness. That proves that the metallic earths differ from other non-metallic earths primarily by virtue of the quantity of phlogiston they contain. Your scientists have already provided clarifications on this subject, but to complete the demonstration that it is to the abundance of phlogiston that the phenomenon for which you asked me for an explanation is due, you can make some observations by means of the following experiment. It will surely interest you greatly.

"An ounce of silver is placed in an earthenware capsule on a fire; one or two ounces of sulfur are thrown on several times over, and allowed to burn. The silver is pulverized as many times as the sulfur is burned; after thus burning two or three pounds, the fire is stoked up sufficiently to make the capsule red hot. Small white dendrites are then seen to emerge from the blackened and granulated silver, and these dendrites have their metallic gleam. The first effect is due to the fact that the acid of the sulfur, in rising, draws with it highly-divided molecules of silver, but, as the acid rises, it combines with a greater quantity of aqueous vapors distributed in the atmosphere. Then it becomes lighter, and the molecules of silver, no longer being of equal weight to it, are precipitated upon one another and form the dendrites.

"The experiment is repeated the following day, and the more silver is divided, the more delicate the branches of the little dendrites are. The silver is boiled in water. Afterwards, the clear water is transferred into two glass saucers; the water from one of these saucers is rapidly evaporated with the heat of a sand-bath. Soon, the silver that the acidulated water holds in solution is precipitated in the saucer as a white powder, with very little metallic brightness. The water contained in the other saucer is allowed to evaporate slowly in the open air. What a difference! The silver is precipitated there in small leaves, and those leaves are extremely bright. Is it not evident that, the acidulated water having an affinity with the ambient phlogiston in the air, taken possession of it, and allows the precipitation of a quantity of highly-phlogisticated silver?

"You see, therefore, my friend, by courtesy of this experiment, that metal precipitates vary in brightness by virtue of the variation in the amount of phlogiston that they retain, because that phlogiston, in uniting the parts, also agitates light and occasions more brilliant reflections. That is what forms the metallic sheen.

"One rather active curious individual, having burned sulfur over the silver for a long time, in accordance with the experiment I have just cited, melted that silver with borax. He then submitted it to dissolution in nitric acid; immediately, he saw a black powder precipitated. He thought that, in spite of the care he had taken in handling the silver, from the outset, some portions of gold must remain therein. To assure himself of that he decanted to the solution, washed the black powder and melted it with borax again. He then obtained a very beautiful and very malleable lemon yellow metal—but what surprised him was that the metal was highly resistant to all solvents. Nitric acid, *aqua regia*, marine acid and vitriolic acid all failed to corrode it, although all metals are corroded by one or several of these solvents.

"He then imagined that the metal was nothing but an alloy of gold and silver, in a singular proportion, in such a fashion that, each being shielded from their respective solvents by the other, it was indissoluble. Now, in order to establish that that was the true principle, it was merely a matter of disturbing the proportion. In consequence, he melted a portion of the metal with a dozen parts of silver—but when that silver, melted and cooled, was dissolved in nitric acid, the same quantity of black powder was precipitated again, and when that powder was heated again with the borax, it reproduced the same quantity of indissoluble metal.

"The curious individual, quite astonished, did not think that agents as simple as sulfurous vapors and water could have brought about such a singularity. He did not imagine that a few portions of silver, extremely divided by sulfurous vapors and condensed again, might have formed a more compact substance, differently combined with phlogiston and giving less access to solvent acids. No, that idea did not occur to him. On the contrary; he tried to form different alloys of gold and silver directly by heating, in order to imitate the metallic product, but he never obtained either its specific weight nor its indissoluble quality. In sum, my dear Nadir, the more you think about it, the more you will recognize the evidence for the principles that I have just explained to you."

"Indeed," Nadir replied, "your principles carry a character of verity that strikes and uplifts me. How many pretended scientists, plunged in a chaos of ineptitude, have forged insipid allegories, drear enigmas, whose subject they did not know themselves! With what enthusiasm those famous Alchemists or Adepts told us about a particular mercury that they had never seen—and that mercury was, according to them, the 'universal principle,' a 'new-born dampness,' a 'radical solvent.' They strove to obtain it by separating the pure from the impure in a substance, obtaining its elements in their final degree of purity, and then recombining them—but as 'pure' and 'impure' are only words to express that which affects us differently, and that pure and impure were both combinations of elements, after having obtained the pure elements they rendered them impure again, since they mixed them.

"No, it was something else. Out of millions or billions of compounds, resulting from various proportions of those elements, the fell upon a proportion that formed, not substances such as Nature presents them, but a marvelous powder, which converted the vilest metals into gold; and that powder, having become fluid, was an admirable oil in which all substances were converted into their first principles. It is certain that such reasoners lacked common sense, for, supposing that these Alchemists had been able to produce such a solvent, first of all, as has already been observed, in what vessel could that solvent have been formed?

"Secondly, since that solvent ought to dissolve all substance and reduce them to their initial elements, the Alchemists would, therefore, have obtained in their marvelous vessels, to begin with, for the first layer, an earth that was not malleable and harder than diamond, since that is the condition of pure earth; for the second layer, frozen water, for water deprived of fire is certainly not fluid; then air, but doubtless very tranquil air; finally, the fire, with is nothing but agitated light, would have floated in the vessel above the other elements, without mixing with them, in spite of its subtlety, and which, therefore, would have produced all its miracles.

"A solvent. Explain the word. A compound of several elements—but that very composite would have separated out all the elements. Ormasis, that picture of the prideful ignorance of several authors presently offers to my eyes al the nuances of their ineptitude."

"I see, therefore, my dear Philosopher, that the work of Nature, in the elaboration of metals, is to combine a great deal of phlogiston with earth. I conceive that the earth, divided by a long circulation of sulfurous vapors, becomes more compact when it condenses again, because, its parts having been more divided, are more susceptible to reuniting intimately, forming masses more deprived of water, and heavier, such as metals are. These truths have a simplicity that astonishes me—but you have promised to explain the formation of precious stones, so let us now examine the operation of Nature in that regard."

"What?" replied the Philosopher, you can't deduce what that operation is? Well, my friend, it's the same one that forms metals. Believe that Nature does not multiply its operations needlessly. The stones that are called precious because of their hardness and their brightness are merely earth divided by less-phlogisticated vapors than those which form metals, which earth, in condensing, retains more water and less phlogiston than that of metals."

"What, Ormasis? Is that the only difference between the formation of precious stones and that of metals?"

"Yes, my friend, and do you not see, in fact, that metals are vitrified when they lost a part of their phlogiston to fire?"

"I agree, but if precious stones only differ from metals by virtue of containing a little more water and less phlogiston, why, can one not form metals with crystals and precious stones, by combining them with a quantity of phlogiston?"

"Nadir, that would perhaps be the least extravagant work with which your Alchemists might have occupied themselves, but imagine the difficulties standing in the way of success, since the Art could not even recall certain vitrified metals to their original metallic state. You know, for example, that tin exposed to violent heat can be converted into glass, but that the glass in question no longer reproduces tin—not, at least, by means of the temperatures that have been successfully generated. It is only in the nuclei of volcanoes in which Nature produces metals and precious stones. Have you ever seen crystal in pumice-stones? On the contrary, violent and long-sustained fires entirely destroy crystals and other precious stones, in the same way that you see crystal from your glassworks that initially acquire a certain hardness from fire, but, when exposed to a more active fire, eventually lose their transparency, are divided, and partly evaporate. Don't imagine that precious stones or metals can ever be formed at the focal points of your best mirrors. I have just explained to you, my friend, the placid work of Nature in that formation; be certain that there has never been another."

"All that you tell me, my dear Ormasis, is very evident, but I confess to you that it is so very simple that I hesitate to believe it. I am in the situation of those people who, having reasoned endlessly about the fastening of a game-bag, can scarcely believe that the manipulation shown to them can be the principle of the trick. I'm presently reflecting on means of refining metals. By following your principles, I see that instead of roasting a mineral at the exit from a mine, it would instead be necessary to expose it to a further circulation of sulfurous vapors and then condense those vapors with water. Would that simple endeavor really suffice to form a large quantity of perfect metal within the mineral?"

"Nadir, in explaining faithfully my observations on the work of Nature, I have not claimed, for the assertion of my principles, to give you the means of imitating all its productions. Why, my friend, would you be happier were you suddenly to obtain that power? Nothing would remain for you to desire. Work, my dear Nadir, gradually draw away the veil that hides great truths from you. Every item that you discover will procure you new delights—and don't you know that, for the human species, the gradation of pleasure is the veritable enjoyment."

Chapter XXV

The eyes become accustomed to the most beautiful spectacles. At first one is transported. Admiration follows. Then one gazes without emotion. Finally, one gets bored. It is not the same with instructive reasoning, which has the most constant impression on the mind. Nadir was silently thoughtful. He was scarcely paying any heed now to the riches that surrounded him, but the Philosopher's explanations uplifted his soul. He still had a few objections to raise, however.

"I understand," he said, "the action of sulfurous vapors in the formation of metals; but if these principles are invariable, why do sulfur mines exist in which one does not find an atom of metal?"

"Remember," the Philosopher replied, "that the formation of metals depends on a considerable division and the great circulation of sulfurous vapors. Now, in less heated terrains, where sulfurous vapors condense almost immediately after their formation, one will therefore only find sulfur and no metal. It is, in any case, a verity adopted and demonstrated by one of your scientists that there is no sulfur and no sulfuric acid whose base is not itself a metallic earth.

"Presently, my friend, you can understand the origin of the continuous transmutation of earths and stones. There is a striking observation in that regard. Have you not seen, in certain places, that water running over stones gradually destroys them? That running water thus takes into solution the earthen parts that it has divided. The more condensed it is, the longer it retains those earthen parts in solution. When that same water runs over warmer terrain, it becomes more rarefied, lighter; then it allows the earths it has divided to precipitate, and those precipitated earths either form masses of the same nature or of a different nature, according to the degree of division they have experienced and the quantity of parts of water engaged in their interstices. That is the true principle of the transmutation of earths and stones. That principle is also that of the petrifaction of vegetables or animal. In effect, the latter substances are sieves that dilate in slightly warmer terrain, and which certain waters charged with earthen matter can easily penetrate. The same waters, having become more rarefied in those little capillary tubes, deposit earthen matter there, which is reassembled and forms stones that are harder in proportion to the degree that they are divided. You see, therefore, how real petrifaction is. At the same time, you can see how such grandiose terms as 'lapidific secretions' are poorly designed to express such a simple and tangible effect."

"Very good," said Nadir. "I can see that minerals, vegetables and animals are transmuted into alone another; I think, however, that the calcareous earth that results from the decomposition of animals does not change its nature."

"In that case," the Philosopher replied, "the entire globe would be a calcareous earth. In fact, calculate the weight of the Earth relative to the weight of a globe of earth one foot in diameter; observe at the same time the approximate weight of all the animals that have covered the earth over thousands of years. According to that comparison of weights, I defy you to present me with an ounce of earth that would not be calcareous."

"Permit me to point out to you," Nadir said, swiftly, "that animals do not contain as much earth as you presume. The proof is that the terrains in which bodies deprived of life are deposited daily do not appear to increase in height after a number of years."

"My friend, that observation signifies nothing. Examine things on a large scale. Remember that the formative earth of animals is singularly volatile, with regard to the quantity of phlogiston it contains. Consider that all the fleshy parts of animals, the base of which is an extremely phlogisticated earth, also communicate phlogiston to the earths that cover them and cause a part of that earth to volatilize, and that the evaporation of that volatilized earth might equal in quantity that of the bones, which is more fixed. That, then, is why, in the space of a few years, one does not perceive any sensible elevation or diminution of such terrains. It also follows that the volatilized animal earth in question rises into the atmosphere, that it is then condensed by cold at a certain height, and that, depending on currents of air, it often falls back several leagues from its point of departure on other terrains, where it serves for the growth of other animals, vegetables or minerals.

"We shall not repeat in that regard what I have already said. Let it be sufficient for you to be assured that all compounds change their nature. The chemist, for example, who had the arrogance to believe that salts were indecomposable because he had not succeeded in decomposing one, was very astonished to see another chemist reduce a mass of alkali salt to pure earth.

"My friend, no substance is immutable. Gold and precious stones are not exceptions to that law, although they require, in truth, several centuries to be subject to sensible changes. In sum, movement changes the constituent forms of substances. Forms change weights and weights change movement. Such is the circular chain in which Nature incessantly shakes up all material beings. If the combinations of the twenty-four letters of the alphabet have seemed innumerable to your calculators, judge how the immense diversity of forms and the different degrees of movement might form combinations in the proportions of elements, the various degrees of which are themselves inappreciable by calculation."

Chapter XXVI

Suddenly, Nadir rose to his feet urgently. "My dear Philosopher, you're rendering me guilty of ingratitude. You were giving me so much pleasure, occupying me to such a degree, that I entirely forgot the object that interests you. My duty is to make you remember it. I promised to help you search for that electric metal, that fatal metal, whose discovery I am far from desiring. Tell me, I pray you, in what form it exists on your planet. Let us go on, let us penetrate into those crevasses not far distant from us. You shall see me expose myself willingly to the greatest dangers. However, you have become an essential being to me. If I lose you, I shall groan, I shall be unhappy, but no matter; I must sacrifice my happiness to gratitude."

"My dear Nadir, my worthy friend, that generous trait would increase my attachment to you, if my heart were capable of receiving new sentiments...but it is full. Let us stay here for a moment longer." He held out his hand. "Come and sit down again. You are now at the point that I desired; you have become curious about the most beautiful knowledge of Nature; it is time I told you the truth about my origin.

"My friend the story I have told you is entirely fabulous. I wanted to capture your attention by means of marvels; I have inspired a great deal of curiosity in you. That was the surest means of giving you the taste, and simultaneously sweetening, the most abstract dissertations. That was my only objective. Learn who I am."

"My dear Philosopher," Nadir interjected swiftly, "you delight me. What...you will always remain with me! Oh, my friend, we shall all be happy. How I forgive you with all my heart for that trickery."

"My dear Nadir, my true origin might perhaps be no less interesting to you. Listen."

Ormasis' Story

My real name is Zirmen; that of Ormasis was given to me by good and honest savages; I keep it out of gratitude. I was born in Aden. That city, as you know, was always the most flourishing in fortunate Arabia. The arts and sciences were held is high consideration there. My father, a great philosopher, had justly acquire a considerable reputation there. He could have extended it further afield, but he never wanted to write, which caused him to be forgotten after his death. Geber, the famous chemist from the kingdom of Fez,[30] and other chemists of the same land came to visit my father several times to instruct themselves, for he possessed sublime knowledge of every sort, especially in medicine. An enlightened physicist, a profound chemist, full of confidence in his ideas, his cures were innumerable. It is necessary to tell all; my father was very rich. The desire to make a fortune had never restricted his genius, and he only undertook to conserve the lives of his compatriots after being assured that he would never cause death.

---

[30] This is a curious reference, as the famous alchemist known in the West by the name of Geber probably lived in the 8th century; his link with Fez was suggested by Leo Africanus, who made him the leader of its Alchemical Society in the book published in 1526 that probably featured among those that Nadir threw out of his library.

As soon as my father became involved in healing the sick, people were quite astonished by his treatments. Often, he went to see patients who were thought to be moribund. He prescribed nothing but distilled water and rest. People looked at him in surprise, and if his disinterest had not shielded him from all reproach, he would have been accused of stealing money. However, the presumed moribunds recovered their health, and woe betide those who demanded more complicated remedies from other doctors. Sometimes, on the contrary, he prescribed violent remedies to patients apparently inflicted by slight indispositions; but in the end he developed a curative method that was helpful to humankind. I shall tell you about it.

That great man accustomed me to thinking early in life. A few agreeable talents that he made me acquire would only serve, he said, to make study unwearisome for me and to enable me to undertake it with more courage. Finally, when I had passed the age of adolescence, he explained his operations to me, making no mystery of any of his secrets. I wish to God that he had put more limits on that confidence.

One day, I was with him in his study. "Zirmen," he said to me, "while all our doctors are busy introducing poisons into the blood of healthy people, let us try, on the contrary, to inoculate them with the antidotes to poisons and destroy the germ of maladies. Various balsamic essences of our plants, introduced directly into a vein, act on the blood with far more efficacy than remedies deteriorated by difficult digestion, which often augment the illness. We shall carry out a few experiments."

Indeed, my father obtained a quantity of liquid plant extracts and numbered them according to the degree of fermentation to which they had been subjected. He obtained freshly-drawn animal blood. While he was making his preparations, he said to me:

"My son, do you know why repose is necessary to all animals? This is the reason. The more exercise a person does, the more his blood is rarefied by heat. The blood that is rarefied necessarily increases in volume. It thus occasions a pressure on the nervous system, and eventually hinders movement. Such is the physical principle that we call fatigue. That is the cause that necessarily obliges humans to rest, in order that their blood might condense again and no longer put pressure on the nervous system.

"Let us pass on now to the principle of maladies. I have demonstrated to you that all the various kinds are related. It is always the blood that becomes defective. Let us suppose a man who overindulges at the table. There is a considerable pressure in his stomach, so a gross lymph passes more easily through the pores, mingles with the blood and disturbs its circulation. That lymph varies in its acidity or alkalinity and its phlogistication, which occasions various accidents. Then diet and water are no longer sufficient to cure such a patient, but the remedies known until now are sometimes not prompt enough. It is therefore necessary, my dear son, to attack the blood directly.

"If, through the pores that serve for transpiration, the healthiest of men pump contagious vapors, which give them the principles of death, why should their lives not be conserved by inoculating them with salutary remedies? Has it not been demonstrated that the sole application of certain plants operates constant cures? For instance, is not a patient tormented by the most stubborn and inveterate fever cured in a matter of days when one applies to his wrists, at the place where the pulse beats, the plant named *cariofilata*,[31] ground up with a pinch of marine salt? That cure is not radical, since it never results in accidents, and is it not evident that the remedy attacks the principle of the malady?

"Now, what might we hope to achieve by inoculating subtle extracts, appropriate to maintain in our liquors a stable fluidity perhaps capable of inhibiting the deposits that form in our joints and gradually impede our movements, leading us to decrepitude?"

At the same moment, my father began his experiments. Blood had been brought to him in a glass vessel with a double bottom. That double bottom only served to contain warm water and maintain the temperature. I soon saw things as surprising as they were instructive.

Sometimes, by means of mucous and alkaline principles, he vitiated the blood, to the point of being very thick and almost black. Suddenly, a drop of a plant extract restored the fluidity of that blood. Sometimes he made it become entirely yellow, divided into layers, and, so to speak, decomposed. Suddenly, another drop introduced into that blood spread swiftly through the mass, mingling those divisions again and restoring the color. Then I saw him put blood under a glass bell-jar, and combine it with phlogisticated emanations; then suddenly halt the agitation and inflation the liquid had experienced.

What astonished me was seeing that he always restored the blood to its natural state, without causing it the slightest effervescence. I told him how surprised I was.

---

[31] Presumably the clove, once classified as *Caryophyllus aromaticus*, but nowadays identified as *Eugenia caryophyllata*.

"My son," he said, "you can see that I am not employing simple acids and alkalis here. Their direct effect would be too active. It's necessary that they be enchained in oily or mucilaginous principles, and that is what Nature provides for us in various plants, of which it is not only necessary to know the principles, but also the changes that those principles experience in the air when they are extracted. I will show you, however, the proportions in which one may add mineral acids to the different extracts.

"At present," he continued, "you ought to understand that warmed blood is rarefied blood and that cooled blood is necessarily condensed. In that regard, here is a liquor whose property will seem singular to you. You'll see the extent to which one can cool and condense blood."

Indeed, my father poured a few drops of it into a quantity of blood that was in its natural state, into which he had plunged a thermometer. To my surprise, I saw that blood diminish considerably in volume, and at the same time, the thermometer went down by eight degrees. Finally, the blood congealed equally throughout its mass.

"That's not all," my father said. "You'll see how subtle the effect of this liquor is on the circulation of a living animal."

He had a bird brought in, and having impregnated a needle with the liquor, he pricked it lightly. Immediately, the bird went to sleep. Soon, it died, without giving any symptoms of pain. Promptly, I opened the little animal up. I found its blood coagulated and almost cold. Surprised by that effect, much more effective than that of non-fermented opium, I asked my father what the remedy was for such a puncture.

"There is one," he told me, "and it always succeeds when it is administered in time. It is concentrated vinegar—but to avoid any accident, let us immediately pass this poisoned needle through the fire, in order that it loses its deadly virtue."

I do not know, my dear Nadir, what fatal curiosity made me ask insistently where that prodigious liquor came from, which poisoned iron with so much subtlety. My father, always having my education and theoretical demonstrations in view, yielded to my insistence.

He told me that it was a mixture of ox-bile with the juice of a plant common in our country; he also indicated the necessary proportions to me. My curiosity, satisfied in that regard, eventually moved on to other objects. I did not doubt, after what I had seen, that my father could inoculate salutary remedies in the most dangerous circumstances.

The opportunity presented itself. Someone came to ask him to visit a patient whom two physicians had despaired of curing. My father, who thought it his duty to attempt to cure a person, in whatever condition he might be, proposed that I should go with him, and that we should take our new remedies. As was his custom, he took a small graduated aerometer, fitted with a thermometer. He also took a glass tube sealed at one end, into which the aerometer fitted easily.

We did not lose a minute. It was a question of a man's life; we walked rapidly. We got there just in time. First, we saw an amiable woman who appeared to us to be overwhelmed by grief, and who had been taken away from the sick man's apartment to spare her the awful spectacle of her dying husband. She held out her arms to my father.

"Alas," she said to him, "man as respectable as knowledgeable, I fear that your cares..." She was unable to say any more.

My father's only response was to hasten to the sick man. He was dying.

The two doctors were present. "Sir," they said, "there is nothing more to be done."

"In that case," my father replied, "let us try a new treatment."

Immediately, while the doctors explained to him the principal symptoms of the malady, he opened one of the dying man's veins and drew into his glass tube about half an ounce of blood.

"What are you doing?" the doctors said. "It's an eruption that can serve no purpose, it would be necessary to push from the center to the circumference, and, on the contrary, you're going to refresh by bleeding. Oh, Sir, what a blunder!"

"One moment, gentlemen. I am not claiming that bleeding might be a remedy in this case."

While speaking to them he had already dipped the aerometer in the blood that was in the tube. He had also exposed to the vapors of that blood and the transpiration of the patient pieces of cloth lightly tinted with a color whose changes indicated degrees of acidity or alkalinity to him.

Finally, after having carefully but rapidly observed the results, he selected one of the little bottles we had brought; he dipped a piece of lint in the liquid it contained. He reopened the patient's vein slightly and applied the lint with a compress.

The doctors, who had not expected that operation, then maintained the most profound silence.

My father, who was observing the patient pulse continuously, perceived that it was becoming less intermittent. "My son," he said to me, "go fetch that woman whose affliction touched us. Tell her not to lose hope and to come back here; I want to show her something interesting."

Imagine, my dear Nadir, how flattering that commission was for me. I went out with a surge of pleasure. A female slave guided me, at a run, although it seemed to me that she was not going fast enough. I reached the room where the woman was, and found her fainted. People were busy trying to bring her round. But what did I see beside her? A young woman—a charming girl—who was lavishing the most urgent care on her mother. She was caressing her, and calling her by the most tender names.

That voice was so agreeable, so touching…my dear Nadir, I cannot describe the commotion I experienced on seeing that young beauty in tears. There are, in life, certain shocks that one can only experience once. Her mother's accident was very minor. I immediately opened a flask full of ether[32] that I always carried on me. You know that no remedy that acts as swiftly and as successfully on the nervous system. I got her to drink it and she immediately recovered consciousness.

_____

[32] This reference is not to diethyl ether, which was later used as an anesthetic and (a trifle paradoxically) as a stimulant, or to any other compound that would now be described as an ether in the terminology of organic chemistry. It is probably *sal ammoniac* ("smelling salts"), which was a standard treatment for fainting, although they would be inhaled rather than drunk, and it is odd that Zirmen does not use the term, as he has referred to the compound by that name before.

"Come, Madame," I said to her, excitedly. My father is hopeful, and he is never hopeful in vain. He sent me to you. The patient, who is doubtless your husband, is not in a desperate state."

"Oh, can it be?" she cried. "Oh, Sir, how grateful I am! How shall I ever be able to thank you? My dear daughter, my tender Azéma, come see your father."

Young Azéma, having recovered from the initial surprise that I had caused, embraced her mother and followed her.

What did we see as soon as we reached the patient's apartment? The doctors on their knees before my father. "You're embarrassing me," he said to them. "These enthusiastic insistences on your part reveal a great humanitarian zeal, and raises you in my estimation. Many of your peers would attribute what I have just done to chance. Get up, then, Sirs; I swear to you that I shall shortly inform you completely regarding this curative method."

Scarcely had I heard these last words than I took Azéma by the hand. "Charming being," I exclaimed, "your father is entirely cured."

The divine Azéma listened to me in shock. She was unable to reply; pleasure prevented her from doing so. She squeezed my hand. She looked at me. Gods, what a gaze! My existence seemed to me to be too feeble for the sentiments I was experiencing. Yes, I wanted the Divinity to multiply my being.

Finally, we advanced toward the patient's bed. He was sleeping peacefully; his wife, his dear Zélis, was contemplating him with tears of joy. She was enjoying, as my father had announced, a truly interesting spectacle. Cador's face—Cador was the patient's name—advertised all the freshness of health.

My father looked at me in silence. He testified his joy to me, and also rejoiced in mine, but he did not know how intoxicated I was. I possessed a delightful sentiment that I had never known before. He looked, however, at the young beauty who was there, examined us, and soon suspected the love in my gaze.

Suddenly, Zélis advanced toward him. "Divine man," she said to him, "how can I testify my gratitude toward you? Your delicate generosity often prevents people from repaying your generosity, which they fear abusing. That is why I only dared to address myself to you as a last resort."

My father replied to Zélis with kind reproaches. "Perhaps," he said, "you will have an opportunity to render a service to one of my friends." At the same time he darted a sly glance at me. He had seen through me.

That conversation might have embarrassed Azéma, and my father too, whom Zélis pressed to explain, but she was interrupted by a no less agreeable scene.

Cador opened his eyes and looked with an astonished expression at Zélis, who went toward him. "What, my dear Zélis, you here! You have, therefore, followed me to this peaceful abode, where…but what do I see? My Azéma…these gentlemen. So I'm still here…I'm alive…and I'm no longer suffering. Tell me, Zélis, to what guardian angel do I owe this change?"

Immediately, Zélis pointed to my father. He recognized him. "You are," he said, "my second Creator…permit me." He took one of my father's hands and squeezed it in his own.

What a scene, my dear Nadir, what a scene of tender humanity! My father embraced Cador. They both experienced the enthusiasm of the benefit. With every movement, Cador felt his strength reborn; he employed it to express what he owed to his liberator. We all had tears in our eyes; they were tears of sentiment. I moved closer to him.

"Who is this young man," he asked my father, in a more assured voice, "Who seems to be interested in my fate?"

"He's my son."

"Oh, the worthy young man; he already has his father's virtues. I want him always to be happy. Perhaps he lacks something?"

"My greatest happiness," I replied, "is to see the change that you have just experienced, and the joy of Zélis, and that of Azéma."

"Worthy young man, if I can ever do anything..."

My father interrupted him, to order him to take some nourishment; he prepared it himself.

The doctors withdrew, very satisfied with the promise made to them, which my father renewed. In the end, we stayed with our convalescent for more than four hours, and only left with a promise to return early the next day. I realized, upon that temporary separation, how much my heart was engaged.

Chapter XXVII

You can easily presume, my dear Nadir, with what vivacity I complimented my father. I was not long delayed in opening my heart to him completely. He was aware of my passion—but what pleasure I took in talking to him about it, in telling him the details he did not know, Azéma's situation beside her fainted mother, her urgent concern, her tenderness, the eloquence of the soul painted on her face, the delight when I told her about her father's cure.

"My friend," he said to me, delightedly, "that filial love always reveals a fortunate character, and in the beautiful Azéma it advertises the happiness that she would procure for a spouse. Be happy. I approve. Embrace me. Tomorrow, I shall make enquiries."

My father had no other children than myself and a sister, with whom I was linked in the closest amity. I immediately told her all about my adventure and confided my passion to her; she took the most sincere interest, and was so curious to see Azéma that my father had to promise her that she could come with us the next day.

My nascent passion was too strong for me to apply myself seriously to other objects. Azéma occupied all my faculties. Finally, dawn came. My father, yielding to my urgency, brought forward the time of our visit.

We arrived at Cador's house. Could I have hoped for a better sight? He was out walking, with Zélis and Azéma by his side. He ran—yes, ran—toward my father, for he was already enjoying his strength. He did not know how to express his gratitude.

"My dear Cador," my father said to him, "I have come to offer the charming Azéma a good friend; this is Zirphile, my daughter; she is worthy of her friendship."

Already the souls of the two young women had flown toward one another; they embraced with an equal fervor, and that expressive kiss was the signal for a harmony that was never troubled.

While I was congratulating my sister on the discovery of such a friend, I discovered Azéma's eyes fixed upon me and thought I saw a great deal of interest therein. I was overwhelmed by pleasure. However, I was listening to my father. He had taken Zélis and Cador to one side. I overheard a few words.

"Imagine," said Zélis, "how much pleasure you are giving us. You are realizing projects that we were discussing before you arrived."

"Yes," my father replied, "but I did not know what Cador intended for his daughter. I confess to you that I might perhaps have been less precipitate..."

"In truth," Cador interjected, "could anyone, my dear liberator, ever suspect you of..."

I did not hear any more because I was following Azéma and my sister, who were gradually drawing further away as they were conversing. I judged that my affairs were making good progress. A short time afterwards we were summoned.

Zélis asked her daughter a few questions in a low voice. Azéma answered loudly enough to be audible. "Mother," she said, "since my earliest childhood I have always known the extent of your generosity. You have allowed me my liberty. You have assured me that is the case that any repugnance moved me...oh Heaven! With what object? The son of our liberator. Him, mother...oh, to prove to you how far I am from being so unjust, enjoy my entire confidence. I have no fear today of making a confession to you. From the moment that amiable young man came into your apartment and restored you to consciousness, I don't know why, but I was delighted to be obliged to him; I was scarcely able to express my gratitude to him. Every word he spoke brought such new sensations into my soul…in sum, let me tell you, he will never be out of my heart."

Azéma perceived that she could be overheard. She blushed.

"Zirmen," shouted me father, immediately, "embrace your bride."

Imagine my friend, with what vivacity and delight I advanced toward the beautiful Azéma—but she escaped my arms and ran to embrace my father.

"It's now," she said, "benevolent man, that I can freely testify all my gratitude to you. I owe you my father's life; share with him, not only that title, which is dear to me, but the sentiments of my most tender attachment."

I cannot express, my dear Nadir, how agreeable was my father's surprise, or rather his thrill. That scientist, that great philosopher, who had been uniquely occupied with his work for fifteen years, did not believe himself any longer susceptible to being affected by what he called "trivial situations," but Azéma, young Azéma, caused him to shed tears of tenderness.

In sum, all my desires were fulfilled. The more I lived with Azéma, the more my sentiments were reflected and the more delightful they were. That charming woman was created for my happiness—but is that something durable? A terrible accident soon interrupted our pleasures.

Scarcely had the charming celebrations that my father and the rich Cador had hastened to give us come to an end—scarcely a month of pleasure had vanished like a dream—when we experienced the sharpest dolor.

My respectable father, the friend of a chemist, a great worker, was invited to come and see a volatilization of gold by a singular method. It was, unfortunately, one of those invitations, welcome to my father, that he could not resist. He therefore went to visit his friend.

There were a few other curious individuals there too. Into his retort, the chemist threw two ounces of previously-treated gold powder into eight ounces of volatile sulfurous alkali. It was by that method, he said, that he had obtained a purple oil whose effects on metal had seemed surprising. The retort having been covered with a stone dome, he lit to furnace.

My curious father and three other individuals moved very close to the furnace, in order to see the first vapors pass into the recipient vessel; they had no suspicion that anything was amiss. Alas, how could they have foreseen that his unfortunate friend, who was also a victim of his error, had mistaken one packet for another and had put into the retort, instead of the gold he had treated with lime-water, a precipitate of ammoniac gold—which is to say, fulminating gold. Gradually, the mixture heated up. Suddenly, there was an explosion more terrible than a thunderbolt...that says enough.

Only one of the witnesses, who was in a corner of the laboratory, was slightly less badly injured, in that he only died four hours after the accident, and it was from him that the details were learned. A portion of the fulminating gold was also found in the laboratory, which was still in its natural state.

There is no need to describe to you the cruel consequences of that tragic scene: our pain and grief. In brief, we abandoned my father's house in order to withdraw to Cador's. My wife and my sister had become inseparable friends. Each of us was suffering; each of us sought to suppress our own pain and distract the others. You know what my principles are with regard to the soul; they were my father's. I communicated them to our society, which adopted them. The fate of a man who has ceased to exist no longer seemed to us so catastrophic. We reflected on that point in conversations as extensive as they were interesting. My dear Azéma, having become wiser, added sublime reflections to that philosophy. My admiration for her increased. Eventually, we succeeded in consoling one another. I confess to you that without that manner of thinking, I would never have been able to resist the further chagrins that fate had in store for me.

My beloved Azéma gave me a daughter, whom she did not hesitate to nurse and raise herself. The pretty child, whom we cherished, was also the object of the caresses of Zélis, Cador and my dear Zirphile. I therefore spent a rapid four years in a circle of happiness. Ultimately, however, it was at the very moment when I was experiencing the delights of my fate with the greatest sensibility that a frightful blow reduced me to despair.

My love for the science was increasing every day. I regretted the precious moments from which I had not profited sufficiently. A man who is too young often has the arrogance to want to raise himself above others, but it is rare that he knows the veritable flight of genius. Indeed, I had the simplicity to prefer the study of petty talents to that of the knowledge of Nature. Sometimes, it was even with complacency that I listened to me father's instructions. Finally, but too late, I realized how much work two months of application followed with that great man might have spared me. He final experiments had opened my eyes completely. I should have collected his lessons then and there and written his methods down— but how could I anticipate that a man who commanded health and had discovered Nature's secrets in that regard would perish so promptly?

It was therefore necessary for me to study the first principles of chemistry. I connected them all to physical principles. It was thus that I wanted to rationalize all my procedures. For example, in examining pieces of colored cloth exposed for a long time to the air, I observed that certain colors subject to being destroyed by acids where more promptly removed in winter than in summer. I therefore concluded that the air was more acidic in winter than in summer.

Subsequently, the reasoning of physics came to the support of that conclusion. The acid, I said to myself, is one of the heaviest salts in the atmosphere. Now, the denser air is, the more of that salt it holds in solution. Then I was no longer surprised that in northern regions, where the acid is more abundant and phlogiston less active, there is less contagious air and fewer pestilential maladies. I finally understood why certain fruits, including oranges, always conserve an acidic taste there, experiment also indicating to me that phlogiston rectifies the acidic taste.

Ultimately, reflecting on the inverse principle, that the more rarefied air is, the less it sustains salts in solution, I ceased to be astonished by obtaining saline combinations in capsules exposed to fire in a current of air, because the ambient air, in being rarefied by the fire and becoming lighter, necessarily allows the deposition of salts, having become specifically lighter than them.

From there I reflected that the same principle occasions the calcination of metals in fire and air; that it also occasions the increase in their weight; and that if certain metals, such as copper, only increase their weight slightly during calcination, it is because they experience such division that a considerable fraction flies away with the lightest vapors.

I convinced myself of that by exposing, for instance, a piece of white paper to the vapors of copper while it was being calcinated and observed that the paper was tinted green. I therefore avoided believing that the fire condensed the air. I saw, on the contrary, that the air, in becoming lighter, allowed to precipitate upon the metal the salts that it held in solution. I also reflected on the variety of weights that might also be occasioned by the absence or presence of phlogiston.

Finally, I applied myself to decomposing plants in order to familiarize myself with their mucous principles and variously phlogisticated acids and alkalis, the changes the plants experience by virtue of different degrees of fermentation, the means of fixing the degrees of fermentation, and the method of forming identical extracts.

Soon, I thought that I was ready to work on human blood. I succeeded in familiarizing myself with the principal constituents of the blood of a healthy man, and also with the degree of temperature necessary to that blood and its absolute weight. Finally, I was ready to undertake my father's curious experiments. I flattered myself that in a short time I would be able to carry out successful trials on my fellows, and that it would be easy for me to conserve for a long time not merely the health but also the charms of my tender Azéma. Great God! How could I guess that in one of my preparations I had, on the contrary, readied the fatal blow that was about to…oh, my dear Nadir, listen to this story; it will bring tears to your eyes. You will weep for your friend; you will groan at his fate. You will shed tears, but those tears will be far from being evidence of weakness. You will feel your soul being uplifted in paying that tribute to amity.

You doubtless recall the singular experiment by which, on mixing in certain proportions the juice of a plant with bile, my father refreshed and suddenly condensed a mass of blood. I repeated that experiment successfully, but I sought to temper the vigor of the liquid in order to compose salutary remedies. I thus soaked needles in various combinations; I pricked small animals and studied the various effects that resulted.

One day, when I was very occupied with these objects, a slave came to knock on my laboratory door. Someone was asking for me. I went out hastily, in order to get rid of the visitor rapidly and return to my observations. In fact, it was a very important matter on which someone had come to ask my advice. I came back as soon as I could. I thought I perceived that one of my needles was missing. However, as I was not entirely sure, and had taken care to close the laboratory door, I did not carry out a very scrupulous search. Alas, I did not anticipate that the fateful needle might have been carried away in one of the creases in my garments, and fallen on to the floor of the room in which I had received the visitor.

I often went to one of our mountains at daybreak to look for certain plants of which I had need. Sometimes Azéma came with me. We went up the steepest slopes, and then rested on the carpets of verdure. It seems that in those blessed places, hearts overflow more influentially. We admired a varied panorama that extended as far as the eye could see. We made reflections on the immensity of creation, and our souls reached out toward the Creator with the sensuality that true philosophers feel.

One day, when I had gone to that mountain, Azéma had not gone with me. I hastened to collect the plants I needed, but as the choice was difficult, I remained there longer than usual. I presume that it was that reason that gave birth to sinister ideas, for I have no faith in presentiments. I came down the mountain at a rapid pace. I was anxious. The haste that I had to fly into Azéma's arms was mingled with dread. I shivered.

At that moment I saw one of my slaves coming to meet me. He was running. A secret horror took possession of my senses. I was fearful of going forward. He arrived. Sadness was painted on his features. I listened to him, trembling.

"Master," he said, "come quickly. Your help might perhaps be..."

"My help? For whom? Explain yourself."

"She's asleep, but she's scarcely breathing..."

"Eh? Who? Speak."

"Alas, your..."

"Oh God! Azéma..."

"My dear Master, she was working at that craft in which one embroiders flowers..."

I didn't hear the rest of his story. I soon deduced that it was the deadly needle...

Yes, I was the murderer of my Azéma. Suddenly, my strength returned; it was violent; it were that of despair. A dart launched by a muscular arm could not have flown any faster than I ran. I flew; I arrived: I took concentrated vinegar from my laboratory, with another liquid. I went into Azéma's room.

Merciful Heaven, what a scene! Cador and Zélis were in tears, beside their dear daughter; my sister was trying hard to get her to take some spirituous water.

"Here I am!" I cried. "Is she still breathing?"

I hurl myself toward Azéma. I lift her up in my arms; her body is cold, her eyes closed, her face pale, and yet the mortal sleep has not yet robbed her of her charms. I make her drink a dose of vinegar; I wait for it to take effect. I place my hand on her heart.

Attentive to my observation, I am motionless myself. Alas, I can sense no reborn movement. I put a piece of polished steel close to her lips. That cold substance, on which the slightest respiration immediately deposits considered vapors, does not show me the slightest mist. One last resource remains to me, though. It is soon put to use.

I decide to open a vein; I introduce into it a little of the solvent I have brought. I perceive. I perceive a few drops of blood resuming their fluidity. A ray of hope seems to gleam, and reanimate my courage. I stare at my dear Azéma. I see her eyelids flutter. Her body is getting warmer.

"O Heaven!" I cried. "Is it an illusion? Will Azéma by returned to me? Will the dangerous trial I have just carried out succeed? May despair, then, has conquered Nature..."

Finally, Azéma opens her eyes. Azéma is alive. She looks at me tenderly. She speaks to me. Alas, how could I have anticipated that the Art would only wrench from Nature the tribute of one last effort?

"Zirmen," she said to me, "my dear Zirmen, you want to recall me to life...there's no longer time...I feel my destiny dragging me away...it's necessary to obey...don't blame yourself...any you, dear authors of my life, and you, my amiable Zirphile, be sure that I shall still exist among you...I commend my darling daughter to you. O Zirmen, my friend, virtuous man, inculcate her as soon as possible with great principles regarding the Supreme Being, those true principles which are today my felicity. Once again, my dear Zirmen, don't blame yourself. Know what I have just experienced...that chaos, that impenetrable void, that eternal night—in sum, all those funereal images with which feeble genius is cruelly afflicted—are merely illusory impostors. The Master of the World only destroys humans in order to ennoble their being...

"Scarcely had a profound sleep numbed my organs that I felt a new existence, a fee existence that I cannot define. My thoughts were elevated to such a point that I understood in an instant the immensity of space and the origin of movement. You cannot imagine what pleasures I felt. That admirable knowledge brought me closer and closer to that of the Supreme Being. What rapture! Oh, my friend, do not mourn me. The Divinity, my dear Zirmen—the Divinity, understand that delightful word...our delights, when we admired one another mutually, were only a feeble prelude to those I am experiencing...

"However, my friend, never hasten the blow that will reunite you with me. There are truths that you cannot yet conceive. The most extensive life is but an instant, a dream; but it is necessary that humans occupy themselves with that dream. The study of great virtues has connections with the Supreme Being—connections that your soul cannot yet discern. Adieu, my beloved friend. Adieu...my strength is abandoning me...kiss me...dear authors of my days, and you, my dear Zirphile, so that I receive your last caresses... Zirmen, your art...your efforts...are futile...let go... Already, I experience...yes, the same state...of which...the Supreme Being... How can I express to my friend...make him experience...delights..."

Such were the last words of my dear Azéma. That scene, although consoling for humankind, only presented shadows of grief to me then.

Let us draw a veil over the crushing condition to which I was reduced. Eventually, I persuaded Cador, Zélis and my sister to leave our homeland. The places that Azéma's presence had rendered so dear to me had become unbearable. We retired to Ispahan. The variety of objects procured some diversion to the grief of my friends, but mine were too intense. My dear daughter, the child I idolized, always recalled to my memory the frightful loss that I had suffered. She was already the portrait of her mother; she had her features, her charms in miniature. Can you believe it? That enjoyment, which ought to have been doubly interesting for me, plunged the dagger ever more deeply in my heart.

I made the decision to travel, and to abandon my child, for a time, to the care of Cador, Zélis and my dear Zirphile. Thos tender relatives consented to the voyage, hoping that it would contribute to my consolation.

I traveled through many countries. My scientific curiosity being excited by continually varied objects, lightened the burden of my chagrin. I wandered through various nations for three years. I received news of my friends from time to time. My sister informed me of the progress of my dear daughter. She assured me that the development of her mind equaled that of her beauty, that she already had sentiments uncommon at her age. I suddenly experienced a keen desire to see her again, and that desire finally offered me rays of joy. I already imagined that I was teaching her, that I was listening to her questions, that she was contesting my replies, that she was applauding them, that I was her friend: my child's friend; is there a title more agreeable?

Oh, my dear Nadir, I was still far from savoring those pleasures. A tempest cast me on to unknown shores. Obliged to live for nine years with savages, with no possibility of sending news or receiving any, doubtless they thought me dead. I shall not enter into detail in that regard. I shall only say that I then learned the consequences of a good education. Indeed, a few useful and agreeable talents, a few ingenious experiments and simple and faithful education earned me consideration among those good people. They had given me the help of Nature; I offered them those of Art; they found them agreeable and were none the worse for it. True philosophy never spoiled the human species.

Finally, a ship that the fury of the winds drove into that region offered me the opportunity to see my friends again, who no longer believed me to be alive. I arrived at Gujarat. O Heaven! What did I learn! Persia destroyed, the city of Isfahan pillaged by the Turks, the inhabitants massacred or taken into slavery.

"In that case," I cried, "if life is a dream, the dream is too cruel; that's enough sleep—it's time to exist. But at least, before vanquishing my destiny, let's taste the pleasure of vengeance. Cruel men, you are stained with the blood of my friends. Cador, Zélis, Zirphile, must have expired under your blows. My daughter, my dear daughter, has perhaps been reduced to a slavery a hundred times more frightful than death. Oh, you idle Ministers, who often form bellicose projects in the bosom of your laxity to satisfy your avarice, it is your cruelty that has guided these mercenary arms. It is you who have caused the misfortune of an infinite number of families. It is you who desolate humankind. It is upon you that I shall avenge myself. Your pompous titles are but the vain expressions of an imbecilic arrogance, or, rather, ironic epithets that censure your conduct and render you even more despicable in my eyes. Nothing can save you. I shall prevent you from causing more unhappiness."

You can well imagine, Nadir, that after these initial transports, I was ashamed of my weakness. Had I even calculated whether that war was just or unjust on the part of the Turks? Was I in a position to decide? But what can you expect? A philosopher is only human.

Soon, I reflected that it was more appropriate to inform myself as to the fate of my daughter and my friends. I had brought some wealth with me. Might I not be able to extract them from servitude? I therefore went to Isfahan. I conducted an infinity of searches. They were all futile. No one could tell me anything. Finally, I wrote to an old friend of my father's, who lived in Bisance. I sent him approximate descriptions of the people about whom I was asking for information.

My friend, my dear Nadir, you shall see the reply. That precious script was the first glimmer of my consolation. I carry it on me. Here it is. Judge whether it is true.

Nadir already had a few presentiments. He opened the letter rapidly and read it.

Ali Hassan to Ormasis.

Our slave-merchants only have vague notions concerning the persons you have indicated to me. The divisions made at Isfahan will surely have occasioned their separation, and they were probably not even sent to this city; however, I am assured that there was a daughter of Isfahan of rare beauty here, about whom a rather remarkable anecdote is told. The Master to whom she had fallen in the division confided to her that she was destined for the Emperor's seraglio.

"Beware," she said to him. "I shall demand your head as the price of my first favor. Beware too of selling me to some Barbarian, the sight of whom will be odious to me; before you complete your bargain, I will have surrendered life and thwarted your avarice. Consider, therefore, consulting my choice before making any promise."

The slave-merchant, whose great passion was that of making money, found himself in the greatest embarrassment, when a young Turk was curious to see the beautiful Persian. He was it was said, very affable and very intelligent.

After a few moments of conversation, the young slave said to him: "You are the first person before whom I feel keenly the humiliation of my status. It is because you sought skillfully to disguise the horror of it from me that you are truly great in my eyes. My pride is abandoning me, my despair no longer sustaining me." Immediately, she burst into tears.

The young Turk took the slave-merchant to one side. Although the latter demanded a considerable price, the bargain was soon concluded.

"Madame," he said, "you are free. A sum similar to the one that man has demanded of me is still at your disposal. Command: it is I who am your slave. Where do you desire to be taken? Alas, if some fortunate lover has made an impression on your heart, you will never hear any complaint on my part; live with him. I swear to you that I will sacrifice my love to your happiness."

"Generous mortal," the young beauty replied, "you merit all my esteem. I have not yet experienced the sentiments of love. I have known those of friendship. I have lost my friends, my relatives; where would you expect me to go? Besides, I tell you this: now that I know my soul, I sense that my existence is drawing me toward you. Yes, I desire you to be my friend; I want to live with you. Come."

She held out her hand in a manner so touching that even the slave-merchant, although his character was ferocious, was overcome with emotion. He has not forgotten the details of that scene in two years, so interesting did it seem to him, but no one knows who that young Turk was. He does not live in Bisance. He left immediately with the beautiful Persian. That is all the information that I am able to give you.

I wish you, etc., etc.

Scarcely had Nadir begun to read that letter than he precipitated himself into his friend's arms. He was that young Turk!

"Oh, my dear Ormasis," he cried, "so you are Mirza's father! What a surprise! What joy! Witness my delight! Mirza, charming being, you do not know that pleasures that are in preparation for your sensitive soul. This man, whose knowledge has elevated your soul, is your father. Oh, my dear Mirza. You constantly refused to tell me the origin of your misfortunes. You only ever wanted to present to my heart the nuances of pleasure. Lover, as delicate as tender, you are not expecting this agreeable surprise. My worthy friend, my respectable father, let us leave this place promptly. Let us fly to Mirza."

Chapter XXVIII

Ormasis and Nadir resumed walking. They followed the easiest route that would take them back to the
chamber where their slaves were. Nadir did not delay in
asking his friend by what fortunate chance he had discovered his abode, and why he had waited so long to
make himself known.

"My dear Nadir," the Philosopher continued,
"scarcely had I received that letter than I went to Bisance
myself. Following false clues, I traveled through almost
all the towns of the Archipelago, and came back via An-
atolia. I thus skirted the borders of Persia again and returned to Bisance. You would not believe how many
ruses I employed, to what dangers I exposed myself, to
gain admittance to various seraglios. The weapon that I
showed you saved my life more than once. Finally, fa-
tigued by the futility of my search, I was on the brink of
despair when a man, who seemed to me to be quite enlightened, succeeded in piquing my curiosity with regard
to a scientific matter, and that curiosity was the source of
my good fortune.

"'Sir,' he said to me, 'I have been in a very interesting quarry situated half a league from Chrysopolis. In
spite of a fearful noise that became audible when I had
advanced some way into the subterranean passages, I
dared to go as far as an extremely curious place—but I
confess that I trembled in trying to follow deeper paths. I
stopped. A few flames that rose up from time to time
inspired me with dread, and I soon resolved not to go
back there.'

"That was enough, my dear Nadir, to determine me to make this journey. Curiosity made me take precautions, but only despair could have made me brave such apparent dangers. My two faithful slaves always came with me as far as the chamber. Gradually, I reached the terrains charged with riches. It was then that I regretted even more sharply the loss of my daughter and my friends. Finally, I said to myself: 'Before quitting life, let us spread good fortune.'

"I had the habit of coming to rest among the good villagers who live fifty paces from this cavern. I gave them presents, careful to make my benefits proportionate to their estate. Soon, therefore, I came to your city. Although Chrysopolis is not far from Bisance, I had always been guided elsewhere. I had not yet undertaken a search there.

Scarcely had I been resting for two hours than I noticed in my caravanserai a man of embarrassed expression. He seemed to me to be grief-stricken. That entitled him to my consideration. I questioned him. I learned that his fortunes had been reversed for a second time, that a young inhabitant of the city had already obliged him once in a manner as noble as it was generous. 'It is for that reason,' the man continued, 'that I dare not make any further claim on his generosity. I would prefer, if necessary, to perish in poverty.'

"You will easily guess what response I made. His thinking appeared to me to be that of a delicate man. I doubled the sum that he desired to reestablish his affairs and demanded no other thanks from him than that he indicate the dwelling of his benefactor. He agreed immediately, and walked with me. My senses had been suddenly excited. Might not this young Turk, so noble and so generous, be the liberator and friend of my dear daughter? I questioned my guide.

Further reasons for hope; further reasons for joy. 'The young Turk,' he says, 'loves the sciences; he also has a library open to scholars. He has a favorite wife whose intelligence and beauty are much praised, but her heart is even more admirable. She has often spread liberality among poor families. She is an accomplished mortal. Her origin is unknown, but it is believed that she is one of the captives of the last Persian war. Here is the house.'

"'That's enough,' I said to my guide. Oh, my dear Nadir, what news for Mirza's father!

"I go into your library. There are a lot of people there. People are calling you by name, talking to you; I examine you, and already feel the impression of the most lively amity for you. Someone asks you about Mirza's health. I hear the name of Mirza, so dear to me, pronounced. I see with what pleasure you are listening.

"There were no longer any doubts to formulate. I was transported with joy. However, I did not want to make myself known yet. I read a book with simulated attention. Oh, my friend, if you had looked at me I would have given myself away. I came to your library for several days, without succeeding in finding you alone there. Finally, the removal of your books procured me the opportunity I desired so much. It was very favorable to my designs.

"I had judged you to be fonder of belles-lettres than to the sciences. I esteem and cherish belles-lettres, but I was desirous of seeing in you a more definite passion for higher knowledge. How could one give birth to it? How could you be inspired in that regard with a taste as ken as my own? Mirza's father would always have interested your heart, but might he not have wearied your mind? A marvelous origin thus appeared to me to be more appropriate to pique your curiosity. You know how hazard served me.

"Oh, my friend, imagine what pleasure I had in seeing you attentive to my dissertations. Imagine what delights I experienced when my Mirza, struck by my ideas about the nature of the soul, came to express her gratitude to me. In sum, my heart was intoxicated.

"It was in those circumstances that, doubtless drawn to cherish my daughter's friend, I experienced sentiments for Fatima that had been unknown to me for a long time. You had confided your way of life to me. I surrendered without scruple to that new situation. It was one charm more attaching me to life. Presently, I no longer despair of finding my old friends again. The strands of happiness multiply themselves like those of misfortune. We shall be able to make a more exhaustive search. I flatter myself that it will not be futile."

"Oh, my illustrious friend," exclaimed Nadir, "count on my must urgent concern; it will delight me to be able to contribute something to your felicity."

Nadir was walking rapidly, a few paces ahead of Ormasis. Suddenly, he perceived several men lying on the sand in various poses. They were fully-dressed. Their physiognomy offered the image of a tranquil sleep.

Surprised by this encounter, Nadir took a step back at first, but eventually drew nearer and saw that the bodies were inanimate. In that moment of surprise, he looked hard at his friend, and that gaze was a question.

"You see unfortunates," the Philosopher said to him, "who were swallowed up in a deep chasm during an earthquake. They have doubtless lain here for several centuries. The circulation of their blood, suddenly arrested at the moment of their fall, caused them neither pain nor despair; that is, in part, what had caused these bodies to retain a more animated appearance. They fell on to these heaps of sand; their limbs suffered scant mutilation and the vaults of these caverns, which had opened up, were doubtless sealed again by a further commotion. As for their perfect conservation, which might astonish you, remember that the stone and sand in this place are filled with salts, which are even contained in the air, that there is less movement here, and consequently more cold. Now, you know that, the air being condensed, the molecules of the cadavers can neither dilate nor disunite; that is why salts conserve bodies. That is another of the laws of gravity. It is because the condensed air weighs more upon the masses, and presses upon them formal directions, preventing them from breaking down."

While reasoning thus, the Philosopher made haste to draw his friend away from the lugubrious spectacle.

Would you believe that Ormasis is retaining that self-composure, even in one of the cruelest situations of his life? Those cadavers advertise a great misfortune to him. In fact, they are the recent victims of an earthquake that has been felt in Chrysopolis. He wants his friend to be unaware of it. He has been talking to him, instructing him, in order to distract him.

Alas, that only delays Nadir's despair momentarily.

Scarcely have they gone a little further along their route than Ormasis notices changes in it: landslides and newly-broken stones; and these accumulated mixtures form impenetrable masses. In sum, he can no longer find an exit.

How can the despondency of his soul be described? Nevertheless, he suppresses his dolor; he still wants to protect his friend.

"My dear Nadir," he said to him, "let's retrace our steps. I forgot to show you..."

"What?"

"Something trivial...and yet...my son..."

"O Heaven! My dear Ormasis, what am I seeing? You've gone pale. Why are we retracing our steps? Explain yourself."

Immediately, Nadir sought to clarify that fatal mystery. He ran to the place where the cadavers lay.

Guided by mortal suspicions, he examines them; he touches them; he searches their clothing. Finally, a wallet, containing papers dated that same day, presents him with certain proof of his misfortune.

"Oh, my friend!" he cried. "I see that we're doomed! In vain, you wanted to disguise our fate from me. These paths are sealed. An earthquake must have...great God! Is the most vivid intoxication by pleasure to be succeeded by all the horror of despair? It is, then, necessary to remain in these abysses. It is, then, necessary to perish...to perish... Mirza! My dear Mirza! I shall never see you again, then...oh, my father...!"

Suddenly, Nadir, oppressed by grief, fell into his friend's arms. Ormasis perceived that Nadir was tottering, and had lost his strength; he hastened to support him, but the lantern providing them with light escaped from Nadir's hand, and the lamps went out.

What a situation for Ormasis! Alone in the bosom of a profound darkness, he is supporting his dying friend. In vain he speaks to him, in vain he calls to him: "Nadir! My dear Nadir!"

No response.

It is in this ultimate crisis of chagrin that a true philosopher finally arms himself with an intrepid courage. Ormasis sits his friend down and, getting down on his

252

knees behind him, he supports his head and body. Thus enjoying the liberty of his arms, he takes the stopper out of his vinegar bottle and presents it to Nadir's respiration. He also thinks about obtaining light. He carries on him a fragment of tempered steel, rock crystal and sulfur-coated strips of card, in order to have everything necessary in that regard. He picks up the lantern and re-lights the lamps.

He perceives that his friend is coming round from his faint; he immediately seeks to light a few glimmers of hope in his soul. That is the best remedy.

"My son my son, don't be discouraged. Summon up your strength."

"Oh, father, is it to die a thousand times?"

"No, my friend; nothing is desperate. Let's follow the same route we have traveled. Believe that we shall succeed in getting out of this place, perhaps through a new exit."

"My dear Ormasis, you're trying to make me feel better again. You're convinced yourself that the chamber that we need to reach has collapsed entirely, and that the shock must also have closed the opposite route that brought us here. No matter; you're reanimating my courage. I'm ashamed of that weakness. Let's go; if it is finally necessary to yield to the fatality of our lot, let's not yield before having contested its caprices."

Chapter XXIX

Our voyagers followed exactly the same route as before. They walked in silence. Ormasis was reproaching himself silently for having imprudently risked the life of his friend and the happiness of his daughter. Soon, the love of sciences and the desire to create happiness, the two respectable guides that had counseled that step, were no longer anything in his eyes but foolish illusions. There were moments when the Philosopher was no longer reasoning as clearly. He was careful, however, not to manifest his dolor; he was only searching for means to reassure his friend.

As for Nadir, the generous Nadir, he was far from criticizing Ormasis; he only cursed fate.

Further anguished thought harassed their minds. Might not the earthquake have swallowed up some of the houses in Chrysopolis? Mirza, Fatima...

That idea made the shiver, but they did not let it show.

Finally, after walking for half an hour, they arrived in the bright terrains charged with riches, at which Nadir had marveled so. "Great God!" he cried, immediately. "I know now, more than ever, the veritable beauties of Nature. What is this combination of dust, imprisoned in their obscure lairs, by comparison with the beautiful crops, the trees laden with fruit, the cheerful greenery illuminated by sunlight? The first man who penetrated into the bowels of the Earth outraged nature. These somber abodes were not made for him."

"My dear Nadir, the situation we're in should not render us unjust. Let's not insult the industry of humans.

On the contrary, one of the reasons that ought to make us proud and make us feel the value of our existence is the perfection of Artifice. Do not the metals imprisoned in the bosom of the Earth serve to obtain multiple treasures on its surface? Without the blade of a plough, how long with it take us to force the earth to render us its productions? Without the scythe, what labor it would require to harvest them! Without the pruning-hook, would we easily obtain from wild trees the fruits whose delicious taste is, so to speak, the creation of industry? Oh, my friend, let us not blame the true characteristics of human genius."

It was while reasoning on these various matters that they reached the fearful location of the narrow and tortuous path to either side of which were profound gulfs.. The noise of the waters precipitated into these abysses further increased Nadir's sadness and penetrate him with horror. It was at that exact moment that the light illuminating them weakened considerably.

The situation was frightful. Ormasis perceived that. "My friend," he said, "I presume that we lost a quantity of oil when you dropped our lamps. Fate is pursuing us, pursuing us cruelly. We need to vanquish it. Let's pause for a moment. We need to refrain from exposing ourselves on this route without taking precautions. Wait."

Immediately, Ormasis picked up a few ferruginous pyrites; he broke them between two stones and gave Nadir the fragments to carry. "Let's walk on now. Follow me. Have no fear."

When they were half way along the dangerous path, the intermitted light of their lamps was dazzling them instead of lighting their way. They stopped. Ormasis opened the flask of oil of vitriol that he carried. He threw the fragments of pyrites into it, and ignited the phlogisticated vapors that were emitted. That faint, blue-tinted but tranquil light substituted for the lamps, which had gone out. How many resources do the science not offer to those who cultivate them!

The ingenious, intrepid Ormasis guided his friend in an assured manner. He succeeded in inspiring him with confidence, From time to time he dropped further fragments of pyrites into the bottle, and the philosophical torch furnished them with sufficient light.

Finally, they emerged from that dangerous path— just in time. Already, the supply of acid, being saturated with phlogiston, was no longer causing effervescence or reaction, and in consequence, less movement. The light disappeared.

"No matter," said Ormasis then. "Don't be afraid. The sparks that the rock crystal will furnish us will now be sufficient to direct our march. But before going any further, believe me, it's necessary to build up strength in order not to be obliged to rest. Let's take a pinch of nutritive powder. Give me your hand. Here's the packet. Good. That trickle of water that you can hear falling ahead of us will slake our thirst. It's necessary that we drink in order that the powder can reanimate us. Let's go on."

At that moment, Ormasis struck the crystal, and Nadir, by the light of the sparks, received in his mouth the water that was falling from the rock.

What a meal! What a situation! What painter would be bold enough to attempt to depict the reflections of light in such a scene?

Very soon, Nadir perceived that his strength was increasing. "My worthy friend," he exclaimed, "in spite of the distress we're in, I cannot cease to admire you. Sublime knowledge, indefatigable patience and invincible courage—that is what characterizes a true philosopher. My father, my illustrious father, what a glory it is to be your son! Yes, I merit that honor. No more weakness. If it necessary for us to die, let us die with courage. Besides, I sense that a more perfect being exists than the matter that animates or bodies. As soon as that being isolates itself from matter, it enjoys all its faculties ecstatically, and all the beauties of the universe. Oh, my father, death is nothing but a frightening curtain that hides a stage of pleasures from us. And yet...Mirza...my dear Mirza...how cruel it will be for me to break your chains."

In order to distract his friend, Ormasis immediately interrupted him with a rather singular dissertation with regard to weighty substances.

"These were," he said, "the first reflections that caused me to quarrel with the Materialists. One day, I wanted to define movement. Yes, I said to myself, I understand that a body in movement is matter, but is the movement itself matter? No. I cannot conceive it, that movement, and yet it exists, and yet it affects my organs. There can, therefore, by substances more perfect than matter, the nature of which we do not yet know. It is thus that, from argument to argument, my existence become precious to me."

The Philosopher continued this interesting dissertation, and Nadir paid attention to it. They had already been walking for a long time, and walking quite rapidly. They took turns to strike the crystal in order to reconnoiter their route. Eventually, Ormasis perceived the opening through which they had to pass again. It had not changed at all.

"Have courage, my dear Nadir. You can see reasons for hope here. Let me go through first."

Ormasis went through the opening. Nadir followed him. They found themselves in the sandy grotto leading to the vast spaces that had formerly been illuminated by fires.

"I see," Nadir said, "that things are in the same state. I also understand why the fires have gone out, but I have no more hope in consequence. And you, my dear Ormasis, agree with me that we were here when the earthquake made itself felt, and that the collapse must have taken place close to the chamber, and, in consequence, in the terrain that remains to us to cross."

Nadir's reasoning was not devoid of foundation. Ormasis too still had the keenest anxiety, but he was careful not to let it show. Eventually they emerged from those spaces. Ormasis was walking rapidly along narrower paths; he wanted to be quickly informed as to his fate. He was a little ahead. He was the first to see a path that was to their right; immediately, he uttered a cry. It was a cry of the most vivid joy. He turned toward his dear Nadir.

"Come on, the route is clear. There's light. It's advancing toward us…it's one of my slaves. Let's run… Well, my friend, you're searching for us—what news?"

"Oh, my Master, how anxious we were. The earth opened up and closed again."

"Where?"

"On the highway."

"Have houses collapsed in Chrysopolis?"

"No, although the villagers among whom I went to look for fodder assured us that people left them out of fear."

"Oh, God," cried Nadir, "you are just! Mirza…what pleasures are in preparation. Embrace me, my father."

Meanwhile, Ormasis continued to interrogate his slave. "Is our sled in the same place, then?"

"Yes."

"You therefore had no fear of coming down here?"

"No, Master. You have always said that there were great dangers in these subterrains, but I presumed that you might need help and I forgot the dangers."

"Tel me my brave and honest servant, what is your comrade doing?"

"He's in the chamber, taking care of the horses. He has surely harnessed them to the ropes of the sled. He wanted to come down in my stead, but we drew lots; I'm the one who had the good fortune to go in search of you."

"My faithful friend, is the path by which I usually return to the chamber in the same state?"

"No, Master, and that was the cause of our alarm."

Nadir listened to this conversation with the liveliest interest. Soon, they arrived at the place where the sled was. The slave tugged it forcibly. That was the agreed signal. His comrade, seeing the ropes move, set the horses in motion. Nadir and Ormasis immediately lay down on the vehicle, and arranged themselves in such a way that there was a place for the slave, but the latter did not want to go up on it. Ormasis and Nadir insisted in vain.

"I won't risk it," he said to them. "Too much weight might break the ropes, and might make you uncomfortable or slow you down. I'll wait for a few hours, and when my comrade has followed you to the cavern entrance, he'll come back to find me."

Already the vehicle was rising with sufficient speed, and climbing the slope, as smooth as it was sheer. There were passages that were almost perpendicular, which obliged our voyagers to hang on to the ropes of the sled. From time to time they stopped, but Ormasis explained to his friend that, after a certain time, it was necessary to bring back the horses and harness them to new attachments, having no capstan.

"How agreeable it is," said Nadir, "to have slaves like yours. They are true friends, and friends of the greatest warmth."

"And yet," Ormasis replied, "they were born into slavery; it's not education that suggested to them the delicacy of which you have been the witness."

"I believe it, my illustrious father, but I understand its origin. It's you who ennoble everything near to you."

"My son, reserve compliments for our tender friends. They are surely anxious as to our fate."

"Oh, my father, my worthy father, we are going to see them again; perhaps we are going to be reunited with them forever."

Finally, the sled reached the chamber. It is easy to imagine the speed with which the voyagers dismounted. The other slave manifested all his joy. He took them with the horses to the entrance of the cavern. The two friends put on their clothes again.

They could have continued along the road on horseback at a fast gallop, in order to return more promptly to the pleasure that was summoning them—but no, they remembered the honest servant they had left in the subterrains; they remembered that he had no light. They therefore traveled on foot, but before emerging from the cavern they instructed the other slave to add lights to the sled. These details, observed in such circumstances, prove that in truly generous hearts, the keenest pleasure never numbs benevolence.

Chapter XXX

You will remember with what apprehension the sensitive Mirza saw her dear Nadir leave. With anxiety in her heart and tears in her tears, she interrogated Fatima. That tender friend made every effort to reassure her. She reminded her of the Philosopher's motives. She suggested to her that a man so enlightened must be possessed of a consummate prudence; that he would surely not expose himself to any danger; that Nadir, tranquil and satisfied, was probably finding objects of amusement in the caverns.

"May he be happy," Mirza replied. "However, love of science is sometimes a passion, and to satisfy a passion, people forget dangers. Have we not seen scientists traveling from one pole to the other, confronting the caprices of a perfidious element, braving intemperate climates, and wandering in frightful deserts, in order to ensure a result of calculation, resolve an astronomical problem or discover a plant. Oh, if a lack of prudence, in such a case, is a fault useful to society, believe me, our dear Philosopher is not exempt from it. And my Nadir...do you imagine, then, that a mind s active and as curious as his will think about dangers? No. You wouldn't believe the shivers I'm experiencing.

"Deadly science, how can I cherish you, you who have caused my misfortunes? Without you I would have had the joy of embracing a mother, that of cherishing a father—a father whose merits and knowledge Zirphile praised to me so many times. Without you, deadly science, that tender father would never have expatriated himself, would not have perished in the bosom of the waters. Finally, my relatives, who loved me so truly, and who took so much care of my childhood, would not have been taken away from me. However, the information that I have been promised might at least allow me to discover where those dear heads are. If I were as happy as Nadir...

"Yes, my fears are misplaced. Nadir will return. I no longer fear telling him about misfortunes that he will be able to remedy. I shall see my good Zirphile, Cador and Zélis again. I shall hold them in my arms. Like love, friendship has its moments of voluptuousness. My Nadir, my generous Nadir, will share my delight; they will be all the more vibrant for that. But my dear Fatima, I wasn't thinking; you don't know about the sad adventures of my family. I'll tell you about them."

Immediately, Mirza embarked on a narrative that touched her amiable friend deeply.

"O Heaven," cried Fatima, "if it is true that you applaud virtue, why have those who gave birth to Mirza been so unfortunate? Well, worthy daughter of such an interesting couple, tell me: so your father, that touching man, that tender spouse of Azéma, ceased to send you his news?"

"Yes, my dear Fatima. Eight years of silence assured us that he was no longer alive. Zirphile, in spite of her efforts to distract me, conserved a secret languor, which I shared with her. I was inconsolable. To complete our misfortunes, you know that Isfahan was suddenly besieged and taken by storm. The mariner whose organs are numbed by drink envisages the fury of the waves coolly. My despair was that drink for me. I suddenly became insensible.

"The insolent victors reached us; they put Cador, Zélis and Zirphile in chains. I saw that frightful spectacle without shedding a tear; they were separated from me. I held out my hand to them mechanically. I did not see them again. Soon, my feeble attractions occupied those ferocious men. I emerged from the lethargy of dolor momentarily. I tried to stab myself. They prevented me from doing so. I was about to be the victim of their brutality, but their avarice proved stronger. They sold me to a Jew.

"Fortunately, that Jew ceded nothing to the avarice of his vendors. He respected me because he dreaded ruining me. Finally, I knew Nadir. A fortunate hazard offered him to my eyes. What a man! What grandeur! What generosity! What streaks of fire also slipped into my heart. Dear Fatima, he wanted nothing but my happiness. Since that time, I have only breathed for him. Can you believe that in those delightful moments, when Nature presents the keenest pleasures to my youth, I sense even more forcefully the possession of a soul like mine. Yes, our dear Philosopher is right. There exists within us a precious being, which is the motor of our imagination, and it is that motor which distinguishes us from animals.

"Oh, my dear Fatima, how much pleasure we shall have in hearing our friend again. We shall make him repeat his lessons more than once. My Nadir is the worthy pupil of such a Master. We shall try to imitate him. Ormasis esteems women, as you now; he loves them, and you know that too, and our questions will certainly never make him impatient."

"Dear Mirza," Fatima replied, "I confess to you that I also experience for Ormasis sentiments that are my happiness, but you cannot imagine how much esteem he has for you, how much amity he has for you."

"I believe so," Mirza replied. "Nadir and I have too much pleasure in knowing him for him not to experience some of our sensations. I think there is a certain mental rapport..."

Mirza was cruelly interrupted. Dawn was beginning to break. Its first rays were suddenly eclipsed. A dull noise was heard. A furious wind was unleashed. The earth trembled. Repeated shocks caused Mirza to totter. She threw herself into her friend's arms. "O Heaven!" she cried. "My Nadir...my dear Nadir...what a frightful signal... It's finished, then! You no longer exist...I sense it. Fatal voyage! Fatal curiosity! Wait...I shall follow you. Cruel Earth, the body of Nadir, the body of my friend, have just been annihilated in your inflamed gulfs. Complete your work; swallow Mirza...

"No, you refuse me. My ashes will not be mingled with Nadir's...the noise is abating...it's all over. It's me, then, who must liberate myself from my fate. Well, dear and sad companion of my misfortune, were my sinister presentiments well-founded? We have been too weak. We ought to have opposed that fatal voyage. We ought to have forbidden it—yes, forbidden it! Tenderness has the right to command. My Nadir would have obeyed me. Our Philosopher would not have been able to refuse your orders. They would be here...they would be here...

"Futile regrets, vain despair...be tranquil, my soul. Soon you will enjoy Nadir. My second existence will become the source of a durable happiness. Dear Fatima, if the moment of transition is painful, reassure my courage. Help your friend; give me death."

What a situation for sensitive Fatima. Tremulous, agitated, overwhelmed by anxiety herself, she made every effort to console her friend. "My dear Mirza, why his despair? What has convinced you that our friends have perished? Are there not places within the Earth where one might be shielded from its explosions? Yes, believe me, we shall soon see them again. I hope that…the interesting Philosopher…that soul, so touching..."

Fatima could not say any more. Tears betrayed her efforts.

"You're deceiving me," replied Mirza, hotly. "You have no more hope than I do. You're weeping. Oh, Fatima, there is a term to pain; we can fix it."

"Listen, dear Mirza—I confess that I'm trembling for our friends' lives, and I don't want to survive them any more than you do, but at least let's make certain of their fate. If, for example, before sunset, we don't see them reappear, I consent..."

"So be it," Mirza replied, shaking Fatima's hand. "I promise you, until that moment, at least the appearance of tranquility."

Such was their last resolution.

Selim and Osman, awakened by the quake, had run to Nadir's house with the natural anxiety of lovers. Laure and Sophie had just come into Mirza's apartment. They too ask to be admitted. They are chagrined to learn about Nadir's absence, and that of the scientist in which they have taken so much interest.

Fatima says very little. Mirza, occupied with conjectures, only replies with sighs. They try to console her. They talk about other things. They also announce that no damage has been done to Chrysopolis.

A short time afterwards, the Physicist arrives. He is introduced into the apartment. He assures them that the shocks have not been very violent, because the fire was surely only slightly compressed in the entrails of the Earth, and that there are probably not many places that have received a violent disturbance.

Fatima interrogates the Physicist. She asks him whether men who were underground and in the vicinity of such an explosion at the time would not be exposed to certain death.

"Not always, Madame," replies the Physicist. "That depends on the elevation of the terrain relative to the direction of the fire. Invariably, during a tremor of that sort, there are places underground where one would be safer than on the surface."

Fatima listens to the Physicist with pleasure. Her heart still has the strength to seek reasons for hope; Mirza's refuses to admit any. She is obliged to go for a walk. The hours that go by are centuries. She looks at her friend from time to time, and repeats the desolate words: 'You'll see that they will arrive.'

What a day! Nadir's house, that palace of delights, was no more than a theater of dolor. Laure and Sophie, anxious for the fate of their generous friend, also shed tears.

It was four o'clock in the afternoon when the old Sangiac appeared. He took a considerable part in the situation. "Console yourselves, though," he said. "If our friends have been running around the city, nothing can surely have happened to them. There has only been one opening on the highway, half a league from here. It's true that three people have been swallowed up, but those people were seen at the moment of their misfortune; they are known, they have been named. Be tranquil, therefore; they were not our friends."

At this unexpected story, Mirza shivers; Fatima goes pale; their eyes meet. What reanimates the hope of others is precisely the blow that overwhelms them.

The old Sangiac continues telling all the stories that the earthquake had occasioned: heroes unseated; princesses deceived; husbands who were not expecting visits from their wives; wives who were not expecting visits from their husbands. In sum, he tries to make his stories humorous.

Wasted effort. No one laughs.

Meanwhile, time is passing; Mirza watches the sun. Already, its rays are beginning to be intercepted by the mountains. She makes a sign to her friend and leaves he room. Fatima understands that fateful sign; sadly, she follows Mirza. Their absence arouses no suspicion.

Mirza only bore the imprint of a tender melancholy. Fatima had already joined her in her apartment.

"Dear friend," said Mirza, immediately. "We're alone...it's time."

"Yes, Fatima replied. "Like you, I have no more hope. In fact, if they were still alive, would they not have come to reassure us? Listen, Mirza, leave that blade where it is. We can, in dying, spare ourselves pain. In the time when I saw my fortune stolen, and my lover had expired before my eyes beneath the Turkish blades, I bought a subtle poison from a slave, resolved to make use of it. You know that Nadir, that worthy friend, wanted to save my life in spite of my determination. But finally, since Nadir is no more, and since that other amiable Philosopher, who was beginning to captivate my soul, has, like him, ceased to live, I shall fetch that poison. Wait a moment. I'm yours."

Fatima, as determined as her friend, runs to her apartment; there she finds the mortal powder.

In the meantime, Mirza was still gazing at the sun, whose last rays were about to disappear.

"So, divine star, I shall not see you again. How many times, with Nadir, have I admired your glare! Oh, if you have ever taken any pleasure in illuminating a generous mortal, you must regret my lover! But your majestic bosom cannot be the palace of those immortal essences that humans cannot define. No, those essences fill all of space. Nadir, dear Nadir, if you are listening to me, tell me: does our soul, separated from our body, wander in the immensity, or does it occupy the point that it desires? Oh, my divine friend, perhaps the point that you occupy at present is very close to your Mirza. I flatter myself...she is worthy of you...if, however, in dying, I am about to cease to be sensible...or if, no longer having the same organs, you no longer love me...oh, cruel reflection, which saddens me and frightens me! Fatal moment...

"But what do I hear? Is it an illusion? No, I'm not mistaken...cries of joy...they're redoubling...the Philosopher's voice...Fatima is speaking to him. O Heaven! My Nadir is calling to me. He's running...it's him. Here he is..."

How can that heart-warming scene be depicted?

Nadir is, indeed, taking his tender Mirza in his arms. The impression of the initial rapture robs them momentarily of the use of speech.

"So one does not die of pleasure!" cries Mirza, finally. "I see you again. I still exist. Delightful friend...yes...embrace me. I would return all your kisses, but I no longer have enough strength to do so. Cruel man, what grief you have caused me. Where were you? What were you doing? The earth shook. The Philosopher has, therefore...why come back so late?"

"Oh, dear Mirza, it is often by means of pain that Heaven prepares us for the greatest pleasures. You shall hear about our adventures but you will never guess what glad news I have to give you."

"Well, speak. Is there anything that can cause me the delights that..."

Ormasis comes into the apartment. He is holding Fatima's hand. Her moist eyes and tender gaze express all her sensitivity. He lets go of her in order to embrace his daughter.

"Oh, respectable friend of Nadir," Mirza said to him, "I ought, yes, I ought to refuse you. To what anguish have you consigned me? I thought that Nadir was dead. It was you who took away my happiness, my life; however, I will tell you that I cannot hate you. I felt the same fears for you. Essential friend, I was in despair at the thought of losing you."

"Oh, my Mirza!" cried Nadir, excitedly, "my dear Mirza, your heart divined it...embrace your father!"

"My father! Oh, Heaven!"

"Yes, my dear daughter, worthy daughter of Azéma, know Zirmen, know that unfortunate father. He has finally ceased to be unfortunate."

"My father, my father...what a surprise! What new pleasures! What raptures! My heart cannot contain them. My dear Fatima, my tender friend, here we are, then, reunited in the bosom of happiness. Oh, my father, my respectable friend's heart is worthy of yours. She wanted to die with me."

Fatima makes a sign to Mirza to shut up. She closes her mouth with her own. Ormasis admires the two friends with tears of pleasure. Soon, his daughter tells him that she has some notion of the fate of Zirphile, Cador and Zélis. The Philosopher's sensitive heart expands again at that news. Nadir assures his dear Mirza that he will punish her for the mystery she has created and that, in order to avenge himself, he will go in person to find her relatives.

"Yes, my dear Nadir, but you will go with me. No more voyages without your Mirza; I will not tolerate that. I have reflected since your absence that tenderness has the right to command. My father, remember that Fatima and I have the same entitlement over you."

Nadir finally remembers that he is carrying immense riches about his person. He displays to Mirza's eyes a quantity of diamonds of the greatest beauty. Mirza scarcely looks at the stones, still gazing at her dear Nadir.

"What, Mirza—you're not applauding? Don't you think that these diamonds are superb?"

"Yes, but they cost me too much. Besides, if you want me to pay attention to them, don't be here yourself."

The cries of joy that the slaves uttered when they saw their Master again were heard by the company. Enquiries were made, and everyone soon arrived in Mirza's apartment. The voyagers were congratulated. They were embraced.

The old Sangiac danced with pleasure on seeing that happy change. "My dear Master," he said to Ormasis, "you've caused us anxiety and distress; it's necessary to compensate us. I shall be your judge. Three allegros on the harp; I won't let you off with fewer. Oh, in return, I'll tell you stories about the earthquake and all the aftershocks that followed it; you'll laugh, I swear to you. These beautiful ladies, whom I strove to amuse, didn't even listen to me. You'll see, however, how excellent the stories are."

"Oh, my dear Governor," Mirza replied, "We promise to laugh wholeheartedly."

"That's good, Madame; I'm content. I declare to you that I shall spend the night here."

"Not on my account. Nadir also has stories to tell me, but I don't want to hear them. Today, it's necessary that the voyagers rest. My father and Nadir interest me too much for..."

"Your father, Madame, really?"

"Yes, my dear Governor, really."

"In truth, I'm not surprised that he has such an amiable daughter. Damn it, I like him even more for it. So, my dear Master, you will stay with us permanently. Oh, I'm quite content. Do you know that I'm becoming a good philosopher? This morning I prayed to God when I heard the racket. I was slightly afraid for myself, but not much; I was much more anxious about our young monarch. I made haste to run to the castle. I learned that no harm had come to him. He was already up and about, they said, and so busy making plans for means to render his people happy that he hardly noticed the noise. I came back very happy. I immediately send an express message asking how my wives were; a satisfactory response came back within the hour.

"You see, therefore, my dear Ormasis, that I'm a good philosopher. I love God, my prince and women. Oh, I'll never forget that. But since your charming daughter doesn't want me to take any new lessons today, until tomorrow, my dear Master. I'll come back at midday and you can throw me out at midnight...with your permission, Nadir. It's not my fault if you and your company enchant me, and I always want to be here...forgive your old friend if he's importunate, forgive him."

"Importunate!" replied Nadir. "Oh, my dear Sangiac, how can you think that?"

"My friend, be frank with me; admit that today, I would annoy you if I were to stay any longer. I'm in agreement with the dear Mirza." He addressed himself to the Physicist and continued: "Listen to me, Sir; I don't know anything about the original causes of electric fires and attraction, but it seems to me that I see beautiful electric fires and great attractions here. Here are four amiable men and four charming women; they never cease looking at one another. Believe me, let's leave together. You can explain the physical phenomenon."

They left.

Meanwhile, Mirza and Fatima ordered the voyagers to go and get some rest. Laure, Sophie, Selim and Osman did not raise a murmur; the health of their friends was precious to them. The customary ceremonies that were to fix everyone's happiness were thus postponed until the following day. Ormasis was taken to his apartment, which had been made ready for him.

Why, one might say, wait for the customary ceremonies, and for whom? For philosophers? Yes, true philosophers are always attached to good social order. They even respect prejudices, the conservation of which maintains laws.

As for Nadir, obedient in spite of himself, to Mirza's tenderness, he forgot twenty hours of fatigue in the arms of sleep—but as soon as daylight appeared, Mirza wanted to know all the details of the expedition.

She goes into his apartment. Nadir was still asleep. She opens the curtains gently; she goes to him. Rosy lips brush his eyelids gently. He wakes up.

Gods, what an awakening! Amour, lend me your brushes; the pencils of voluptuousness are too fragile.

The flowers of pleasure that sentiment can bring into bloom never fade. Nadir and Mirza breathe in concert. The same delight uplifts them.

Twenty times over, Nadir commences his narrative; twenty times over he interrupts himself. His tongue is caught in a chain of caresses, unable to pronounce anything but Mirza's name.

The tender Mirza, too occupied to be curious, ceases to ask for details that she can no longer hear.

Nadir, Mirza—those two names, repeated rapturously, are more expressive for them than any of the lascivious phrases with which indolent hearts strive to reheat their cold existence.

Finally, the term of one pleasure is for them the commencement of another.

Mirza escapes from Nadir's arms. An old man is asking to speak to her. They do not know what he wants. He is insistent, imploring.

She goes down; she sees him; she runs. It is Cador.

To cover him with caresses and questions, to take him by the hand and lead him to her father's room, is for her the work of an instant. Oh, hearts sensitive to amity, paint that tender recognition for yourselves. See Mirza in the midst of such friends.

Ormasis' joy is also in its final phase. Cador tells them that Zélis and Zirphile belong to a very humane Master, but he lives thirty leagues from Bisance.

Nadir has come to rejoin Mirza. He embraces his new guest enthusiastically. The departure to go in search of Zélis and Zirphile is fixed for the following day. As for Cador's Master, he is an interested Armenian presently in Chrysopolis. Nadir finds out where he lives, and takes one of his beautiful diamonds. He goes out and returns with the liberty of his dear relative. This prompt exchange causes Mirza to feel more acutely the utility of the riches that Nadir has brought.

Finally, everyone is happy. Soon, Zélis and Zirphile augment that felicity.

Scarcely has that charming society been reunited than Fatima and Mirza order multiple celebrations. It is a natural opportunity to spread benefits, without charging the recipients with the burden of gratitude. They go in search of all the poor artisans in Chrysopolis who have families. They affect to be very difficult and very meticulous about their adornment, although intimately convinced that they have no need of it. They continually change fashions. Hard-working seamstresses are kept busy. Mirza and Fatima check the work, in order that it is begun again; then they pretend to be very content, in order to pay more generously without anyone being annoyed by it. Censorious imbeciles and insipid moralists, you would have criticized that apparent levity. Oh well—our true philosophers will only see virtue therein.

Ormasis and Nadir go to their library from time to time, but a physics workshop and a laboratory are soon necessary. "It is not sufficient," said the Philosopher, "merely to speculate about the work of others. It is necessary to do experiments oneself, to produce new work, to scrutinize Nature.

One can easily imagine the progress that Nadir will make under such a Master. Our Philosophers' wives will become very knowledgeable, but they will not believe so. True beauty is never eclipsed by ridicule.

Nadir was soon able to put aside a number of productions. He finished reforming his library. Finally, he dabbled in writing.

"My dear Nadir," Ormasis said to him then, "you know that our ideas do not fit in with a number of received theories. Believe me, it's not with a dogmatic tone, nor with ill temper, that it's necessary to refute the sentiments of others. Present our opinions with simplicity and in an amusing form. Let everyone decide for himself whether to adopt them; never become demanding in that regard. Above all, don't cease to hold those people in esteem who, enslaved by old prejudices, will perhaps refuse to admit what they call singular novelties. Let us be content to admire the verities we perceive, and remember that our philosophy must be unpretentious.

SF & FANTASY

Henri Allorge. *The Great Cataclysm*
Guy d'Armen. *Doc Ardan: The City of Gold and Lepers*
G.-J. Arnaud. *The Ice Company*
Charles Asselineau. *The Double Life*
Cyprien Bérard. *The Vampire Lord Ruthwen*
Aloysius Bertrand. *Gaspard de la Nuit*
Richard Bessière. *The Gardens of the Apocalypse*
Albert Bleunard. *Ever Smaller*
Félix Bodin. *The Novel of the Future*
Alphonse Brown. *City of Glass*
André Caroff. *The Terror of Madame Atomos; Miss Atomos; The Return of Madame Atomos; The Mistake of Madame Atomos; The Monsters of Madame Atomos; The Revenge of Madame Atomos*
Félicien Champsaur. *The Human Arrow; Ouha*
Didier de Chousy. *Ignis*
Captain Danrit. *Undersea Odyssey*
C. I. Defontenay. *Star (Psi Cassiopeia)*
Charles Derennes. *The People of the Pole*
Georges Dodds (anthologist). *The Missing Link*
Harry Dickson. *The Heir of Dracula*
Jules Dornay. *Lord Ruthven Begins*
Alfred Driou. *The Adventures of a Parisian Aeronaut*
Sâr Dubnotal *vs. Jack the Ripper*
Alexandre Dumas. *The Return of Lord Ruthven*
Renée Dunan. *Baal*
J.-C. Dunyach. *The Night Orchid; The Thieves of Silence*
Henri Duvernois. *The Man Who Found Himself*
Achille Eyraud. *Voyage to Venus*
Henri Falk. *The Age of Lead*
Paul Féval. *Anne of the Isles; Knightshade; Revenants; Vampire City; The Vampire Countess; The Wandering Jew's Daughter*
Paul Féval, *fils. Felifax, the Tiger-Man*
Charles de Fieux. *Lamékis*
Arnould Galopin. *Doctor Omega; Doctor Omega & The Shadowmen*
Léon Gozlan. *The Vampire of the Val-de-Grâce*
G.L. Gick. *Harry Dickson and the Werewolf of Rutherford Grange*
Edmond Haraucourt. *Illusions of Immortality*
Nathalie Henneberg. *The Green Gods*

V. Hugo, P. Foucher & P. Meurice. *The Hunchback of Notre-Dame*
Michel Jeury. *Chronolysis*
Gustave Kahn. *The Tale of Gold and Silence*
Gérard Klein. *The Mote in Time's Eye*
Louis-Guillaume de La Follie. *The Unpretentious Philosopher*
Jean de La Hire. *Enter the Nyctalope; The Nyctalope on Mars; The Nyctalope vs. Lucifer; The Nyctalope Steps In; Night of the Nyctalope*
Etienne-Léon de Lamothe-Langon. *The Virgin Vampire*
André Laurie. *Spiridon*
Gabriel de Lautrec. *The Vengeance of the Oval Portrait*
Alain le Drimeur. *The Future City*
Georges Le Faure & Henri de Graffigny. *The Extraordinary Adventures of a Russian Scientist Across the Solar System* (2 vols.)
Gustave Le Rouge. *The Vampires of Mars The Dominion of the World* (w/Gustave Guitton) (4 vols.)
Jules Lermina. *Mysteryville; Panic in Paris; To-Ho and the Gold Destroyers; The Secret of Zippelius*
Jean-Marc & Randy Lofficier. *Edgar Allan Poe on Mars; The Katrina Protocol; Pacifica; Robonocchio; Tales of the Shadowmen 1-9*
Xavier Mauméjean. *The League of Heroes*
Joseph Méry. *The Tower of Destiny*
Hippolyte Mettais. *The Year 5865*
Louise Michel. *The Human Microbes; The New World*
José Moselli. *Illa's End*
John-Antoine Nau. *Enemy Force*
Marie Nizet. *Captain Vampire*
C. Nodier, A. Beraud & Toussaint-Merle. *Frankenstein*
Henri de Parville. *An Inhabitant of the Planet Mars*
Gaston de Pawlowski. *Journey to the Land of the 4th Dimension*
Georges Pellerin. *The World in 2000 Years*
Ernest Pérochon. *The Frenetic People*
Pierre Pelot. *The Child Who Walked on the Sky*
J. Polidori, C. Nodier, E. Scribe. *Lord Ruthven the Vampire*
P.-A. Ponson du Terrail. *The Vampire and the Devil's Son*
Henri de Régnier. *A Surfeit of Mirrors*
Maurice Renard. *The Blue Peril; Doctor Lerne; The Doctored Man; A Man Among the Microbes; The Master of Light*
Jean Richepin. *The Wing*
Albert Robida. *The Adventures of Saturnin Farandoul; The Clock of the Centuries; Chalet in the Sky*

J.-H. Rosny Aîné. *Helgvor of the Blue River; The Givreuse Enigma; The Mysterious Force; The Navigators of Space; Vamireh; The World of the Variants; The Young Vampire*
Marcel Rouff. *Journey to the Inverted World*
Han Ryner. *The Superhumans*
Brian Stableford. *The New Faust at the Tragicomique;The Empire of the Necromancers (The Shadow of Frankenstein; Frankenstein and the Vampire Countess; Frankenstein in London); Sherlock Holmes & The Vampires of Eternity; The Stones of Camelot; The Wayward Muse.* (anthologist) *The Germans on Venus; News from the Moon; The Supreme Progress; The World Above the World; Nemoville; Investigations of the Future*
Jacques Spitz. *The Eye of Purgatory*
Kurt Steiner. *Ortog*
Eugène Thébault. *Radio-Terror*
C.-F. Tiphaigne de La Roche. *Amilec*
Théo Varlet. *The Golden Rock. The Xenobiotic Invasion; Timeslip Troopers* (w/André Blandin); *The Martian Epic* (w/Octave Joncquel)
Paul Vibert. *The Mysterious Fluid*
Villiers de l'Isle-Adam. *The Scaffold; The Vampire Soul*
Philippe Ward. *Artahe*
Philippe Ward & Sylvie Miller. *The Song of Montségur*

MYSTERIES & THRILLERS

M. Allain & P. Souvestre. *The Daughter of Fantômas*
A. Anicet-Bourgeois, Lucien Dabril. *Rocambole*
A. Bernède. *Belphegor*; *Judex* (w/Louis Feuillade)
A. Bisson & G. Livet. *Nick Carter vs. Fantômas*
V. Darlay & H. de Gorsse. *Lupin vs. Holmes: The Stage Play*
Paul Féval. *Gentlemen of the Night; John Devil; The Black Coats ('Salem Street; The Invisible Weapon; The Parisian Jungle; The Companions of the Treasure; Heart of Steel; The Cadet Gang; The Sword-Swallower)*
Emile Gaboriau. *Monsieur Lecoq*
Steve Leadley. *Sherlock Holmes: The Circle of Blood*
Maurice Leblanc. *Arsène Lupin vs. Countess Cagliostro; Lupin vs. Holmes (The Blonde Phantom; The Hollow Needle); The Many Faces of Arsène Lupin*
Gaston Leroux. *Chéri-Bibi; The Phantom of the Opera; Rouletabille & the Mystery of the Yellow Room*

Richard Marsh. *The Complete Adventures of Judith Lee*
William Patrick Maynard. *The Terror of Fu Manchu; The Destiny of Fu Manchu*
Frank J. Morlock. *Sherlock Holmes: The Grand Horizontals; Sherlock Holmes vs Jack the Ripper*
Antonin Reschal. *The Adventures of Miss Boston*
P. de Wattyne & Y. Walter. *Sherlock Holmes vs. Fantômas*
David White. *Fantômas in America*

SCREENPLAYS

Mike Baron. *The Iron Triangle*
Emma Bull & Will Shetterly. *Nightspeeder; War for the Oaks*
Gerry Conway & Roy Thomas. *Doc Dynamo*
Steve Englehart. *Majorca*
James Hudnall. *The Devastator*
Jean-Marc & Randy Lofficier. *Royal Flush*
J.-M. & R. Lofficier & Marc Agapit. *Despair*
J.-M. & R. Lofficier & Joël Houssin. *City*
Andrew Paquette. *Peripheral Vision*
Robert L. Robinson, Jr. *Judex*
R. Thomas, J. Hendler & L. Sprague de Camp. *Rivers of Time*

NON-FICTION

Stephen R. Bissette. *Blur 1-5. Green Mountain Cinema 1; Teen Angels*
Win Scott Eckert. *Crossovers* (2 vols.)
Jean-Marc & Randy Lofficier. *Shadowmen* (2 vols.)
Randy Lofficier. *Over Here*